From the time Carrie Taylor discovered the magical worlds of romance novels, she devoured them one right after the other. She not only thrilled to each new hero, one more dashing than the one before, but Carrie clearly saw herself as each beautiful heroine waiting to be rescued by each daring hero. And then one day, she brought home a photograph. A very special photograph and suddenly her imaginary hero turned into a living and breathing man. Or did he?

At one time Black Eagle scoffed at the girls of his village wishing on a falling star. And yet his one great wish, that of a woman of his own, was never realized. And then one night, he wished upon a star. Can the love of a man from the past help a modern woman with her modern problems in a modern world?

The Photograph
Copyright © 2020 Regan Taylor
ISBN: 978-1-4874-2694-1
Cover art by Martine Jardin

Published by eXtasy Books Inc or
Devine Destinies, an imprint of eXtasy Books Inc

Look for us online at:
www.eXtasybooks.com or www.devinedestinies.com

THE PHOTOGRAPH TREASURES ANTIQUE BOOK 1

BY

REGAN TAYLOR

CHAPTER ONE

He backed her against the door, holding her firm in his embrace. "You are mine, Cassandra, mine and mine alone."

As the stunningly handsome blond-haired man took the dark-haired beauty in his arms, his oh, so sensuous lips coming closer and closer to her own, Cassandra knew he would take her in a passion that only grew hotter and hotter with each taking. She felt him hot and hard against her, leaving no doubt what he wanted of her. "Yes, Erek, yes. Now and always."

He reached for her, pulling her into his embrace, knowing this was the love he had waited a lifetime for. No man, no army could keep them apart. Never again would they be torn from each other. This would be a love for all time. "I love you, Cassandra. I will love you forever."

Carrie Taylor sighed and closed her eyes as she held the book to her chest. "Why don't they make men like that in real life? Why can't I meet my own Erek? A man who's not only totally gorgeous on the outside with a fabulous chest and nice butt, but a really nice guy on the inside? A guy who you can tell anything to and he'll listen and help you do whatever it is you really want to do?"

While good for company on a dark, cold, rainy winter night, Taister's 'meow' didn't really answer her question. She scrunched the long-haired black cat's ears before turning off the light beside her bed. As she snuggled under the covers, she heard Taister's purr from the foot of the bed. At least he

1

was faithful, not like that jerk Dean. "Dean Welman — what an absolute loser," she told the cat. "The porker. Taister, tell me this, just because I hung out with him — all right, dated him — am I a loser?"

When the cat didn't respond with more than a louder purr, Carrie thought back on the man she'd recently broken up with. Dean had come on all charm and kisses, promised her the moon and then went and two-timed her. Such was the story of her life. "Hell, he wasn't even that hot in bed!" Chalk up number — well whatever number he was. And come to think of it, *he* was definitely the loser. "I'm well rid of him, Taister, that's for sure."

Drifting off to sleep, Carrie replayed the last few chapters of *Her Knight* in her mind, seeing herself in the role of the heroine, Cassandra. Erek, of course, looked just like the model on the book cover. She could almost feel the soft velvet of the deep burgundy gown worn by Cassandra on that same cover, her cheeks warming at the thought of the bare-chested Erek with his long blond hair flowing over his shoulders, his powerful hands kneading her breasts. Erek was the best hero she'd read in a long time. As a dream lover, he was ideal. At least in her dreams someone loved her.

The alarm jarred her awake long before she was ready for it to be morning. Even the music from her favorite oldies station sounded way too loud when she wanted a few more minutes in the big four-poster bed in the castle with Sir Hot Bod Erek. Unfortunately, or fortunately for the pocketbook, her sense of doing the right thing and holding down a job demanded she get up and head into work.

Padding towards the kitchen, she found a note from her roommate Molly, who worked for a police department in the next county.

She read the note and sighed. "Man, Taister, things are getting worse at that job of hers instead of better. I really thought—well, hoped actually, that one of these days things would get better. It appears not."

Taister meowed up a storm while she tried to read the note; so much so that she was sure he was telling her if he didn't get his breakfast ASAP, life on planet Earth, as they knew it, would end.

"Okay, okay, little man, let's keep Earth in orbit another day. One can of the stinky, wet, fishy food coming up. Molly wants to get together for dinner. I sure hope it's good news for a change and not more BS from her supervisor. She needs to be catching a break and soon. Did you hear her talking about that crazy supervisor of hers the other day?"

The black cat continued his own little diatribe on how he was missing out on some of life's greatest joys because she had slept till the alarm *and* taken a shower instead of rushing to make his breakfast. After all, he had some serious cat things to do.

"Sounds like you didn't catch the entire 411 on it and, that you don't much care, either. I'm hurrying, I'm hurrying and just so you know, I've thought about it, long and hard and here's a news flash for you: Life as we know it will not end if you don't get something to eat, right here and now."

Taister grumbled, or at least that's what it sounded like and she couldn't miss the look he shot her. "And some people think cats don't know how to communicate. If there's one thing you can do, and do well, it's communicate."

Carrie finally put the dish down on the floor. Taister ate his requisite two bites and went off to engage in his own morning ablutions. "You sure have a tough life, Taister, a real tough life." He only gave her a quick glance before returning to his grooming. Carrie grabbed her coffee and headed off to get ready for work.

Just a few short hours later at work, Carrie looked up from

yet another mailing project and to her surprise, there stood Erek—in full knightly garb. While seeing his bare chest would have been mighty pleasing, the shining metal of his suit of armor and the way that metal triangle piece kinda sat there up front between his thighs sure conjured up some pleasant thoughts. "Sweet Carrie, I hath been looking for you."

"*Erek?*" The sight of her latest mental lust–break made her glad she'd chosen to wear her favorite sheer ivory shell under an ashes of roses blouse and thigh highs in lieu of pantyhose.

"Yes my love, 'tis your Erek." He took a step towards her, his hand outstretched in a courtly gesture. "I've come to take you for a ride, a short one because you are at your labor, so we will think of it as a prelude to our time tonight."

"Oh, yes, Erek. I like the way you think."

He turned to shut the door and began to divest himself of his knightly garments while he boldly strode to her desk. Seeing his intent and knowing the type of ride he planned, Carrie unbuttoned her blouse. Erek's eyes lit up in anticipation and he reached out a hand to cup her lace-covered breast. "Ah, sweet Carrie, I like this corset much better than those of yore." He lowered his lips to hers. At first he brushed them ever so slightly, tasting the sweetness there. "Ah my love, your lips are like the freshest berries. I hunger for the full meal."

His hand kneaded her breast as she reached upward to partake of a full kiss. His warm tongue was like honey and she melted to his touch. His hands pulled up her skirt, murmuring against her lips as he did so, "I love these hose you wear. The memory of them when we are apart makes me crave you all the more."

Carrie acknowledged to herself that she felt pretty sexy in her thigh highs along with her 'come do me' red pumps, but she wasn't going to bother Erek with that trivial knowledge.

"Carrie. Carrie?"

What the hell? She turned to find her co-worker Maria

standing beside her, hand on her shoulder and no sign of Erek in the room. "What's going on? How long have you been here? Where's . . ." *Oops, better not ask about Erek. I don't need anyone thinking I'm crazy 'cause I imagine my romance heroes being with me in the flesh. It was bad enough when I called out that one character's name when I was in bed with Dean right before we broke up.*

"I've been standing at the door calling you for the past two minutes. Man, when you get into your work you really get into it. Although I can't imagine stuffing envelopes is *that* absorbing."

"It's not. I mean it is. Well not absorbing, you just need to be really sure you get them stuffed just right. And well, I was just thinking."

"Well, think on this, girlfriend. A bunch of us are trying out the new café up the street, Gazillios, for lunch. Wanna come?"

"Yeah, sounds good. Let me grab my purse."

During lunch the group shared the usual good laughs about some silliness that happened at the office in the morning with one of their co-workers. "Okay, so what did Visa do now?" Carrie asked referring to their co-worker who lived up to the credit card slogan—everywhere you want to be.

"I can't believe you missed it!" Debra told her.

"Sorry, you know how it is when you get totally involved in work."

"Right. More like thinking about your latest romance novel," Maria whispered to her.

She play-slapped her friend. "So what happened?"

"Well, you know how Visa's been on this total man hunt?"

"Yeah. That's not exactly news. She's always sniffing out a new guy."

"This morning she comes strutting in wearing this bright red sweater two sizes too small for her and the reddest lipstick ever on her lips."

"I thought she was going to fall out of that sweater." Macy

put in.

"Who's she after now?" Carrie asked.

"Anyone she can get!" Doug answered.

"Like you'd know." Maria jabbed him in the ribs with her elbow."

"I so would. She was after me a few months ago. Never wore that sweater, though," Doug mused.

"So if she did, would it have turned you straight?"

"Probably not. Still, it is something to watch." Doug chuckled.

"Why do you call her Visa?" Sandy, the new girl asked.

"Because like Visa, she's everywhere you want to be. Invited or not, there she is. In fact one time she even showed up at this funeral. Didn't know the guy who died or his family, just showed up because a bunch of people she knew were going."

"So do you give everyone nicknames?" Sandy sounded a bit nervous waiting to hear what they called her.

"Actually, no. Just Visa."

Downtown Napa—if you could call it a downtown—is a city full of quaint shops, charming restaurants and has an overall enchanting aura to it. Not too far from San Francisco, Napa sports every variety of eatery, but with the magic of a small town. The shops look like Christmas through the entire year. Little lights peep out of windows with pretty curtains, trees dotting the curbs, with full bushes in open spaces. Even though considered a city, it has all the ambiance of a long ago small town . . . quaint and cozy. The café they went to had the best quiche and smoothies, some of which Carrie saved to bring back to work with her for an afternoon snack.

As the group passed Carrie's favorite store, the Treasures Antique Shoppe, she made her excuses. "Maria, I'll be along in a few. I want to see if Mr. Merle has anything new in the store."

"Looking for some new treasures in Treasures?" She laughed.

"Yeah. Even though I split with Dean a month ago I still feel like I need something comforting or to do something special for myself."

The people who wandered into the quaint shop were always friendly and interesting, each with their own story about what they were looking for and why.

The owner, Mr. Merle, seemed to enjoy talking to each person, hearing their story and helping them find just the right item. He was an elderly man, seventy-five if he was a day. With his snow-white hair and twinkling blue-gray eyes, when Carrie spoke with him it was like speaking to a beloved grandfather or great-uncle. There was something magical, for lack of a better word, about him. It was almost like he came from another time and place. He always had a kind word, good advice and knew some intricate detail about every item in his shop. Maybe it was because he seemed to have this thing about bringing couples who really loved each other, like soul mates, together that Carrie believed him when he told her there was a wonderful man out there for her, just waiting to appear, even though all she ever seemed to meet were jerks like Dean.

They exchanged waves of greeting when she walked in, before he turned to complete whatever it was he was working on. The kindly old gent was always busy tinkering with something or other. She quickly spotted a large old trunk towards the back of the shop chock full of what looked to be some fascinating bits and pieces. Tea cups, ribbons, a few leather bound books, a spindle of yarn and papers filled it to almost overflowing. It reminded her of one of her pirate stories where the kidnapped maiden finds just the object she needs to escape her captor when they arrive in port.

She stood, gazing into space a moment trying to remember

which it was, "Oh yes, *Captive of the High Seas*. Captain Black Jack Walters, wasn't he a hunk and a half?" she asked no one in particular.

The author described one of the most passionate love scenes she'd ever read when Black Jack and the heroine made love during a storm while at sea. She'd re-read that scene over and over and tried to entice the guy she'd been dating at the time to rent a boat during a storm so she could find out for herself just how intense sex could be under those conditions. He thought she was crazy and that was the last she saw of him. When she asked the next guy she dated about it Carrie had to settle for a waterbed in a hotel up in Reno to see if the rolls and pitches added to the experience. It didn't.

Digging deeper in the trunk, she came across a photograph. No ordinary photograph, this one was very, very old, one of those ancient tintypes used way back when. Like in the old west . . .which reminded her of a western she'd read a few months before about a woman who pretended to be a mail order bride and ended up married to the town's sheriff.

"They sure don't make em like Sheriff Rick Hansen, that's for sure." She drew a curious look from one of the other women in the store, causing Carrie to make a mental note to stop talking to herself, especially about her romance novel heroes.

She studied the old, faded photograph for a few minutes, unsure if it was truly so blurry or if it was just that the picture was kind of cloudy. Interestingly, one of the people in it seemed to stand out. He was either a proud Indian warrior or someone made up to look like one. Truth be told, it wasn't his firmly muscled chest, those pecs that made you want to reach out and touch them, something that almost always drew her attention. No, it was his eyes. Carrie had never seen such compelling eyes in her life. They were dark, like molasses, warm and comforting. Even in the photograph, they seemed to hold her, to reach out to her and make her want to be with him.

It wasn't like in her imagination. This felt so real. As if he called to her through time and space. Nor were they the same kind of feelings she had when she looked over the hunky models on the covers of the romances she devoured like candy. No, this felt different, far different than anything she'd ever felt before. Taking the photograph, she headed to the register to ask the Mr. Merle about it. At some point she'd heard he had an abiding interest in paranormal type happenings, not that she felt there was anything odd about the photograph itself. After all, it was just an old photograph. She appreciated him because he'd talk to her about the things that interested her. Mostly she talked to him about her romance problems — he always seemed to make her feel better.

"Hey, Mr. Merle. How are you doing today?"

"I'm good, Carrie, I'm good. And how's my favorite treasure hunter?"

"I'm just fine."

"That no-account fella Dean hasn't been around bothering you, has he?"

That was another thing she liked about Mr. Merle, he listened to her and remembered things she said. Too bad he wasn't forty years younger because he'd be the perfect date. Sir "D", her pet name for Dean, so named because he was — in a word — dickless, had dark hair and brown eyes and while he had a chest that made any red blooded female want to run her fingers over it, when it came to personality, his was non-existent. While it didn't bother her, he didn't deal too well with his Napoleonic height, or his scrawny butt and legs. His being so short didn't faze Carrie.

For that matter, his lack of height didn't seem to bother anyone but him. He seemed to think the world owed him for being short and he tried to be such a Casanova to make up for whatever lack he thought he had. He wasn't even that good in bed. It was always all about him. Talk about getting the old one-two punch. That was Dean. One thrust, two thrusts and he was done.

"No, he hasn't. It's really over, finally. At least I hope it is. He was calling a lot in the beginning, after we broke up, but he finally seems to have backed off."

"Well, I'm glad to hear it. Never did like that fella. There was something about him that just didn't seem right. I tell ya, Carrie, somewhere out there is the right man for you. He may just pop out of nowhere like a bolt of lightning."

"It would be nice, but so far nothing. So, Mr. Merle, I found this photo while I was poking around. I'd like to buy it."

Mr. Merle leaned over the counter and took a look at the photograph. It could have been Carrie's imagination, but it looked like he made some kind of hand signal over it, kind of like what a magician did at a party she went to as a kid passing his hand one way and then the other.

His smile seemed luminous when he said, "I'll tell you, Carrie-girl, one of my relatives took that picture years and years ago, back in — oh, I guess around the mid-1850's or early 1860's thereabouts. He was all up for being a journalist and then those tintype cameras came about and he just knew there was a career in that. Taking pictures. I always did like that picture."

"Oh, so it's not for sale?"

"No, I won't sell it to you, but I'll *give* it to you. There's something about it that makes me feel it should belong to you. It's yours if you promise to care for it real close."

"Oh, I will. Are you sure? I don't mind paying for it."

"Yup, that photo's been looking for a home for some time and I believe it found the right one with you."

CHAPTER TWO

Carrie happily brought the photo back to work and carefully placed it on the corner of her desk. She told herself she was being so totally cautious with it only because she'd promised Mr. Merle she would take care of it and remember to take it home with her that night. He had been most determined she immediately bring the photograph home with her. Yup, it was because she promised Mr. Merle she'd bring it home, certainly not because Carrie already imagined the Indian in the photograph coming to life and carrying her away. Several times during the afternoon, though, she picked it up to study it. Try as she might to take in all the elements in the picture, she always came back to the warrior. So much so that when she prepared to leave work for the day it was the first thing she picked up to bring home. With plenty of time before meeting Molly for dinner she stopped off at the local gift shop and found an antique-looking frame for her new picture.

They picked a little Italian restaurant with great antipasto for dinner. With its red-checkered tablecloths, wooden chairs with plump cushions matching the tablecloths, and old wine bottles with the basket-type bottoms holding multi-colored candles, it was, for Carrie, like she'd really gone to Italy. At least that was how her books described the cafes there.

She showed the photo to Molly as soon as they sat down to dinner, asking her roommate, "Isn't this the coolest photo ever? I found it at Mr. Merle's and he gave it to me."

"That's a pretty old photo. Carrie, look how funny the people look. It's like they all have bug eyes."

11

Carrie giggled in response to Molly opening her eyes so wide all of the white seemed to show. "Yes, but it's so cool. Look at the Indian, isn't he gorgeous? No, wait. More than gorgeous, there is just something so, so, so . . ."

"*Uber* hunky?"

"Yes! That's it . . .*uber* hunky about him."

Molly studied the photo a moment longer before replying. "You know, there is something kind of cool about him. Too bad he's not around anymore."

"Yeah . . . a guy like that would be a once in a lifetime kinda guy."

"Uh huh. Only I'd want him to be coming here, not me going there—I wouldn't want to live back then: no microwave, no electric coffee pot, no lattes, no pizza. Much as I'd like to be hanging with a gorgeous guy, I'm not about ready to give up my creature comforts."

"Mmm, I'd have to agree with you on that one, maybe."

"Maybe? Girl, think about it—no hot showers, no coffee pot with an automatic turn on in the morning, no cars, no cell phones . . ."

"Less stress, more time to have, well . . . quality time, cleaner air."

"Rough work-hardened hands, no sunscreen."

"Men who aren't afraid to be men."

"Ah . . .right . . . marital rights, you don't get the vote."

"Yeah, well I guess. Still, sometimes I do wonder what it would have been like to have lived in another time."

"From the faraway look in your eyes I can see you're already mentally traveling somewhere other than the present," Molly told her. "I suspect even with all those historical romances you've read you don't know what it would be like."

"No, not really. After all, the books are all made up. Well, yeah, there's historical research and such. But to have really lived it, not just imagined it would be so incredible."

"Is it the times or the men you are interested in?"

"Ooo-la-la, the men." Carrie paused a second before mentioning to Molly, "You'd also have no Julie Prince to deal with."

Molly sighed and spun her fork around her angel hair pasta. "That's true, although, I'd rather send *her* to the dark and dirty past. Life would be so much better, at least the work life, if I didn't have to deal with her."

"Which brings me to your note this morning. What did she do now?"

"Same ole, same ole," she sighed.

"Want to talk about it or let it go?"

"You don't mind hearing me bitch about her again?"

"Bitch about the Bitch? Hell. No. It makes me appreciate how easy it is at my job and besides, that's what friends are for. If it helps you deal with it, I'm all over it."

"Thanks. I do need to vent. I sound like a broken record. She just did what she usually does, again, yesterday. I go on my days off and someone else—that stupid blond bimbo badge bunny, Kris Harris, the skinny one who does all the officers, screwed up again."

"The one who if she stood sideways and stuck her tongue out would look like a zipper?"

Molly giggled. "That's the one. The Zipper."

"Why don't they do something about her?"

"Because the guys like her . . . well not like her personally, but I hear she does amazing things in the patrol cars when she's out on ride-a-longs. Do you know she's slept with twenty-one out of thirty-three straight male officers in the past two years and broken up two marriages?"

"Sounds more like a suck-a-thon."

"You got that right. Someone needs to put a leash on her."

"Or a chastity belt."

Molly snorted. "I knew I could count on you."

"So bimbolina screwed up again, and . . ."

"Of course I got written up for it. Eventually I'm going to remember that if the Zipper blows it, rather than blowing an officer, I shouldn't point out that I wasn't there on a particular day because Julie will write me up for not being able to take criticism and heaven forbid I show her that *twit* did it because then I'll get in trouble for trying to blame co-workers, even if it is their mistake. I gotta get out of there."

"Did you hear anything yet from the application you filed with county?"

"No." She sighed again, "The problem is, with all the bogus write ups chances are I won't get another job. Julie gets off on writing up those bullshit log entries, and since she hates to lose staff, it keeps anyone who wants to leave dispatch from finding a better job. I swear if someone took up a collection to get her laid I'd contribute twice the going rate. I'm just a bummer, aren't I?"

"Absolutely not."

"Bitching aside, I do have some good news."

"Give!"

"Since Shannon is about to finish her probation and her graveyard rotation I'll be going back on graves in a few weeks."

"And that's good because?"

"I won't see Julie or I'll hardly ever see her. Maybe a few minutes before my shift on Fridays and Mondays, but otherwise I won't have to see her. And, working nights, there's less chance of someone doing something I can get blamed for."

"I know you've always preferred graves, but I like having you around to do things on the weekends. Does Vincent know? Have you told him?"

"Not yet."

"Will it bother him?"

"You mean me working Friday and Saturday nights? Who

knows? I mean, he knew I worked for the police department and did shift work when we first started dating. And I've covered a few graveyard shifts the past few months since we met. We'll see how it goes. Since I'll have seniority, of a sorts, after Maria and Sally, I can always move back to swings for the next rotation if it's a problem for us. Although our relationship better be moving to the significant other stage for me to put up with Julie through a weeks of swings."

"Well I'm glad you'll be out of Julie's radar for awhile." She drew in a deep breath and shook her head, "We're just a pair. I've got boyfriend issues and you have job ones. Somewhere between the two of us is someone who is issue free."

"Well let's hope we find her soon."

"Speaking of someone who is issue free, Visa pulled one of her stunts today."

"Oh, no. What did she do now?"

"Red sweater, two sizes too small, spiked heels—hooker heels—and this red lipstick that looked like something out of a bad 50's B movie."

"She so doesn't get it, does she?"

"No. I'll tell you, Mol, sometimes I swear the woman has no self-respect. She's like a cartoon character. Doug Mitchell said she was sticking her chest out trying to make it look like she had more in the cleavage department than is actually there. It was pretty funny."

"Any guys around to pick up on her show?"

"No." Carrie giggled. "We must have been her dress rehearsal."

"Well at least you have something to laugh about at work."

"Yeah, we do. I'm really sorry that things are so shi-tay at your job."

"Thanks. Carrie, I swear that woman stays awake at night thinking up the next hair brained thing she can come up with to disrupt someone else's life. Usually mine. Right now I just want to look forward to the weekend."

"I wish I had an answer for you. Short of just quitting, I can't think of anything. Although, hmm, you know, I have an idea. Let's fix Julie up with Dean and they can take off on a wild and wacky weekend together . . . and forget to come back. Maybe they just both need to get laid, you know?"

"That, my friend, was a visual I just didn't need. I do feel better for talking to you, though."

Later that night, Carrie grabbed one of her newest romance novels—a steamy regency she'd picked up the day before and headed to her room. Reading a bit before going to bed was a habit she had started back in junior high. Back then, it was Dickens and Dumas that held her attention. Especially Dumas. In high school she first 'discovered' historical romances and was hooked on Rogers, Woodiwiss and a host of others, buying each book as they came out. Of course, she had to hide them between her mattress and box-spring when she was at school because her mom would have had a hissy if she found out she read what she called "those smut books."

Even now she liked to read a bit before going to sleep and found when she read a good romance it definitely left her with sizzling dreams. Only tonight, when she climbed into bed to read her newest regency with a to-die-for viscount, she found she couldn't get far. Talk about a total first.

Instead she kept glancing over at the photo now sitting on her light pine nightstand. Tearing her gaze away from the picture, Carrie looked over her room.

It was everything she had always wanted . . .girlie and at the same time very sensual and conducive to sweet dreams, if not a few romantic nights. When she was dating anyway. It was a study in contrasts and yet the epitome of all she was. Pale lavender satin sheets covered the bed beneath a fluffy white down comforter. Bunches of pillows in all sizes and shapes, along with several stuffed teddy bears that reclined on them, decorated the head of the bed when she had the time to make it. The bed itself was a pine four-poster with matching nightstands, a dresser and an armoire she couldn't resist buying when she saw the mini-closet it held. Stained glass nick-knacks hung from the center curtain rod, covered by sheer lacy curtains on the windows. A bookcase — a very large and very full one — took up almost one wall.

Her favorite pastime was sitting in bed, vanilla votive candles scenting the air with herself dressed in a sexy nightgown, propped up against the pillows reading before she fell asleep. She usually drifted on to dreams of the hero in whatever book she was deeply engrossed in.

Tonight, however, she just couldn't stop looking at the warrior in the photo. Finally giving in to impulse, she picked it up and, after studying it for quite some time, placed a kiss on his image. She held it to her breast and thought about the fact that not since high school, when she'd read her first romance novel, had she done anything like that. Who kissed a picture? She set it on the nightstand, then picked it up again, giving the man in the photograph another quick kiss and could have sworn she felt . . . warmth . . .warmth? . . .coming from it. As she set it down, she wondered if she really saw the photograph give off a flash of light.

"Okay, I'm becoming certifiably weird. No more antipasto for me."

CHAPTER THREE

T"ake that, Sir Dickleth," was heard over the clash of swords as Sir Erek, a companion of the Round Table, advanced on the heartless jerk, err, mis-knighted knight. Amid the thrusts and parries and parries and thrusts, Sir Erek avoided the pathetic blows Sir Dickless tried to strike him with. "Lady Carrie-etta deserveth mucheth bettereth than you, you dicklesseth wonder."

"I am not dickleth, Sir Erek . . .merely a shrimp of a jerk with not much in the package and I will win back the fair Carrie-etta."

"I thinketh noteth thir Dickleth, err Dickless."

Lady Carrie-etta stood by on the sidelines, musing over how her hero had suddenly developed a lisp.

Carrie woke and shook her head, realizing it wasn't a lisp at all, but her dream hero, the ever charming Erek, was merely speaking in a Shakespearean type dialect which was definitely out of place if he was one of Arthur's knights. "Well it was a dream so he can talk anyway he wants as long as we get to the good part."

Trying to avoid looking over at the photograph, telling herself that she wasn't about to become obsessed with it, she glanced at the book she had been reading the night before. Why were there no heroes like in her books out and about anymore, only guys like Dean? She really, really did try to avoid looking at the photograph, but somehow it seemed to call to her. It was like the man in the tintype was somehow a part of her. Finally giving in to the urge to look at it once again, she picked it up and gazed into the enigmatic eyes of the warrior within.

Sighing, she asked aloud, "Why aren't you real and here with me?"

Not expecting an answer, she put it down and rolled over to go back to sleep and resume her dream . . .but not at the sword fight—at the part where Erek had vanquished Sir Dickless and she and Erek got to the good part.

Somewhere in the Mid-west, 1850

Meanwhile a hundred and sixty years ago, an Indian warrior and his friends stood before a white haired man with a camera. One of the warriors told the tall, good-looking man, "Don't do it, Black Eagle. Don't let the magic box take your spirit."

"Black Eagle, that's hokum. The camera doesn't take your soul or spirit. It's just an image of you, but it's not you. I promise you, nothing will change for you. You'll still be you," the white haired man assured him.

"I am not afraid. The magic box is nothing to me. Go ahead, Arthur Merle, take my photo-graph."

Chapter Four

Black Eagle stood, tall and proud, beside the *Sihásapa, Lakota* warriors on the dusty street of James River for the 'photo', as Mr. Arthur Merle called the paper with images of himself and other men from town. He had fought *mato* and *shunkaha*, what the whites called bears and wolves, hunted buffalo — there was no reason to fear the box the man before him used. A mere box could not take his spirit. Only *Nagi Tanka*, the Great Spirit, could do that, and hopefully that would only be at the end of a long, fruitful life.

The one sadness in his life rose from the thought that despite his bravery as a warrior his feats had not brought him a bride. There were maidens aplenty in his village who sought his eye, but none spoke to his heart. Perhaps if the box took a piece of him, that piece would bring him the bride he sought.

The box seemed most wondrous. Mr. Merle would point it at someone and in a short while their image would appear on a piece of paper. He had seen the pho-tos after some of the townsfolk had their pictures taken. They would change their hair, their clothing — the pho-to remained as they were on that day.

"Black Eagle." Running Elk tugged at his arm trying to pull him away. "You will be forever trapped in that position."

"I think that is not so. Look at how many of the town had their pho-tos taken and still walk about free. Who knows, maybe the maiden of my dreams will find her way to me from this taking."

The sound of Manfred Mann singing Doo-Wha-Ditty extra loud jarred Carrie awake once again the next morning. Usually, she relied on the alarm because she'd be up reading till all hours of the morning. Today, she needed it because sleep had eluded her. She couldn't stop thinking about the nameless Indian warrior.

With a vengeance she hit the snooze for the third time. Taister, however, was a firm believer that at the first tinkling of the alarm his female person should rush from the warm bed to the kitchen to prepare his breakfast. He alternately meowed — right in her, ear of course — that plaintive meow that clearly indicated he was going to starve in a matter of moments — and pawed at her ear. Giving up on any hope of continuing that oh-so-lovely dream, once she'd fallen asleep, with Erek making love to her, Carrie crawled out of bed. Much to Taister's obvious chagrin, evidenced by his loud yowl and spitting at her slippers, she showered before making his breakfast.

Placing his dish in its appointed place she asked him, "Think maybe you can manage three bites this morning?"

The cat didn't even spare her a glance before he took his ritual two bites and strolled out of the kitchen for his first nap of the day. He temporarily stopped when Molly joined them in the kitchen and reached for her own cup of coffee

Peering over her coffee cup at her roommate, Carrie greeted her, "Ready to face the Red Queen today?"

"Yeah. Just a few more full days of her. I'm glad I worked four days over the weekend this week and I've got the next three days off. So how's Mr. Picky Pants?" Molly asked with a smile towards the big black cat. "Hmm, it's not that he's that picky, he's just . . ."

"A cat. What was it the Egyptians said?" Molly asked as she pulled milk from the refrigerator to go with their coffee.

"That cats were gods?"

Together they finished, " . . .and still believe we should continue to treat them as such." They both laughed, much to Taister's annoyance. He was sure to let them know as he stalked out the door to another busy day of doing 'cat things', starting with napping, followed by looking out the window and preparing his list of other 'cat things' to discuss with Carrie when she got home that night.

"He's got a lot on his mind this morning."

"I think it has something to do with me hitting the snooze three times."

"Well, I gotta get going. Vincent wants to go to dinner tonight so I'll see you when we get back."

"Where you guys going?"

"I have no idea. He's kind of spur of the moment when it comes to eating."

"I'd rather that than what Dean used to do."

"Which was?"

"Oh man, I never told you? He had his calendar set up so he'd eat at certain restaurants or eat certain foods on certain days during the month. Like the fifth was always Mei Lings, the tenth was Chico's Mexican."

"Dang. How anal."

"Tell me about it. I'm glad we broke up for more reasons than you can count. Oh! By the way, there's an antique show this weekend. Want to go if your work schedule allows?"

"Maybe, where is it?"

"Over in Miwok actually."

"Sure, I'll see if I can go in either a little late or leave a little early Saturday. Never know what, or who, will turn up, huh?"

"Try to get off early and we can hit that new sushi place you mentioned for dinner," Carrie told her.

"Sounds good to me. You looking for anything in

particular at the show?"

"No. Just want to check it out."

Molly glanced at the clock and rose. "Gotta go. See you later."

Carrie rose at the same time and headed to her room, intending to only grab her purse, when she felt drawn to her new photo. Giving in to the urge, she sat on the bed, picked it up and traced the contours of the warrior's face. It felt warm through the glass, almost like she touched a living man's cheek.

"I'm losing it, I'm really losing it." She moved to put it back on the nightstand, but just couldn't. "Who were you? Why am I so drawn to you?"

She held the photo to her chest and again warmth seemed to emanate from it. Snapping herself out of a fantasy before it could begin, she gave the man in the photo a quick kiss and put it back on the nightstand, convincing herself she was just being fanciful. A flash of light came from the photo.

"Probably just a ray of sunlight hitting the glass," she mumbled to herself.

Unable to check it out further right then, she rushed off to work. Carrie knew she was way over-qualified for the receptionist position she held at the Hastings Insurance Company, but she enjoyed what she did there. Far better than what Molly dealt with every day at her job. For years, Carrie had taken jobs that other people thought she should do, or she'd be good at, but she didn't enjoy them. Just because she was smart and good with computers didn't mean she had to work with them. She had enough money from her parents' trust fund that she didn't even really have to work, so when she saw the ad that Hastings had an opening for a receptionist, she took it. The job turned out to be exactly what Carrie wanted. Low stress, she didn't bring the work home with her, either physically or mentally and it gave her time to either read, or relive the books she read in her mind.

That was also where she'd met Dean. He was an associate attorney with Turnberg & Jeffers, the biggest law firm in the area with close to fifty attorneys working either in Napa or the surrounding counties. He'd come into Hastings one day to pick up some documents they needed for an insurance defense case that was going to trial, and wasted no time in asking Carrie out. She had agreed and the rest was history. Now, she hoped it stayed history. Now she wanted nothing further to do with Sir Dickless.

He was sweet enough to begin with, calling regularly, taking her to nice restaurants and fun events. He listened to her and even asked questions about the books she read. Then he began to show up late for dates, or not show up at all, calling later, telling her, "I'm sorry hon, I had to work late". Carrie told herself that the working late excuse was only a ploy in romance novels, but she learned the hard way slimeballs like Dean used it in real life, too.

Once again as she went about her day, answering phone calls from people who wanted to know their business hours, insurance claims, photocopying, faxing and the never ending envelope stuffing. It was easy to imagine herself in another world. Today it would be that Indian warrior whose face topped the bodies of her long ago heroes. Problem was, she didn't know his name.

"Well shoot, I'll have to come up with one. Hmmm."

Riding behind Erek on his stallion, she firmly gripped his waist as they picked up speed. He'd promised her he would come to take her for a ride today and that they would have what he called a 'sweet interlude' in a secluded glen he knew. As she grew comfortable with the pace the horse set, she brazenly moved her hand down his trim waist down towards his groin. Taking his member in a firm, yet gentle grip, she squeezed and then began to stroke . . . only to realize Erek wasn't wearing his usual clothing. No, it was some kind of leather or hide type fabric . . . and his legs were bare and . . .

Oh my!

His back and chest were . . . why they were bare too! And he no longer had long blond hair . . . it was black, black as night!

Carrie gasped the moment she realized she was no longer with Erek, but with the unknown Indian warrior!

"Carrie! Hellllooooo."

As with the day before, Maria stood in the doorway, her expression clearly concerned. Carrie quickly ran a finger over her lips and across her chin, hoping she wasn't drooling while lost in her fantasy. "Oh yeah, I'm fine, why?"

"Well, you called out, 'Oh no' pretty loud, like something really nasty happened and when I got here you were just kinda staring out in space. Did Dean call or come by to bother you again?"

Everyone at Hastings knew about her and Dean and, of course, his cheating on her. At first they thought him asking her out was romantic, with several of her co-workers talking about marriage looming on Carrie's horizon. When Carrie first realized that all with Dean wasn't so rosy, she'd kept it to herself. When Maria found her crying in the ladies' room one afternoon, the story came out—Dean had been sleeping around. Maria wasted no time spreading the word and Dean immediately became *persona non grata* at the agency. Maria became her self-appointed guardian.

"Oh yeah, sorry, no, no Sir Dickless, thank goodness. I just remembered, uh, I remembered that I needed to get something from the store on the way home."

Maria giggled, "O-kay. Umm, so Friday night we decided to go to Brady's after work for a drink. See if Vincent and Molly can join us, okay?"

"I will. I know she likes Brady's."

"Great."

Great, great . . . At least I'm only saying simple things when I call out like that. I can just see it "Erek, Erek, take me now! That would

25

sure raise some eyebrows. Finishing up her paperwork for the day, Carrie's mind again went back to her afternoon fantasy. Normally she'd think about the hero of the book she'd been reading just here and there . . .not like an ordinary event. But what happened today — it was like he was really there with her. Like her arms were really around him and stroking that soft, warm skin of his and that when she stroked his member — as they referred to a guy's cock in the romance books — it really did feel like it hardened with her touch.

She headed home, but found herself at Treasures and wandered in.

"Hey, Mr. Merle!" she called out.

He answered her from behind a shelf towards the back and she followed his voice through the rich assortment of treasures from other times and places to find him. "What's up, Carrie-girl?"

"Oh, nothing. I just wondered, well the photo you gave me yesterday . . . do you know much about it? About the men in it?"

"Well, let's see."

He took her arm, led her into his back office and offered her a cup of tea. It appeared to be an ancient Chinese tea set. She was sure that like almost every object in the shop, there was an intriguing story to go with it. That would wait for another time. Right now, the photograph completely occupied her thoughts.

Pouring the fragrant brew, he asked, "What exactly do you wanted to know?"

"I guess mainly about the Indian, the warrior. Do you know who he was? Did your ancestor ever tell you much about him, or anyone in the photo?"

"Well, let me think. He told me about it long ago . . ."

"So the relative that took it is still alive?"

"Alive? Well, not so you and I could actually sit and talk to him together now."

"I see. Can you remember anything he told you about the Indian?"

Mr. Merle thought for a moment or two, his eyes getting that faraway look he usually got when he told Carrie stories from long ago. It seemed the kindly man had an endless cadre of relatives who traveled the world over.

Once he mentioned a sister or cousin or some woman who wasn't the nicest person around and how pleased he was she never came to visit. Another time he briefly mentioned another sister who was really cool. When Carrie tried, out of politeness, to ask about them, Mr. Merle quickly changed the subject. His other relatives made their lives collecting the most fascinating items and objects all of which eventually ended up in Treasures. Each object he sold in his store seemed to have a spellbinding story to go with it. There were only two objects he wouldn't talk about. One was a really old mirror and the other a beautifully decorated sword kept in a glass case, the faint image of a mountain or rolling hill framed behind it. With the case mounted on the wall, way out of reach from anyone who entered the store it was hard to tell for certain just what that background was.

"As I recall, the Indian was one Black Eagle, a Lakota warrior of some renown in his tribe. Led lots of buffalo hunts, fought a few big bears, served as a guide with a few groups going west on the Oregon Trail. He was a tall man and a good lookin' one, too. But, from what I recall about hi — my ancestor sayin' that is — Black Eagle never married. He said that the one thing that Black Eagle really wanted for himself was a wife. Yet it was also the one thing that seemed to elude him. Word was he'd think on doin' most anything, anything at all, if it would bring him a bride.

"Now it wasn't that he didn't have women aplenty looking him over and letting him know they were interested. They just weren't the right one for him. I seem to recall hearing that he would have rather died of a broken heart than to have never known the love of a good woman. Story is he never did meet that special woman and died alone and lonely."

A tear trickled out of Carrie's eye and she sniffed, "That is so sad. Too bad he wasn't alive today. He'd have plenty of women to pick from, and would definitely find the right one."

"I'm thinking someone like you, Carrie. From the stories I heard about him, you would have been the perfect wife for him. But well, one hundred and sixty years is one hundred and sixty years, not like you could go back there and be with him, now is it?"

Carrie sighed, "That's so funny. Last night Molly and I were talking about living back in time. Wouldn't that be something, to be able to go back in time to be with the man of your dreams?"

So lost in her own speculation, Carrie missed the gleam that entered Mr. Merle's bright blue eyes. Before he could answer, the bell on the front door jangled announcing a customer. Carrie stood and told him she would see him soon and headed on home, thoughts of Black Eagle swirling in her head. Now she had a name, his name. When she kissed his photo goodnight tonight she could say his name.

Oh now I am really thinking crazy. I can't believe I'm already planning to kiss the picture good night again tonight!

A thought struck Carrie. Mr. Merle said she couldn't go back in time, but could someone come forward? If Black Eagle could come forward . . .okay, *I'm being totally fanciful now . . . time travel . . .only in my books, only in my romance books.*

Chapter Five

When Molly came in from dinner Carrie told her about the plans for Friday night and that the gang was hoping she and Vincent could join them.

"Yeah, sure. What the heck? Even if Vincent doesn't want to, I'll go."

"Great."

"If he's going to come, do you want me to see if he has a friend to set—"

"Absolutely not! No how, no way. I know you mean well, but right now I just need time for me. You know, kinda alone time before I get back into the dating thing."

"Carrie, it's been over a month and Dean was no great shakes. The guy is an ass and there's no reason for you to—"

"No reason except I really don't want to get back into the dating thing right now. I'm having fun just hanging with friends. I suppose since his butt was nothing to write home about, he had to be an ass to make up for his ass. Besides, I thought we were going to fix him up with the Red Queen?"

Molly snorted, "The Red Queen? That's a good one. Are you sure?"

Carrie knew Molly meant well. Since high school they had always been fixing each other up with dates. It amazed Carrie that they were never interested in the same guy. Right now though, Carrie wasn't ready to return to the dating scene. Then again, Molly was the reliable, practical, studious one and Carrie was the adventurous one always finding trouble. "We've had this conversation before."

"I know, I know. Well, let me know when you're ready."

"I will, but I don't think it's gonna be with a friend of Vincent's."

She headed for bed, and despite her best intentions, picked up the photo and traced Black Eagle's cheek, enjoying the warmth emanating through the glass. "Black Eagle," she whispered. "Why can't I meet someone like you now, in my world today? Why can't you be here to find me and be with me?"

As with the night before, she kissed the photo and this time looked for the flash, but it didn't come. She turned off the light and as she closed her eyes . . .*No, that was my imagination . . . there was no light coming from the photo last night and I didn't see it.* Carrie fell asleep, with fantasies of a romance novel starring herself and Black Eagle running through her mind. Images of him sharing her bed, his head on the pillow beside hers, his body curled around her, she couldn't help but feel someone like him would make her life complete.

Black Eagle lay on his back, staring up through the smoke hole of his teepee.

Last night he had a dream of a *winyan*, a woman with long brown hair and green eyes, dressed differently from even the white women of the nearby James River town. She called to him in the dream. He felt her arms around him, her cheek on his chest, sighing softly just before she raised her head, lips formed for a kiss. Then again today, while he rode on the hunt he could have sworn he felt a soft body leaning against his back, arms reaching around to his front, a hand on his manhood, a small, yet firm hand, stroking him to hardness. Yet he knew he was alone on his horse.

Unable to sleep, Black Eagle left his home and wandered out towards the edge of the village, his gaze focused at the stars. Near the river he chose a large rock to sit on and looked up to see a falling star. He had heard the *wichasha wakan*, the medicine man, tell some of the young women of the tribe that if they wished on such a star their wish would happen. *If it will work for a young woman, why not me?*

The fearless, brave warrior offered up his wish to the star. "End my lonely search . . . if the woman for me cannot find me, bring me to her."

The star seemed to suspend in space, to just hang there a moment as if it stopped to look down on the warrior, before it continued its descent to earth.

CHAPTER SIX

With a yawn, Carrie managed to tell Molly and Vincent, "That was a blast!" as the threesome walked into the house Friday night.

"You guys are totally crazy." Vincent answered her.

"Umm hmm, however, you have to admit we do have a good time when we're together." Molly told him.

"Oh I'm totally behind that. I love the Pink Shrimp, especially those cheese rolls." Vincent rubbed his stomach.

"I know." Carrie quickly glanced around their living room as if she had a great secret to share. Reaching into her purse she pulled out a baggie with several of the muffins—smooched, but still edible.

"Oh my God, you didn't!" Molly laughed while reaching for them. "These are the perfect post schnockering snack."

"And schnockered you were . . . are . . ." Carrie laughed.

"Who started that whole business of having a shot of schnapps after each strike?" Vincent asked.

"I think it was Manuel from accounting. If I remember correctly, he had the worst time of all of us bowling with skates on and decided that having shots would make it easier," Carrie told him.

"Uh huh. When Molly first told me about the roller bowling I thought she was messing with me. That's insane." Vincent shook his head.

"Rockin Lanes has been having roll-n-bowl nights for years." Molly smiled up at him.

"Well, I've still got a buzz going so I'm going to grab a few aspirin and hit the sheets. Night Mol, Vincent." Carrie waved and started down the hall.

"Night."

Looking at her reflection in the dimmed down bathroom light as she brushed her teeth, Carrie thought not about the night's festivities, but wondered — not for the first time — what made guys think she was a push over. *Good thing marriage isn't a priority for me at this point.*

Still, she wondered, why she couldn't find a decent guy like Vincent. He clearly liked and cared for Molly. He was cute, too. Now, his friends were . . . well they weren't Vincent. They were nice guys, but went off on these diatribes that she just couldn't relate to.

One friend, Fred, had gone on about how the stories about aliens in the *Truth Now* newspaper were about real life events. He really believed there were three headed men or that Elvis was still alive and living at some other singer's ranch in Southern California.

Pushing aside thoughts of Fred's alien beings Carrie set her dream thoughts on a knight named Erek and how one day he might just ride into her life.

But it wasn't the virile and dashing Erek who rode through her dreams. Instead it was fleeting glimpses of a man with long, dark hair, holding her close while stars peeked through the velvety sky that took her through the night. She most definitely did not welcome the alarm the next morning.

Molly left a note that she couldn't get off from work and for Carrie to enjoy the antique show if she went. That was fine with Carrie, because she had some things she'd been meaning to do but had put off. The rest of the weekend breezed by, with all the usual events including a few harassing phone calls from Dean. He'd stopped making them for awhile, but suddenly this weekend he started up again.

"Must be that time of the month for him."

Their arguments were escalating and before she hung up

on him, he yelled something about marrying her. She wondered, not for the first time, if the guy was totally certifiable. He had started the constant calling right after she dumped him and after the first week of it, she called the police.

They said there wasn't much they could do, since he wasn't really threatening her and he'd eventually get tired of it. They suggested caller ID, which helped if she remembered to use it. They did call him and tell him to back off and he had for a time. Now, here he was again.

Of course, there was always the answering machine. He'd finally stopped leaving long rambling messages after Molly picked up a call in the middle of him leaving one, and made fun of him on the phone. If there was one thing Dean hated, it was people making fun of him. Now he just called and called and hoped she'd pick up.

"What a loser," she muttered.

"I think I'm becoming a staid old maid." Carrie told Molly over breakfast a week or so later.

"How come?" Molly asked, brushing a crumb of oatmeal from the corner of her lip.

"I'm falling into a pattern."

"Um, well you already have a routine, more or less."

"Mm-hmmm. I guess I'm adding to it. It's not like I *want* to be a creature of habit or anything like that. Like some old fogey."

"Shudder to think! You're not an old fogey. You're just, well, organized."

"Not as much as you are. My life is boring. It's gray, gray, gray and not even shades of gray. Think about it, unless it's a holiday, five days a week I get up for work, feed Taister, go to work, do my job, come home, have dinner, check email and play on the computer and then read until I go to sleep."

What she didn't mention was that as she fell asleep, even when she was dating someone, she'd fantasize about the hero of whatever romance she happened to be reading. It was really wonderful, truth be told. With each book she traveled to ancient Egypt, rode across the Scottish Moors, traveled to the old West, saw the sites of modern day Paris and flew in spaceships to planets not yet discovered. Every adventure was done in the arms of the most gorgeous, most hunky, and most considerate and loving men imaginable.

Too bad none of them were real.

Of course, when she dated someone, the routine changed. Then the guy she dated slipped in to be part of the fantasy. She always knew when the relationship was running its course, about the time she began to imagine the hero from her latest novel vanquishing her date. And she had some good times with those dates — miniature golf, bowling, in-line skating, skiing — you name it. When they made love, it was good, sometimes really good. A few even had those cover model perfect bodies . . . but when it ended, it ended and she still had those hot romance novels to turn to.

"You do stuff on weekends, we have a blast when we've got the same days off. You've always been the one thinking of new things to do. Think about it, since high school and college, we've doubled dated a lot. If you're seeing someone and I'm not, we fix each other up. And we've had some crazy times, like when we went on vacation in Virginia Beach and went to Oceana naval base and went to the big Wednesday night party. Remember when you got up on one of the speakers and danced?"

"*That* maneuver got me in big trouble with the MPs."

"Uh huh, however you *did* meet one very, very hot jet jockey who was, to say the least, yummy."

"That's true." Carrie smiled in remembrance of the F/A-18 pilot she'd met on that outing. "Or how about the time we decided to run the Bay to Breakers Race and left home like about 3:00 a.m. to be on time for the race?"

"That's right! And you brought along a nice hot beverage to keep them warm while we waited. Those hot toddies had more butterscotch rum . . ."

They walked half the race, met some really hot guys and — well — they made it to the finish line, but not the one out at the breakers. Or the time they had been out partying and took a short cut home and ran into the . . .well, never mind. Weekends were always something new and different and a break from the monotony of the week.

"So, you aren't dull."

"Maybe it's the backlash of the Dean thing. You know, when I met him, it looked like he might have been the one. When we first met he wined and dined me, sent me flowers at work, called two or three times a day and took me out every Friday and Saturday night. He seemed so considerate when he said he wanted to wait for us to go to bed until we were ready to think about a commitment. Although, Sir Dickless never said exactly what kind of commitment he thought about." She looked back on the beginning of the end of their relationship. Actually, once it began to end, it had died pretty quickly. "From what I saw the few times we double dated anyway, he's a born negotiator."

"Yeah. As a candidate for partner in his law firm, he always talked about finding situations where both sides could win. That was well and good, but it wasn't long before I noticed that whenever I disagreed with him he would tell me it was 'just my perception'. Like my feelings weren't real or didn't matter and that when I saw things differently I was the one who didn't get it."

"Now though, you do see he was loser and that your, ah hem, 'perceptions' were, and continue to be, right on target."

"Yeah. Mol, I gotta tell you, when I found him in bed with

Jolene Crane there was no question of perception on that one. She was flesh and blood and laying in his bed. The best though," Molly continued, "was when Dean did the down on the knee thing on the front steps and you walked past him, putting your hand on his forehead and pushing him backwards down the steps, at the same time telling him, 'You come near me again and I'm calling the police and reporting you as a stalker'."

"You do my voice pretty well." Carrie laughed, remembering how Dean got up and backed away and then had the nerve to call her that night, again asking her to marry him. It seemed he did that every time he called or ran into her lately. Marry him her patooti. Sir Dickless had a definite perception problem. "So what's going on now? Why so suddenly down on yourself?"

Carrie thought about her answer. Since 'La Pictura', as Carrie called that fateful day when she found Black Eagle's photograph, she had added a bit of spice or sugar to her routine. Now she not only kissed his photo good morning and before turning to him in her dreams at night, she fantasized about him throughout her workday. He was never far from her thoughts. Not like a romance story character, but more like the way a real live man should be. It was foolish, but she couldn't stop thinking about him and she really needed to.

"Nothing, not really. I just need to focus more on the real world, not the world of my books."

Deciding the best way to do that was to get to the bottom of the enigmatic Mr. Black Eagle, Carrie set about trying to find out about the warrior in the photo. Sitting at her desk Monday morning, she considered how best to begin.

"So what do I know?" Starting a dialogue with herself she began . . ."Let's be logical about this now, what do I know? He was an Indian . . . okay . . .what tribe? Mr. Merle said Lakota. What year? No clue. What state? One of the Dakotas, maybe. So what do I know? Mr. Merle's relative took the photo, which means a trip back to Treasures to see what, if anything he knows."

Stopping in after work, she brought her favorite shop owner a peppermint mocha and a pumpkin scone. When Mr. Merle saw Carrie enter, he put up the closed sign for the night and they sat in the little kitchenette in the back to talk.

"Mr. Merle, I got to tell you, every day it seems I get more and more interested in the man in the photograph — Black Eagle. Are you sure you don't know more about him?"

"Like what?" he asked around a bite of the scone that he was clearly enjoying.

"Well, do you know what year the photo was taken?"

"Hmm, off the top of my head, no, I can't say. But let me check through my family's papers and such and see what I can find out for you. Will that work?"

"It sure would. Mr. Merle, can I tell you something in confidence?"

"Of course, Carrie. Of course. You can tell me anything any time."

"Well, this is going to sound really weird. I'm sure it's just my imagination but, Mr. Merle, sometimes I think that there is more to the photo than just, well, just the photo. Like he, Black Eagle, is alive."

"Now that's interesting."

"It is? Why? You don't think that's crazy talk?"

"No. Not when you understand what he and his people probably believed."

"Which was?"

"Back when that photo was taken, the Indians thought that the camera would capture their spirits and keep them in the box. It would have been very brave of Black Eagle to have his picture taken. And who knows, maybe a part of him stayed with that photo."

"So you think he's stuck in the photo?"

"Oh no, no, not that he's stuck, just that maybe a small part of his. — now what do those psychics call — his energy — might be attached to it. Not a bad thing, but you just may feel that."

"I think I see. Well, that helps, I think. I would appreciate it if you could, when you get a chance, look through your papers, though, and see if you can find out any more about him. For some reason the man just fascinates me."

"I will, Carrie, I will. You have a good night now." Showing her to the door she glanced up at a sword, stopping suddenly just in front of where it was mounted on the wall. "Something wrong, Carrie?"

"Err, no. Must be the light."

"What do you mean?"

"The sword in the case. I know it's been there for as long as I've been coming in here."

"Indeed it has. What about it?"

"Like I said, it's probably the light."

"But?"

"Well the picture behind it. It looks brighter, you can see the hill behind it a little better. It's like there's more light in the picture. Anyway, I gotta go. I'll talk to you soon. Thanks, Mr. Merle."

"Sure thing, Carrie. Sure thing."

CHAPTER SEVEN

As the door closed behind her Mr. Merle turned to look at the ancient sword. He narrowed his eyes and studied it, looking for what he thought was only a glimmer of light. Shrugging when he didn't see anything different, he tidied up a few items. Carrie seemed such a sweet, kind and generous young woman. It's too damn bad none of the men she's dated ever saw what a treasure she was. Merle figured she deserved someone strong and brave and who would cherish her for herself. A man with the courage of his convictions who wanted a wife he could love and share his life with."

He shuffled over to the sword case, looking beyond the gleaming metal and sparkling jewel encrusted on the hilt to the image behind it.

"Didn't work out? That, dear friend is an understatement, don't you think?"

Startled by the appearance of the one person who truly knew him, he managed, "Vivianne. What brings you here?"

"You. Your—work, and things not working out."

"And why would you think I was thinking about something not working out?"

"I know you. You don't spend all the time together we have and not be able to read each other's thoughts. That first relationship you tried to bring together and then salvage was a disaster. You must admit it."

"That was long ago. A past best forgotten."

"Best forgotten? When you stand before the remembrances of that time, how can you speak of forgetting?"

"They remind me to forget."

She crossed to him, the gossamer thin white gown that flowed around her like a cloud gave the illusion of revealing, yet concealed so completely. Dark hair, worn loose, reaching past her knees adorned only with a slim silver circlet, a heady contrast to the purity of the gown. She reached out and laid a hand on his cheek. "Do you truly think it would please them to be forgotten? Lying as they do, awaiting the time to return?"

"At times I wonder if they could, would they do it in a different manner."

"How different? What the gods set in motion . . ."

"So you say. You must admit since then, I have made some good matches."

"Hmm, good matches. That is akin to 'What good is having magic if you can't do something fun with it'?"

"Your idea of fun, and mine, are two totally different things."

"Another understatement."

"So Vivianne, my dear, why have you come? Do you miss me?"

"Miss you? How can I miss you when in the blink of an eye I can be with you? Ah, do not look so sad, dear friend. I know what you hope for. You hope to bring couples together in love; it cannot always be."

"So you say. Would you care for some tea?"

"Yes. Thank you."

She followed him into the small kitchen, seeming to float above the ground.

"I think you would like this time. There is all manner of teas available and some of the most tasty treats."

"I think you have said something to that effect in each time you have lived." Her laughter floated across the room like an otherworld chime.

"Yes, well, it's true," he grumbled.

"Come, come. T'was just a joke."

"A poor one. So, which would you like? English Breakfast, Earl Grey, Chai?"

"Surprise me."

He turned and winked, "Don't I always?" He put the water on to boil and considered the different blends of teas, finally selecting a spiced apple brew. While the water boiled and tea steeped he asked, "So, tell me, what does bring you here?"

"I told you, I missed you."

"And?"

"And I saw you with your young friend. Is she really a sweet and caring person?"

"Very much so. And before you ask, I had nothing to do with her recent break up. He found and courted her on his own, and she made the decision to send him packing on her own."

"I am glad you have made such a friend."

"Thank you. And?"

She shrugged. "Sometimes I wonder that you do not see what is in front of you."

"Not everything is seen in a glass or pool of water."

"No. 'Tis true. I am speaking of what is in front of you. Has anyone inquired about the sword?"

"No. Not recently. A few people over time have asked about it, as well as the mirror. They were curious about its history, where it came from and as they couldn't buy it, where could they find a similar one. I do not say much."

"And they are pleased with your answers?"

"I explain that it has been in my family for years and years, a few centuries and selling it would be a wrong to my line." He knew she knew he was always very careful with it, making sure to cover it each night. "Of course it would be easy to just store it elsewhere, but to do my work I need it close at hand."

Picking up her cup, she took a tentative sip. "Mmmmm. You are right, this is the finest I have had."

He handed her the container, "Then please, take this with you when you go. Unless—will you stay a spell?"

"No, dear friend, I cannot. I only came to see how you fared and to see if you had any news. We will see each other again soon. I feel that times are changing and we will be in each other's company more often."

"I'd like that. I miss you."

"That, my dear, is your choice. You are the one who chooses to travel from place to place, unable to forgive yourself for one small error."

" 'Twas not that small, Vivianne."

"In the history of man, yes. Keep an eye on the Tor, my friend. I feel a restlessness." Container and cup in hand, she faded as if she were never there. Tidying up the kitchen, setting all to rights, he gave one last look around the shop, making sure the mirror and sword were well covered before locking up for the night. It was good to see Vivianne, and he hoped, one day, she would stay longer and really talk, not just flit in and out of his life. People came and went; Vivianne was always somewhere there, in his heart, his mind, and his life. As he walked up the steps to his small apartment above the shop, he looked to the sky through a small captain's window and saw a falling star tumble its way to Earth.

There's always something magical about those falling stars, always something magical.

"Hey girlfriend, what's up?" Molly asked, as she turned on a light.

"Hey, Mol," Carrie answered without looking up. "Not much, just doing a little research."   Pulling up a chair, Molly looked at the page on the screen. "Black Eagle, huh?

Who's he?"

"You're going to think I'm crazy."

"I already *know* you're crazy. It's part of your charm. So who's Black Eagle?"

"The man, the Indian, in the photograph I got a couple of weeks ago."

"You still on that? Girlfriend, we gotta get you a new man! A real one, not one that lives in an old picture or one of your books."

Carrie debated with herself a few moments before deciding that if Molly had survived some of their earlier antics, she'd survive this. If nothing else, she'd think it was just the break-up with Dean causing her to be a bit irrational. "Yeah, I'm still on it. So, Molly, listen. There's something weird about that photo."

"Nothing weird about the photo. The weird is you. It's part of why I've been your friend all these years. You make me look sane."

"Fine." Carrie turned back to the computer, her shoulders stiff.

"This is really serious for you, isn't it? Wanna tell me what's going on?"

"Look, I know this is going to sound bizarre. Even I think it's weird. But, well, when I got the photo I thought that the Indian in it stood out. And, well, okay, this is totally juvenile, but I couldn't help it. A few times at night I held the photo and a few other times well I . . . I . . . ."

"Carrie, did you kiss the photo?"

"Yes! How did you know?"

She chuckled. "I know you. It's completely something you would do. So you have a thing for an Indian in a photo that's like a hundred and sixty years old. Carrie, he's gone, dust. Kaput. We need to find you a living man. Not some guy in a picture. Not some guy on romance novel cover and certainly not some wimpola like Dean. You need a for real, solid, decent guy."

"I know, I know. I'll get on it. So listen, though, I talked to Mr. Merle about it—the photo, not my lusting after a guy in the photo—and he said that the Indians believed that if someone took their picture that the camera would steal their spirit. He also told me that this Black Eagle was just a really sad guy 'cause he never met a woman to marry and fall in love with. Can you imagine a guy like him not being able to find the right woman?"

"Carrie, like I said, this guy was alive like one hundred and sixty years ago, you don't know the first thing about him and even if you did, he's gone. There's no way you can meet and fall in love with him. Besides, for all you know he could have been a major jerk. Even jerkier than Dean."

"No one is jerkier than Sir Dickless."

"I like that—Dickless. So his . . ." She wiggled her index finger in front of Carrie. "It was sized to fit his shrimpy bod?"

"Totally."

"Well, what's done is done. I think it's time we thought about you meeting a new guy. Let me ask Vincent if he's got a friend we can double date with this weekend."

"Uh, I don't think so. I'm glad you guys are getting along well, but the last two friends of his that he thought would be great dates for me were, well—I don't think so."

"Yeah. We are. Good together. Although sometimes I think he's getting tired of the crap from my job."

If her blush was any indication, they were doing more than getting along well. Vincent was a keeper. "Mol, Vincent is a steady guy, one you can count on. He's not going to change friends 'cause he's dating a terrific woman. I know he sees beyond Julie's crap." Molly stood. "I've got to get going. I'll see you in the morning."

"Night," she called as Molly headed off to bed. As Carrie

prepared to turn off the light, she vowed that tonight she was not going to pick up the photograph. She was not going to hold it to her chest and she was not going to kiss the man in the picture. She was not.

She simply was not going to go there tonight. She turned out the light and lay there and lay there and turned her head. Just for a second—and knew, without a doubt *knew* a light flashed in the photograph—almost like a falling star had passed over the man standing there.

Chapter Eight

"Shit!" Dean Welman spat. He'd been hoping to get out of work early this Friday afternoon for a long weekend. Not that Dean ever really put in a full day's or week's work. In fact, his whole life he only put into school or work whatever he had to. He just skated by. He learned early on how to manipulate people—read all the big motivation gurus and acted like he believed in their theories.

To date, his biggest claim to fame seemed to be being an expert in quoting anything and everything from Covey and Dr. Phil. If he wanted someone to do something, he would bring up the platitude master of the hour and quote whatever fit, for what he wanted to get.

Someone once told him he had the Tom Sawyer thing down because he could pretty much get anyone to do anything for him. Best part about that was if the project came out wrong, he could blame someone else. His parents tried to get him to take some personal responsibility, with little or no success. Even his teachers at school were taken in by his apparent charm. If the clichés didn't work, he managed to allude to how hard it was for a short guy to get far in a tall man's world. The ploy worked every time. If people didn't buy into his peacemaker act, he had them feeling sorry for him.

That's why things with Carrie frustrated him. At first she fell for his line, but she got wise to him. He figured if she fell for his win/win arguments once, she'd do it again. All he needed was some time to talk to her. Today, he hoped to leave work physically—as well as mentally—earlier in the day. His wish, however, was not to be granted. Just as he logged off his computer, Mr. Turnberg called him into his office.

"Sure, Mr. Turnberg, no problem, I hoped for some time to chat with you, so this works out great." He worked to make his voice warm and appropriately enthusiastic about the meeting.

That wasn't quite how he felt. Turdberg probably wants to talk to me about getting married again. Shit. Why can't they just leave me be, just give me the damn partnership and let it go? As if being married makes money. Hell, I bring in more business and bill more hours than anyone else in this stupid firm. Works out great my ass.

Stopping at his doorway, he closing the door halfway and looked into the mirror he had hung on the back. Giving himself a close look, he opened his mouth and peered inside before clamping his teeth together. He checked to be sure none of the greenery he ate for lunch was in his teeth. There was, in fact, a piece of broccoli between his front teeth.

After picking it out, he turned his head this way and that a few times while double-checking the expressions he planned to use. Carrie had caught him practicing his expressions one time, which embarrassed him to no end. She said she believed him when he said he learned in his trial techniques class in law school, but he could tell from the doubt in her eyes she didn't really think it was so.

Carrie's intelligence amounted to a double-edged sword — he liked her being smart enough to help him figure things out, but not that she could figure out his motives. Giving himself one last appraising look, he headed to his meeting with Mr. Turdberg, admonishing himself yet again to be very careful to call him *Turn*berg and not his favorite nickname for his immediate boss.

When he knocked on the door said boss summoned him into the office. "Dean, how are you?"

"I'm well, Mr. Turnberg and you?"

"Fine, fine. You and that lovely Miss Taylor have plans this weekend?"

"Of course."

"Good. Glad to hear it. Have a seat, have a seat."

The office smelled of stale cigar smoke, something old man Turnberg told his associates was a sign of wealth. Dean thought it was a sign of a date with the porcelain god because it turned his stomach. As Dean sat in the under-stuffed, stiff backed, incredibly lumpy leather chair that had him sitting below eye level from Turnberg he tried to mentally prepare for whatever the busy body wanted to talk to him about.

"What are you two planning to do?" Turnberg asked, catching Dean off guard.

"Planning to do?"

"Yes. You and Carrie. What are your plans for the week-end?"

Well crap, he would ask that. Why would he care? How the hell do I know? Now I not only have to explain why we aren't married yet, I have to make up something really incredible we're doing.

Dean cleared his throat, "Um, well, I'm not too sure. Carrie had some things she was interested in doing—she—she's a real fan of antiques, you know."

It was antiques she liked, wasn't it? He thought back over the conversations he and Carrie had, as well as the few times he brought her to company events, and was pretty sure she'd said something about antiques. Hopefully it was because she liked, rather than hated, them. Knowing Turnberg, he would remember if it was modern art or some other type of things she liked, so he hoped he had it right.

"Yes, I do remember her mentioning something about that at the holiday party. She likes to go to those antique shows, and all?"

"Definitely. In fact, our wedding will probably be real old fashioned, you know, like those re-enactments. The Civil War era is one of her absolute favorites. Knowing her, she'll have me decked out as a Union officer or some such thing."

"That would be very charming. Say, listen, you ever take her out Mendocino way? There are a few places out there I can't keep my Beth Anne out of. They've got some shops up there that have a lot of the items that'd go with that kind of period wedding."

"Well, you know how it is up that way," he sought for the right word, "very romantic."

"Yes, yes it is. The more romantic the better." Turnberg looked down at some papers on his desk for a moment. Picked them up and tapped the up and down to align the pages. "So, I spent the better part of today looking at your stats for last quarter."

"Yes, sir?"

"Your billable hours are up, but it seems your cases aren't moving along real well. Seems you aren't getting your discovery out in a timely manner."

"Ah, yes, well, I spoke with Lisa about that just the other day. She was — well, you know how it is for a newlywed, planning the wedding and all. Even when she was at work she was, ahhhh, you know, doing wedding plans."

"So you are telling me Lisa was neglecting her work to plan her wedding? And doing it on company time?"

"Ah, yes, sir. I didn't want to say anything, she needs the job and all, you know?"

"I do, Dean. And as much as we like our employees to be married, we really can't allow our private lives to interfere with work. Image is one thing. Productivity is the bottom line. I understand if it's awkward for you, so if you like, I can have Jolene let her go."

Jolene Crane — Head chopper extraordinaire. She came across as all warm, friendly and caring, but was a cold-hearted piece of work. The woman would fire her mother if it would get her something she wanted. Dean knew the secretaries hated her — he wasn't too fond of her himself — however she definitely knew how to please a man between the sheets. *Someone ought to let Jolene go — to the moon.* "Sir, I'm not sure that letting Lisa go is the right thing to do. After all, she is a newly — "

"Dean, we can't afford to drop things like this. Business is business."

"Begging your pardon, sir. No statutes were run by the delays, and since she's married now, all the brou-ha-ha is over, right? If we want to make this a win/win situation, how about I talk to her and make sure she's back on track and if she can promise to get back on top of things we give her another chance?" Dean smiled to himself at his perceived cleverness bringing up a Covey-ism.

"You sure?"

"Yes, sir, I am. And, you know, Carrie is fond of her and if we were to lose Lisa, well . . . ." Dean put on his best 'the little lady will put me in the dog house' look, glad he'd practiced before going to Turnberg's office.

"Fine, fine. You got a little time before the end of the day, so why not take Lisa out for a coffee and explain to her about paying more attention to her job?"

"Great idea, Mr. Turnberg, great idea." *You dumb chauvinistic slob — take Lisa for coffee, my ass.* "We'll have this all worked out in no time."

"Good. Good. You keep Carrie happy and those billables up now, you hear?"

"Yes, sir. Have a good weekend, sir."

"You and Carrie do the same. You tell her I think that re-enactment idea is great and I'm looking forward to that wedding reception."

"I will, sir."

Walking back into his office, it was all Dean could do not

to slam the door.

That was close. Good thing that stupid broad Lisa got married. Man, if she hadn't he wouldn't have anyone to blame for not getting that discovery done. Damn, doesn't old man Turdberg realize that pursuing a woman who dumped you takes time? Hell, no. Bet he never had a woman walk out on him. Now he had to waste time and money taking Lisa for a coffee and getting her on board with pretending she was busy with her wedding. Gees, all he wanted to do was get out a little early. Now he had to do a bunch of work this weekend and pretend he took Carrie up the coast. *Knowing old Turdberg, he's gonna want action photos of our romantic weekend in Mendocino. If the guy were on Twitter, he'd want hourly tweet updates. Crap, crap, crap.*

Checking his face in the mirror once again, practicing a series of smiles, he made note of how his jaw and cheeks felt with one particular smile and headed out the door to Lisa's desk. Standing in front of his secretary, Dean plastered on the smile he'd practiced. If Lisa thought he looked odd or funny when he moved his jaw side to side a couple of times while he drew his lips back to reveal he had clenched teeth in a grimace-type grin, she gave no indication. "Dean?"

"Lisa. Yes, I'd like to take you for a coffee."

"Now? It's Friday and almost four. I want to finish up a few things before the weekend."

"Yes. Well, they can wait till next week. Why not think of it as an early start to the weekend."

"Well, all right." She was clearly reluctant to leave with him.

When she leaned over to log off her computer, he stopped her, "We'll be back before five. Just a quick coffee."

"Sure."

Looking at the clock as they left, Dean did a quick mental calculation on how much time he'd have to waste while pretending to talk to Lisa and still be able to leave at a reasonable hour. Not as reasonable as he planned, but reasonable enough.

Entering the café, he ordered their coffees, grousing to himself that of course she'd want one of the expensive lattes. But with a receipt he could put it on a client's bill and get reimbursed. "Wanna go find a table for us, Lisa?"

"Sure."

Coming to the table, coffees in hand, he put on his best 'friendly boss' persona as he sat down. "Well, congrats again on your wedding, Lisa."

"Thanks, again, Dean. It *was* two months ago."

"Yeah, I know, but you know how we at Turnberg and Jeffers feel about marriage and all and I'm all over that. I think the right people should be married to each other and you and your, um, your husband sure are."

"Craig."

"Excuse me?"

"His name. My husband's name is Craig."

"Right, yes, Greg."

"Craig." She shook her head and huffed. "Did you need something, Dean?"

"Oh, right. So when you were getting ready for your wedding I didn't want to put a lot of pressure on you and wanted to be sure you weren't stressed from work." He paused, waiting for her to thank him for his consideration. When she didn't he continued. "So anyway, I just wanted to warn you that I'll be doing a ton of work this weekend to catch up, so don't be alarmed on Monday when you walk in to a stack of files."

"Oh, sure. No problem. Is that all?"

"Yup. Just wanted to let you know that I had been holding back on the work and that I'll be catching up this weekend."

"Okay."

"And, of course, to congratulate you on your nuptials as

well."

"Well, thanks. So I guess we should be getting back now, huh?"

"Yeah, we should. I know I want to get out on time. Drink up your coffee, huh? Don't want to waste an expensive drink like that."

Dean strolled into his office, pleased with himself that he had avoided a fiasco with Turnberg and had gotten Lisa on his side. He wasn't pleased he'd be spending the weekend working, but such was life. As soon as he made partner he'd have some entry level associate taking on all the hard work, so he could do what he did best—nothing.

CHAPTER NINE

A s with many nights since the day he allowed Mr. Merle to take his photograph, Black Eagle woke again in the dark hours. Something or someone called to him. He felt it. It was as if a force reached out to him.

He had a fleeting remembrance of a dream where he saw a *wiwasteka*, a woman, with long brown hair and eyes as green as a meadow in springtime beckon to him. She stood in a strange place, with buildings of stone and strange *maza*, or what the whites called metal, objects that appeared to contain people moving on the ground behind her. Her clothes were strange for other *wasicun winyan*, white women. Her legs often showed when she wore a dress, or he would see her in the pants some men heading further west wore. Women in nearby James River never wore such clothing. With her, often in her arms, was a small black *igmuwatogla*, perhaps a panther cub, and she would feed it from a small tin. Her own food came from either a small black box or a larger white one. In the glimpses of the *wiwasteka* she always seemed to smile with genuine warmth.

At other times he would see her in a room with white walls that held many pictures, not at all unlike the photographs Mr. Merle took. She would sit behind a metal box and move papers around.

Sometimes she would be deep in concentration, yet the warm smile would often appear. Then there were occasions when it looked as if she had somewhere better to be and other times she would seem so sad he would want to reach out through the dream to hold and comfort her.

Each night he would have dreams of her and in each one he would see her do something strange and wonderful. Yet for all the wonderful things he saw around her, despite her welcoming smile, she herself seemed so sad. He wanted to help the *winyan*, but she lived only in his dreams. She was not real, only a *winyan wanagi*, a dream woman. Yet something about the dark haired woman called to a deeper part of him.

Dreams held messages. He believed this completely. They told of the future, gave warnings, showed he and his people things that needed to be known. Was she a *winyan wanagi* spirit come to show him the future? Or, was she in fact his future?

He'd held off approaching the *wichasha wakan* about the dreams for the past few days, mostly because he did not want to appear a fool. After all, who was he to receive such signs? Yet if they held an important message for his tribe, if the woman were trying to tell him something important through the dreams, did he not need to seek guidance?

He decided that if three more dreams came to him he would seek that guidance. That way he would give the *wanagi*, if indeed the woman were one, a chance to convey her message more clearly to him. Another dream came to him again this night. Like the wispy clouds on a summer's day, tendrils of thoughts wove their way to his mind. Again to-night he left his warm teepee and stepped out into the cool-ness of the night.

Once again as he sat on the flat rock near the water's edge, the *peta* now holding the chill of the dark. He sat in contem-plation but a moment before he saw a star streak across the sky.

This time, however, there was a difference. As the dazzling light flew across the sky it was not with a sudden brilliance that faded as it tumbled to earth. This time it seemed to stop, as if gazing down on him, watching him, before it fell to the earth. In times before a star's descent was a pleasure for his eyes, a reminder of the vastness of the sky. This time, however, he felt a crushing weight on his body just before he felt lighter than air. Then he was falling, falling, falling like the star. His body moved through the darkness of the night, just before he felt as if he was shrinking, getting smaller and smaller, as small as the pho-to of himself that Mr. Merle had taken. He looked up and saw what at first he thought was another shooting star and then fell into darkness.

For the first time she could remember doing so, Carrie woke before the alarm. It was even still a little dark outside. Gees, she woke even before Taister! And he was prince of early wakings. This was a total first.

Maybe she only heard Molly coming in early from her job.

She put a hand out to smooth Taister's silky fur and yup, there was Taister, his furry little head on the pillow next to hers — yup, his furry little . . .

Now wait just a minute — .where is Taister's furry little head?

She groped the warm bodying lying where Taister should have been. Either something happened to Taister's fur or there was someone with long silky hair in her bed with her. As her hand moved down through the soft hair she came in contact with warmth. The warmth of someone's skin. While satiny smooth at first, there was a small indentation, a rough spot or two — clearly someone's arm. She slid her hand down that arm before allowing it to travel back up, seemingly of its own accord, to connect with what had to be the chest of whomever was beside her in her bed. Flat. Well, not exactly flat. No, more like well defined — like the guys that graced the covers of her romance novels.

Curiosity took over and she slid her hand further down, across his abdomen, over his hip, down his thigh, stopping just at the point where what felt like well-defined muscle sloped downward towards his knees. This was clearly not Taister. Not unless the fluffy black cat suddenly learned to shape shift and that wasn't likely. Heck, she didn't even read those kinds of books so her imagination wouldn't conjure up one now, would it? Could it?

Like a bolt of lightning searing her brain she realized what she was feeling *Oh my God! It's a naked man in my bed! Oh my God, oh my God, oh my God!*

Suddenly wide awake she told herself, "Okay, don't panic — It's okay, Carrie, it's okay, you haven't lost your mind, just somehow a naked man got into your bed."

Sitting up half way, in the dim pinkish light of dawn cresting the horizon, peeking in her window, she looked over at the man sleeping peacefully next to her. He was tall, easily over six feet, powerfully built and had that long silky black hair that just seemed to call out to her to tangle her fingers in it.

Either I'm having a really, really, really good dream or I've totally lost it.

Opting to find out which it was, she reached out a hand to touch him once again and then stopped. It crossed her mind to wonder just how touching the naked man could tell her whether or not he was real or a figment of her obviously delusional mind. But still . . .

Glancing towards the foot of the bed she saw Taister sitting there, his demon yellow eyes calmly focused on the sleeping man. Now that in and of itself was interesting. Taister never had much truck with the men she dated. In fact he'd be outright, well, catty. He'd express his displeasure from something as blatant as clawing a shirt to pieces to something as subtle as peeing in a shoe. He did that to Dean, peed in his shoe, on more than on occasion. Carrie figured she'd sleep with Dean one more time if there was a guarantee Taister would pee in another shoe or two. Belatedly, it occurred to

Carrie that the man in her bed was not someone she'd had a date with. He just sort of showed up in her bed. Now that wasn't possible, right?

So clearly this man, this naked man in her bed, was a figment of her imagination because if Taister was okay with him . . .

Carrie looked closer, taking in his long dark hair, the handsome face with eyebrows that begged her to reach out and trace them, the smooth powerful chest, the loincloth, the . . .

Loincloth?

Okay, so he wasn't totally naked. After all a loincloth, no matter how skimpy it was, was still an article of clothing. Like a bikini or a thong, right?

Definitely awake Carrie bolted upright and twisted to look at the photo. Something was wrong with the photo. Something was missing. Black Eagle was no longer in the photograph. He was in bed with her—he was the naked man in her bed!

Black Eagle's eyes fluttered open just as Carrie collapsed, unconscious, beside him.

CHAPTER TEN

Black Eagle lay still, not daring to move, looking through barely opened eyes to take in the room around him. He quickly acknowledged that he no longer sat on the large rock near the river. He was in a room and not a room he could remember being in before.

It was a very feminine room with pale lavender walls, frilly white curtains with purple flowers and he was lying on something that felt softer than anything he'd ever laid on before. His quiet perusal of the room ended abruptly when he came eyeball to eyeball with a baby *igmuwatogla*!

The panther kit had slowly crept up his belly and now sat on his chest licking its paw while looking down at him with its yellow eyes. He felt somewhat relieved when it seemed to be the panther cub from his dreams. It must then be his totem! The little panther stopped its licking to take full measure of the man it sat on. Nothing would have convinced Black Eagle the little panther was not grinning down at him, as if he had just played some wonderful joke on someone. Knowing how sharp their claws could be, Black Eagle lay perfectly still. The little one couldn't really harm him, but if its mother was around, she surely would. So he would simply lie still and hope the mother cat called to her kit, and that the kit would leave before he was injured.

But where was he? He shifted his gaze to his right to see the *winyan* lying beside him. Her long brown hair was a silky veil covering a voluptuous body, her breasts full and straining against her shift, almost the whole of her legs exposed where the shift had ridden up. He groaned to himself — a *wasi-cun winyan,* a white woman. If he was not mistaken, it was the same one from his dreams. How had he ended up in an unknown bed in an unknown room with not only a *wasicun winyan,* but also a panther cub?

Could this be a wondrous dream with messages for his people? Or was he really with the woman and baby panther from his dreams? To his surprise, even with all the unknowns, just the sight of the woman caused his groin to tighten. Then it struck him.

Mr. Arthur Merle. His *colapi,* what the whites called his friends, were right, Mr. Arthur Merle had not only taken his spirit with his magic box. The old man had somehow managed to put him in a bed with a white woman. He wasn't sure if he was relieved or not when she began to stir, her hand reaching out and connecting with his arm held closely to his side.

Her hand slid slightly up that arm before moving across to his belly, over his abdomen and again continuing its path upward to his chest. If he thought his manhood had hardened at the sight of her he was surprised to find himself hardening even more at her touch. She shifted slightly, leaning upward to gaze down at him. At her movement the panther kit jumped down with a rather loud meow and to his relief, seemed to leave the room. The woman gazed down at him, her green eyes reminding him of a meadow in springtime, her lips begging for his kiss — but she was not for him.

No, this was a joke of Mr. Arthur Merle and his black box. Of that he was sure.

"Boy, did my imagination go the distance this time." The woman spoke, sounding quite pleased by his presence. "You are a heck of a lot better looking than any cover model on any book I've read, and even better looking than the Indian in my photograph." She leaned over a bit more until her lips touched his. At first tentative, she feathered light kisses over his, her tongue peeking out to taste the crease where his met. "Mmm" she sighed, "You taste so good. Who knew an imaginary lover could have a flavor and taste so good."

Seemingly of their own volition, his lips parted and she quickly plunged her tongue into the warm wetness of his mouth. At first she gave the inner cavern of his mouth a quick sweep, as if to be sure it was indeed there, then began a slow exploration of every nook and cranny of his mouth. Her slow, sensuous assault caused him to harden even more, his balls drawing tightly up and that was just with her kiss. His body demanded he respond to her and his tongue began its own pleasurable dance with hers. Toying, tasting, savoring the gentle play, he fought to keep his arms at his sides lest he scare her away — not that the bold woman would frighten easily.

As if reading his thoughts, she shifted again for better access to him. Little noises of pleasure escaped her lips while she explored his body with her hands. With one hand, at first so softly he wasn't even sure he felt it, she stroked his chest, taking its time to rub his *chante*, her thumb caressing the nipple, causing it to harden to her touch. The other hand had moved to his hair, her fingers tangling in it while she stroked its length. She slid her leg over to cover his groin, possessively skimming along the length of his muscled thigh, teasing the length of his proud standing manhood. His manhood clamored for him to take what she offered him.

She broke the kiss and looked down at him, her eyes drugged with her need for him. She sighed, drinking in the sight of him. "Wow! I've never had a fantasy feel this good before. Some pretty hot ones but nothing like this." She moved to give him a kiss and stopped just as her lips met his again. "You *are* a figment of my imagination, aren't you?"

"*Wasicun winyan*, I fear I am very real, but have no answer as to how I come to be here."

She froze in place.

He wasn't sure she was even breathing. Would she cry out rape and have him killed before he could even begin to discover how he came to be in this place?

"You're—real?" She slid off him, moved slightly away and studied him a brief moment before turning to the table beside her bed. She picked up what appeared to be a flat box-like object that he quickly realized was a photograph in a frame. The woman studied it for what seemed a long time before glancing down at him, back to the photograph and back to him. "Oh, I don't think this is good." She turned the photograph to him. "He's gone. I thought maybe I didn't see so right before, you know, that with there not being a lot of light in the room I might of missed it—him—you. Oh crap! Oh no, oh no, oh no! Black Eagle isn't in the photo anymore. He was last night, but he's not now, so if he's not in the photo . . ."

Debating with himself only a short moment, he chanced speaking to her. "Black Eagle is gone from the paper, but he lives and is here in this bed with you. Who, *winyan,* are you?"

Carrie's mouth flew open and again she looked back and forth between Black Eagle and the photograph. "Oh my god—.it can't be—it can't! Tell me you aren't real!" Although whispered, her voice filled the room, the fear evident in her voice.

"I am not here to hurt you, wo-wo-woman." He stumbled over the word, tried to use their language. "I am as confused as you. Please, do not call out. I have no wish to die, at least not until I know how I came to be here." He reached for the sheet to cover himself.

If nothing else, Carrie saw the fear and confusion on the man's face. "Hey, it's okay." She sat on the edge of the bed and raised her hand up to caress his cheek, a motion meant to soothe. "I think we both kinda caught each other off guard, you know?"

He lay perfectly still, as if moving would cause his demise. "You, then you would not, it would not, frighten you if I were to sit up?"

It hit her—*It's a joke.* Either Molly got one of Vincent's friends to sneak in here and play like a big Indian or . . .

Oh nasty – what if Dean put him up to it? Dang he's good. Molly or Dean, whichever one put him up to this sure coached him well – but, how could Dean have gotten him in here? Then what happened to Black Eagle in the photograph – how did they do that?

She raised her arm in an upward gesture, "No, have at it. Far be it from me to make a man uncomfortable."

As he shifted his arms to push himself upward to a sitting position Carrie couldn't help but admire the way his biceps bunched and stretched with his movement and just how good his hip looked as it peeked out from the sheet he'd just tugged up to his thighs, the thin strip of rawhide or whatever it was, just on the curve and she didn't miss that delicious dip of joint where his hip, butt and thigh came together. Rawhide—okay, so he wasn't a totally naked man in her bed, but naked enough. This was far better than anything she'd ever read in any of her books, that was for sure.

"So give. Molly put you up to this, right?"

He settled himself, leaving his hands at his sides, before speaking, "I know no Mol-lee and I am sorry, woman, I have nothing to give."

"I'm sure you do. She's about five foot, six inches, reddish hair, blue eyes?"

"No, I am sorry, I do not . . ." His voice trailed off.

Apparently hearing their voices, Taister ventured back into the room, paused at the doorway and took in the man still in his person's bed.

"Woman, the little panther is back. Its mother will surely

64

come looking for it. Do you not think you should release it?"

"Little panther?" Carrie looked down and Taister looked up at her, giving every indication that he was sharing a private joke.

Who said cats don't have thoughts and expressions?

Taister was no doubt a human trapped in a cat's body. Or maybe he chose to be in one since he was treated like a king.

"Taister's a regular house cat, not a panther — although I'm sure he likes to think of himself as a great kingly cat."

"House cat?"

"Yes, a pet, you know. Like a-a-well he's a pet."

"He appears like the cub of a panther."

"I'm sure he likes hearing that. Little guy fancies himself quite the mighty hunter."

Taister cast her a look over his shoulder as he sauntered to the side of the bed Black Eagle was on, jumped up and climbed onto the man's lap.

Carrie pondered *that* action a bit. Taister had *never* warmed up to anyone quite like that. He'd study them for worth and accept whatever treats they would give him, but climb in someone's lap? Unheard of. Maybe Mr. Naked rubbed catnip on himself. That sounded like something Molly would encourage someone playing a joke on her to do, to catch her off guard.

"Yeah," she continued, "he has his moments, but he's a domestic house cat. Forget the darn cat! What did Molly promise you for playing this trick on me?"

"I told you the truth. I know no Mol-lee."

Taister settled, then just as quickly, unsettled himself to undertake his morning grooming. He had that wonderful perversity shared by most cats of not only finding the focal point of a room to start grooming — and Carrie's mind *did* give a passing thought to the piece of Mr. Naked's anatomy just under where Taister had parked himself — but like every other cat, he would start grooming his most private parts as soon as he had the attention of everyone in the room. By his loud purring, it was clear Taister enjoyed this, and if she didn't know better, she'd think it was her little furfaced child who invited in Mr. Naked.

"Fine, then that asshole, Sir D, put you up to it. He wasn't any great shakes in the looks department and sucked in b—" She stopped abruptly. Dean was always a little uptight about the fact he topped five foot five at most, and while he tried to work out, it never quite happened for him. He certainly wouldn't send a skyscraper-tall hunk like Mr. Naked to her house, so that left . . .

"All right, so where did you come from?" she demanded of the man in her bed.

"My wicoti mitawa."

"Your what?"

"My *wicoti mitawa*." He squinted in thought. "My village."

"Right." She rolled away from him and tugged down her nightshirt. Or rather tried to. The over large tee shirt wasn't all that over large and it barely hit her mid-thigh. Making her way off the bed and taking a step back she stood, glaring at him. "Look, we're getting nowhere. You and Taister have a nice visit. I'm taking a shower."

Carrie walked off into the bathroom and stepped into the shower. Usually she waited until the water heated a bit, but this morning she was more than a bit distracted by the strange man in her bed. When the first blast of warming water hit her, it occurred to her that she might be totally certifiably insane to leave an unknown man wearing nothing but a loincloth in her bed. Either that or she was hallucinating. What was she thinking? For all she knew he was an escaped killer who liked to dress up like Tarzan. But Taister seemed to like him. That in itself was quite novel. Her shower done, she pulled on an oversized sweatshirt, sweat pants and her bunny slippers and padded back into the room. Mr. Naked was still sitting there with Taister sound asleep in his lap.

Trying to act like a buff hunk showed up sans clothing in her bed on a regular basis she casually asked, "Still here?"

"The little panther fell asleep. I did not wish to disturb him."

"Yeah, well, 'little panther' sleeps twenty-two and a half hours a day, so don't worry about waking him. So, look, as long as you're here, you want a shower? And while you're in it, why don't you think about telling me who put you up to this? Or, if you're a serial killer, maybe you should go kill someone else."

It was clear from the look on his face that the man in her bed had no idea what a 'shower' or a 'serial killer' was.

"Thank you, yes."

Carrie gestured to the bathroom, pulled out a towel and stood back to watch Mr. Naked walk across the room and stop at the bathroom door. Then patted herself on the back at how calmly she was handling whatever this situation was.

"Woman, how am I to call you?"

"I'm sure you already know. It's Carrie. Carrie Taylor." She thought a moment and glanced at the photograph before asking, "Are—are you really Black Eagle? The guy in the photograph?"

"Yes, Car-rie Taylor, I am Black Eagle."

While his loincloth hid the essentials, there was still an eyeful to enjoy. He had the most incredible legs—his skin, the color of honey, over the tautest muscles. The piece of cloth in the back swayed just enough to show off a part of his butt and—oh, my—what a nice piece of eye candy *that* was. She licked her lower lip, thinking about running her tongue into that little indent where his butt cheek met his hip. The man was a walking turn on. She realized he'd stopped and that her eyes were no longer ogling his butt. She had a full frontal look and she could only see the outline of what the front of that little piece of cloth hid, but he sure did look—healthy. Her blush grew as her eyes traveled upward, past that magnificent chest of his to meet his eyes. She probably looked like Christmas with her green eyes and the blush that warmed her face.

Carrie instantly felt contrite when she saw the mixture of fear, embarrassment and pleasure in his eyes. The man was afraid of her, that was for sure, but he liked her looking at him. "Yes?"

"I do not see a bucket."

"Bucket?"

"To bring in the water."

"Bring in the water?"

"You offered me a show-er. That is a bath, yes?"

At Carrie's nod, he went on to explain, "I need water to . . ." Carrie stepped forward and brushed past him, trying her best not to rub up against him but, oh, the temptation was so there to just sort of accidentally on purpose slide against his chest. "Did you want a bath or a shower?"

"Shower?"

She wasn't sure if he was asking her what a shower was, or if he could have one, but she was in no mood to play any games, either. She waggled her finger to have him join her at the tub. "Here's the hot water, here's the cold. Be careful with the hot, it warms up real quick and I don't want you to burn yourself, okay?"

She demonstrated how to turn on the faucets, pointed out the soap and shampoo and left him to figure the rest out for himself. If he was pretending, he'd get a free shower out of his night of lying in her bed. If he was real, well, she'd cross that bridge when they came to it.

Carrie went to the kitchen while he bathed, and noticed there was no sign of Molly having come home yet. Deciding her roommate was probably hiding from her wrath, she started making coffee and pulled out the fixings for pancakes, bacon and eggs. The coffee started, she headed back into her room, just as Mr. Naked emerged again wearing only his loincloth. "Um, you can stop the charade now and put on your clothes."

"Woman, these are my clothes."

Certain she was really fully awake, after all, she had taken a shower and she still couldn't wrap her mind around the fact that the man in the photograph was apparently now in the flesh and in her house. Carrie grabbed onto some basic, every day concerns, like: where were his clothes?

"Oh, come on, you agreed to play this joke on me and didn't pack a change of clothes? How gullible do you think I am?"

"Woman . . ."

"And enough with the 'woman' thing. My name is Carrie, Carrie Taylor. Now get dressed, would you?"

When he didn't move, she stalked into her room and over to the bureau. It seemed he was unsure of what he should do, because he followed close on her heels. She could tell he knew she was angry now, but whatever forces, if it weren't Molly or Dean, had sent him here did not send him with his clothes. Before he could speak, she pulled out a drawer from the bureau in the room and snagged a hefty tee shirt, tossed it at him and then stalked to the closet. Emerging a moment later with a pair of jeans, she also tossed those in his direction.

"Clay left those here about two years ago and hasn't been back. They're clean and I think they'll fit. So get dressed."

"Woman, believe me, I truly have no idea who this Clay is but if he is your man I do not want to anger him, even if he has not been home for two years."

"Just put the pants on, would you?"

Carrie couldn't tell for sure but it sounded like the man muttered, "If I make it out of this *yata* alive, I will thank *Nagi*

Tanka the rest of the days of my life, and will never again ask for a woman. If I am destined to live my life alone, so be it."

Under her breath, just in case she did hear what she thought she heard, Carrie mumbled, "Talk about drama — whatever the heck a yata is."

While he dressed, Carrie moved to sit on the bed and picked up the photograph.

With the shirt and pants on, Black Eagle moved to sit beside her. "Carrie Taylor, I am sorry, I do not know this Mollee or Dean or how I came to be here. I would return to my home in a breath if I could, but I do not know how." He glanced at the photo in her hands and sucked in a breath. "Mr. Arthur Merle."

"What? You know Mr. Merle?" She was stunned. It didn't seem like the elderly gentleman to just up and send a man to her house and certainly not one that would crawl in her bed without any clothing.

"I know Mr. Arthur Merle, a photo-graph-er."

"He sent you? Mr. Merle put you up to this?" She stood, dropping the photograph on the bed, hands on hips she repeated, "Sweet, kind Mr. Merle put you up to this?"

"No, Mr. Arthur Merle is the one who took that photograph. He said it would not take my spirit, but I saw when he was done that there was a small image of me, Black Eagle, and I knew my spirit lived in the photo-graph. Now my spirit no longer lives in the photo-graph. I know not where it is, but I am here."

Carrie couldn't miss the look of despair in the man's eyes, the utter hopelessness that something precious had been taken from him. That squelched any thought that Mr. Merle had sent the man to her house for any nefarious purpose. At the same time she recalled what Mr. Merle had said about the Indians believing that a camera would steal their spirit. How frightening for this man, if he really was Black Eagle, and that was really what he thought had happened. She swallowed. She swallowed again.

Her mouth suddenly without any moisture, she managed, "You, you're really Black Eagle? That's why he's—you're not in the picture anymore? It's not a joke and Molly or Dean didn't figure out a way to take your image out of the photo?"

"Yes, that is how I am called."

"When, err, when did your Mr. Merle take the picture?"

"About two, maybe three weeks ago."

Carrie held her breath, "What year?"

"1860 . . . what year is this?"

CHAPTER ELEVEN

"Vivianne! Back so soon?" Mr. Merle greeted his friend.

"And you are surprised?" Her royal blue cloak, the color more vivid from the contrast with the dark, hardwood floor, billowed about her in the small space of the antique store.

"Of course I am. Usually I only see you once every so many years. Not that I am complaining. Have you come for more apple and spice tea?"

"No. No." She stepped over to the sword and looked it over. "The Tor glows brighter. I think you may have done something to bring about the parting of the mists. Either that or its time is coming on its own."

He stepped over to where she stood. "Hmm, does it look all that different? Are you sure it is not the morning light?"

"Morning light here or there. Come with me now and see what is happening."

If Carrie was disconcerted by the revelation that Mr. Naked — no, that was now officially being unkind if, in fact, this was Black Eagle sitting in her room — she could only imagine how he felt. The poor guy was either very mentally ill, or he traveled through time and woke up, not just in a strange woman's bed, but also in another time. Could Molly have figured out a way to take his image out of the picture and find someone who looked a lot like him to sneak into her room last night? Nah, Molly might like to play an occasional joke on someone, but not quite like this.

She thought about it for a few minutes. In one of her favorite books with a character that time traveled, there was always a bit of confusion after the time traveler arrived, and they always wanted to go home. It didn't matter if they were men or women. They always wanted to go to their own time, at least at first.

It never took long, however, for at least one of the characters to discover an attraction to the other. By the next chapter they were crazy in love with each other, but didn't want to talk about it. It was the whole tension thing she read about in a writing magazine. The conflict they called it.

Whatever it was she sure enjoyed reading them. Of course the sex was always very hot and the guy always had an impressive package.

She smiled to herself. Dean would never cut it as a time travel hero—too short and not much in the package department. She realized that was a mean thought, and realized she enjoyed having it.

As the story went on, they fell in love and had a happy ever after, usually staying in the time that the traveler came to. From what she'd seen under that little loincloth, this guy had a pretty decent package. That was a nice plus.

In Carrie's imaginings, when she had time travel ones, they always got to what she thought was the 'good part' pretty quickly. Now that it appeared to have actually happened to her, she was plenty confused, and while the 'good part' with Black Eagle might be really, really good, she wasn't quite ready to jump into bed with him. Well, that wasn't exactly true. She *had* been in bed with him, but hadn't exactly jumped in with him and she wasn't about to have sex with him. At least not . . . She mentally slapped herself. *Don't go there. The man is probably as baffled as I am.*

It was time to get down to basics. "So what do you say we have some breakfast and we'll talk a little more while we eat, okay? Who knows, maybe even Molly will be home and have some ideas about all of this."

He nodded, rose and followed her into the kitchen, with Taister running beside him, his little black fur-face looking trustingly up at the tall man. Taister was through the door before him, immediately embarking on his morning demand for breakfast—and considering this morning it was much later than usual, he was actually quite decent about waiting for it. But Taister, being Taister, had his priorities. He had no sooner started on his meows than Black Eagle stepped into the room.

Black Eagle stood frozen at the doorway, his hand gripped at his side as if there was some sort of weapon there that might help him, instead of just a belt loop. "My dreams. These are the things of my dreams."

Carrie stepped over to him. "It's all right, you can come in. There's nothing in here that can hurt you."

He stumbled to the closest chair and sat down.

"I'm just going to make us some breakfast, okay?" Carrie tried to reassure him.

At the word 'breakfast', Taister first looked up expectantly at the man, as if to say, "yeah, breakfast, it's good, the most important meal of the day", and offered a little meow as emphasis.

"*Winyan*, where am I?"

As soon as he was seated, Carrie picked up a can of the cat's food and handed it to him along with his dish. "Uh, um, like I said in the bedroom, can we drop the *winyan* thing and just call me Carrie? And as to where you are, well, um, we'll get to where, and when you are in a minute. For now, here. Your little panther will love you all the more if you feed him."

She turned back to start their breakfast, glancing over her shoulder a few moments later just in time to see Taister jump on the table and tap Black Eagle on the hand as the man turned the can over in his hands, tapping it on the table and trying to figure out how to feed the cat.

Evidently the little guy tried to help and clearly the man wanted to feed him and obviously it wasn't working out. Carrie reached for the can, held it so Black Eagle could see what she did and popped the top.

The man was either a very good actor or clearly amazed.

Taister was elated . . . food!

Just as Carrie turned back to start their breakfast, Molly ambled into the kitchen and sniffed the air with appreciation and made a beeline to the coffee pot. Cup firmly in hand, she reached for the pot and stopped. Turning slowly she retraced her steps with her eyes and allowed her gaze to rest on Black Eagle. Black Eagle watched closely as she gave him what seemed to be an approving once over from the top of his long black hair, to his cheeks, to his shoulders and his chest, that was just about bursting out of the t-shirt Carrie had found for him.

It seemed she did not give much thought to her coffee, which she put down and moved over to him. Thrusting her hand out, her voice just a hair above giddy, she told him, "Hi! I'm Molly Hudson and who might you be?"

Caught off guard by the bubbly young woman, Black Eagle hesitated a moment before tentatively offering his hand.

Just as he opened his mouth to speak, Carrie, who seemed to be planning to closely watch Molly's response, and to cover up just who her visitor *could* be, interjected, "This is Blake, Blake Eagleston. Blake — my roommate, Molly."

Molly took in the man's confusion at Carrie's introduction and with a gimlet eye towards her friend, answered, "Well, good to meet you, Blake, you drop in for breakfast?"

"Yes, yes — breakfast, I dropped in."

Carrie studied the exchange between the two and she still couldn't tell if Molly had just become an academy award-winning actress, or she really didn't know this guy who looked a whole lot like Black Eagle. Maybe he was one of the police officers she worked with, or a friend of Vincent's Molly convinced to play a joke on her. Of course, that wouldn't explain where the man in the photograph went in the middle of the night. It wasn't as if Molly could walk into her room, take the photograph, scan it into the computer, alter it and put it back in without waking Carrie. Could she? Could a photograph be aged exactly that way? And there was no blurring of lines in the photograph where Black Eagle had been. It was as if he'd never been there. The sky behind where he had stood was seamless.

"Well, great. Carrie makes the best pancakes and bacon, although I'd pass on her eggs—"

"Since you're up, Molly," Carrie cut her off, "I won't be offended if you make the eggs."

"Sure, sure. How do you like yours, Blake?"

"However you wish, I am not—I am not a difficult man to feed."

"Cool." Molly turned back to the stove to start the eggs as she continued. "Great. So, interesting accent. Where are you from?"

Black Eagle glanced at Carrie for guidance, and at her shrug, answered, "The Dakota Territory."

"Territory?"

"Oh, he means North Dakota. You know, near South Dakota."

"What? I'm just making conversation. It's not every day you bring a guy who could be a real live cover model straight off one of your books in for breakfast. Or at least a really hot looking guy who could be one." She glanced over her shoulder. "So, are you a model? Where'd you guys hook up? Do you have any friends you can hook me up with?"

"Molly, don't you know him?"

Molly turned to study the man sitting at the table. His look clearly showed uncertainty about just what the two women were talking about.

"No, I can't say I do. Give me a hint. Oh man, he *is* a model, isn't he? Where did you guys meet? When did you arrive? Why didn't you tell me? If I'd known, I wouldn't have been trying too hard to fix you up with someone. Man, do I feel like a total goober. This is totally awesome! So where did you meet? Which one of your books is he from?"

"He's not a model or anything like that. He's a regular guy that . . ."

"Oh, so what do you do? How'd you meet Carrie?"

"Molly, like you said, you've been trying to fix me up. You know, meet a new guy. You really don't know Bl—Blake?"

"Girlfriend, if I knew this man he wouldn't be having breakfast with you, he'd be between the sheets with me."

"Between—Fine. Never mind about Vincent." Carrie needed to digest this. She really did. It just wasn't possible. He couldn't be Black Eagle. It had to be some sort of joke. "No problem. First we eat. Then we talk."

Black Eagle looked expectantly between the two women. A loud rumble from his stomach let them know which option he'd vote for.

Carrie dished out the pancakes and bacon, while Molly grabbed the eggs and coffee, and the threesome fell to eating. As they took their last bites, Carrie picked up her coffee, took a long swallow and decided, from the little conversation they had over the man and the way Molly kept looking him over, she was being honest—her roommate didn't know Black Eagle.

Deciding to test the waters with what appeared to be the

truth, Carrie asked, "So you ready to hear how we met?"

"Sure am. It sounds like one of the secrets of the universe."

"Molly, doesn't he look familiar to you?"

"Didn't we already talk about this? No, I'm sorry, Blake, I don't recognize you. Carrie reads so many books they kinda go by in a blur, so if you graced one or more of them, I'm not getting it."

"Remember the photograph I bought?"

Molly studied the man sitting across from her, taking in each detail. She giggled a beat, "The one you — you know . . ."

"Molly . . ." Carrie's tone carried the unspoken warning.

"So are you an ancestor of that guy, or was the photo a fake? Or *are* you a model and that was like a sales or portfolio shot?"

"Neither," Carrie told her.

"Say what?"

"Molly — well, this is crazy — It's going to sound totally crazy — but hear me out. Remember how I told you that sometimes at night I'd see like a light, like a camera flash coming from the photo?"

"Yeah . . ."

"Well, last night I kinda saw it again and when I woke up, well, the Indian in the photo, Black Eagle, well ah, he's not in the photo anymore. I woke up and, well . . ." Knowing just how crazy she sounded, she clamped her mouth shut.

Black Eagle drew a breath before speaking. "I am the man in the pho-to-graph and I believe Mr. Arthur Merle brought me here through his magic box."

"What? Are you two nuts?" Molly looked from one to the other. "What's the punch line?"

"No, Molly, I wish we were — or maybe we are — but it's true."

"Yes, Molly. What Carrie says is true."

At Carrie's nod, he continued. "Several weeks ago Mr.

Arthur Merle came to James River, near my village and with his magic box took my pho-to-graph. He promised me the box would not take my spirit, but it did. I saw my spirit on the paper. After he took it, I found sleep did not come to me in the night. Several nights I went to the river near the village and watched the skies and each night saw a star fall, like the light from Mr. Arthur Merle's box. Last night the light was different, brighter, more like the light from the magic box. I woke up in Carrie's bed."

"*Your* Mr. Merle, Carrie?"

"No, of course not, it was his ancestor, I'm sure."

Turning to Black Eagle, Molly continued, "Okay, I'll bite. So where is your village?"

"Well that's the thing, Mol," Carrie began, "I think it's somewhere in the mid-west, like maybe North Dakota and — one hundred and sixty years ago."

Carrie watched as her roommate looked around the room, as if searching for the answer on the walls before speaking. "Are you telling me this man, Blake, is really an old Indian warrior and he traveled through time to be here?"

"Seems that way."

His look somber, Black Eagle nodded and answered, "I am called Black Eagle, but I was not old when I walked to the river last night. In the looking glass this morning I did not look old, but . . ."

"Gees." Molly whistled through her teeth. "So what are we going to do with him? You?"

Carrie answered, "I don't know. I think maybe we need to talk to Mr. Merle. Remember I told you he told me an ancestor of his took the photo in the first place? He might know how this happened. But Black Eagle, you need to know, the camera doesn't take your spirit or anything like that. It's just, well, just a picture. You are still you, and you still have your spirit. He didn't take anything from you."

"Then how did I come to be here, in your *tiyata*?"

"Our what?" Molly and Carrie said together, looking at each other.

"*Tiyata*," Black Eagle repeated, raising his hand to indicate the house around them.

"I don't know the answer to that, but I think maybe if we talk to Mr. Merle, the one I know, we may find some sort of answer."

"That sounds reasonable," Molly interjected, "so when do we leave?"

"I'm thinking as soon as we can—maybe first stop to get Blake some clothes, shoes, stuff. He didn't have any on when he—er—arrived. Are you sure you want to come? You just got in from work?"

"I wouldn't miss this for the world."

CHAPTER TWELVE

A s they prepared to leave, Black Eagle followed Carrie out the door and stopped before he was ten steps outside. The fear and confusion were back in his eyes. Carrie reached for his hand. "It's okay, trust me. It's okay."

The resignation in his gaze and relaxation of his jaw told her he would, but only because he had to trust someone. They found an old pair of men's flip-flops in Molly's closet. There definitely was something to be said about old boyfriends. They didn't exactly fit right and Black Eagle had a bit of a time adjusting to using them, but they worked out okay, at least for the trip to the mall. Even if Mr. Merle had a way for Black Eagle to go back to his home that day, he at least had to have something decent to wear until they got to Treasures. The problem was getting him there.

The walk outside the house from there went fine.

Getting in the car was not quite so fine.

The 'metal box', as he called it, really seemed to unnerve him until he saw a few other cars and a truck drive down the street. A big red Ford F350 that roared down the street definitely appealed to him and he immediately wanted the women to trade Carrie's conservative black Honda Civic for it, or one just like it. The idea that people didn't really barter much any more, or that trading cars just didn't happen, didn't set all that well with him.

Once in the car she saw his nervousness return, and it wasn't just from the Saturday tourist traffic through the city. Carrie began to wonder why she said they'd go to the outlet mall outside the city limits, instead of a shop in town. He resisted the seatbelt, insisting it trapped him in the box, and told them if they meant to do him harm they should at least let him die like a man. A fairly lengthy discussion, and many assurances later, that the seatbelt was really for his protection, they drove off—only to have Black Eagle begin to hyperventilate from fear of the car moving. Even having the window open didn't ease his fear. Carrie pulled over, stopped the car and got out, asking Molly to drive so she could sit in the back seat.

Once there she leaned forward and put her arms around his shoulders, her lips near his ear to assure him he was all right, that they were safe and Carrie wasn't going to let anything happen to him. In other circumstances, Carrie would have thought of holding onto Black Eagle as she was, whispering in his ear, as something romantic. But, with how frightened he seemed, romance was the last thing on her mind.

The outlet mall coming into view was a welcome sight. Stepping out of the car, Carrie deliberated about bringing Black Eagle inside the mall at all, and finally decided there was no other way. While she could pretty much guess his sizes, leaving him alone in the car or parking lot probably wasn't the best idea she'd had.

"Okay, we're here and we need to call you Blake, okay? And for now, it might be best if you let me do the talking, at least till you know the lay of the land, so to speak. Tell me if you don't like something, but otherwise . . ."

"I understand, Carrie Taylor. You are right."

His extraordinary good looks drew attention from virtually every woman in the mall, but not so much that anyone came up to them. They picked up jeans, some dress slacks, shirts, shoes, socks—when it came to the choice of boxers or briefs—well, Carrie figured she'd make that choice—briefs.

They stopped for lunch at one of the quieter restaurants just outside the mall. At least he'd seen cafés back in his own time, so it wasn't quite as startling to him as the food court would have been. The variations of coffees, from cappuccinos to lattes to the mochas, were more information than he seemed to be comfortable with. However, he seemed to enjoy the mocha she ordered for him, telling the women repeatedly that it was truly a gift from *Nagi Tanka.*

It was Molly who suggested maybe it was time to go see Mr. Merle. "Before we all get too attached to each other, maybe it's time, you know?"

CHAPTER THIRTEEN

Crouching behind some low bushes just outside the café, Dean watched as Molly, Carrie and the tall man climbed back into her car. The scent of fresh baked quiche and chocolately mochas filtered out to him making his mouth water. The thought of going in for some lunch himself crossed his mind, however he wasn't sure Carrie would buy a story that he just happened by. He hadn't followed Carrie around as much lately as he had after they first broke up, but after the meeting at work yesterday afternoon, he felt time was running out for getting a wife and he needed to amp up his pursuit. That meant rather than sitting home hitting his favorite x-rated Internet sites, he had to be out here trying to figure out how to win her back. To do that he'd gotten up early this morning, driven to Carrie's house, parked around the corner and then hidden in the bushes along her porch. Kneeling in the dirt with all those damn flowers he had to fight to keep from sneezing for the better part of the morning until she, Molly and that big guy left. Popping into the restaurant right then didn't seem like the best plan.

When they took off down the street, he tried to run as inconspicuously as possible for his car so he could follow them. A few steps down the street he tripped over a crack in the sidewalk and fell splat out down, tearing his jeans while he scrambled to keep his face from hitting the ground. It was only by sheer luck he got to his car without Carrie or Molly seeing him and was able to pick up their trail as they drove down to the outlets. A few people walking by gave him the once over, clearly wondering what he was up to. After the first couple of people, he pretended to be tying his shoelace while still trying to keep an eye on Carrie.

He'd perfected his skills following people as a kid. Since he wasn't all that popular with the neighborhood kids, not because of his small stature, but because he was just mean-spirited, he was left out of a lot of the neighborhood games and such. So he'd follow the other kids and pull mean tricks on them. None of the adults seemed to catch on to his antics.

In school, he enjoyed starting something with two or three of the other students and getting them set at each other. Then, just as the teacher or yard guard would approach, he'd raise his voice to make it sound like he was the peacemaker. His arms would get all tingly with excitement at putting one over on the adults. When the other kids would try to tell whatever adult happened on the scene that it was Dean that started it, no one would listen. After all, Dean could quote from the Bible, was up on all the latest self-improvement books—the 1970's and 80's sure had a lot of them—and it was all about everyone coming out feeling like they got something.

Mostly it was Dean who got something out of it, because the adults all thought he was so wonderful. As to tracking people—when the kids figured out what he was doing, they stopped playing with him. So Dean took up following them wherever they went. Early on they would spot him and they would all pretend to go home, but Dean found out they would just regroup at someone else's house. Deciding to get back at them and make a winning situation for himself, he learned to follow without anyone seeing him. He'd watch what they were up to and then call their parents, or the police, anonymously and make up some outrageous story about what they were doing. Dean never gave his name, of course and worked really hard to hide his voice.

Now, as an adult, heart racing with excitement he was able

to follow Carrie without her knowing about it. Because he seemed to read so many adult books—not adult with sex and romance, but adult like how to be a better person—teachers thought he was well read and studied his heart out. The reality was that he listened to his parents talk and as to doing well in school, well, that was due to him being really good at reading other students' papers.

Dean admitted to being a schemer only to himself and up until Carrie dumped him, he'd done all right with his plots and plans. How many other guys could claim to have graduated law school with honors without attending half their classes? Ruminating about Turdberg calling him in yesterday, Dean settled in to watch and wait for a chance to talk to Carrie. *Maybe the big guy belongs to Molly . . . he's not Carrie's type at all . . . big, brawny, right?* He cursed silently to himself yet again about yesterday's meeting. He had hoped it was to discuss his becoming a partner without that stupid marriage stipulation. That partnership was his goal from day one and four years in, he was more than ready to discuss it. Discuss it? Hell, he wanted to hear it was his.

"Damn you and your stupid rules, Turdberg."

Looking back at when Turnberg & Jeffers first hired him, Dean wanted to spit at their attitude about marriage and family. Their whole thing about promotions and candidate selections was just bunk. One requirement to become a partner was to be married and have at least one kid. A baby on the way would seal the deal, but it had to be definite.

The first two years, Dean had worked his butt off in hopes that the marriage issue would go away. Not that he minded marriage. Wedded bliss to the right woman—that would be one with money who would look the other way while he did what he wanted—would have been fine. Carrie had money from that trust fund of hers, but she wouldn't spend it. She wasn't cheap. In fact she was very generous with her friends.

It was major expenditures—like treating herself and him to a first class week in Hawaii—she wouldn't do.

In time he saw one of two things happen at work. Those members who were married got promoted, those who didn't take the stroll down the aisle were lucky if they weren't fired. They might get raises, but not as high as the guys who were married. More often than not, the unmarried men were invited to leave the firm—there were few, if any female partners. So Dean went in search of a wife. Anyone would have done, really. He just needed someone to get married to and make a baby with. After that, it didn't matter what happened one way or the other.

It didn't take long till he met Carrie. After all, when you are on a bride hunt how hard is it to find a likely prospect? Carrie met all the basic requirements . . . she was female and single.

Okay, and she had money. The bonus was that she was really smart and able to give Dean advice and insight on how to do his job better. Of course, that bonus was also a problem because that made her hard to manipulate. At first he'd hoped that simply dating her would satisfy the partners, but they said, again and again, that they wanted anyone they promoted to be married.

So he began to earnestly pursue Carrie, while at the same time refusing to give up his other enjoyments. Things were going really well until she showed up unannounced and uninvited at his apartment that day a few months ago when he was enjoying Jolene's questionable charms. It was one thing for him to just show up at her house without asking ahead of time. It was something else again if she thought she could just show up at his.

Now he had to waste his time trying to get her back and pretend to the company they were still an item and things were moving along. At one point, he thought he could convince Carrie about a marriage of convenience, like she read about in those juicy romance books of her. After all, if she could enjoy reading about some old Scottish guy in a skirt marrying the enemy's daughter and having a baby, why wouldn't she agree to that for herself? The few times he brought it up she went off about marrying for love and how *she* could never marry because her father told her to.

In what he felt was a Herculean effort, he actually read one of those books and was surprised when it wasn't too bad. At a minimum, it gave him some cool ideas about what Carrie might want. But, first things first. He had to get her to marry him, but even when he brought up the idea that if they did marry for convenience, they'd fall in love, Carrie held firm on the love before marriage thing. When Turdberg called him in yesterday Dean hoped it wasn't to once again ask about his pending nuptials.

Sadly, he didn't get his wish. So far Dean had found ways to explain the delay in marrying Carrie, but it was looking like he wouldn't be allowed to stall much longer. Coming out and telling the truth that Carrie dumped him wouldn't do. The bosses liked Carrie and really wanted her to be one of their partner's wives. So now here he was, up at the crack — make that the *crap* — of dawn, following Carrie and her little entourage, squatting in the dirt and hoping against hope to get her alone and maybe even pop the question.

If she said no, he figured he'd find a way to get her in trouble with the police and then bail her out. After all, what good was being an attorney if you couldn't bail someone out now and again? Besides, if he did that, he'd be the hero, she'd be grateful and they'd rush off to the justice of the peace.

Unfortunately, it appeared she had met someone new, unless, of course the big guy was Molly's. From the way Carrie was acting, though, her hand on the guy's arm and how he looked at her, it appeared he belonged to Carrie. Rising a bit and running low behind the hedges, his back aching from the awkward crouch, he hoped she wouldn't spot him as he got back into his car. Climbing in, he banged a fist on his steering wheel in anger and frustration.

"Ouch! Damn it! That hurt."

Nursing his hand as he followed the threesome to their next destination, fleeting thoughts of drugging Carrie, kidnapping her and heading to Reno for a quickie wedding ran through his mind. He just needed to wait until the big guy with them took off to wherever he came from.

Pulling up in front of Treasures, Carrie immediately saw the bright red *Closed* sign on the door. Jumping out of the car, she ran up to the door and even though the store was dark she jiggled the door handle. "Oh crumb, it's not only closed for the day, the sign says Mr. Merle is on vacation for the next two weeks."

"What?" Molly and Black Eagle asked together as they both joined her at the door. Like Carrie before him, Black Eagle immediately tried the door.

"Sorry Blac—Blake, it's locked and it looks like for the next two weeks it's going to stay locked. He's on vacation."

"What is vacation?"

"It means he's gone away for a bit, taken a trip or something. But why did he have to go now?"

"Did he say anything to you when you stopped in the other night?" Molly asked.

"No, not a word. Molly, you don't think . . .he wouldn't . . . he couldn't . . ."

"Carrie, the Mr. Arthur Merle I knew was a kindly enough man, but he had his secrets. I could see that clearly in his eyes. They twinkled with happiness, yet one could see a secret hid behind them. Perhaps his descendant shares those secrets. Perhaps your Mr. Merle knew my Mr. Arthur Merle put my spirit in his magic box, and knew your Mr. Merle or another family member would release me to be with you," Black Eagle told her.

Carrie peered into the shop. Chewing on her lower lip, she looked for any sign the proprietor was inside and would either magically materialize or jump out and say he was playing a joke on her. But there was nothing. It was dark and no one was inside. Seeming to have his words finally register she muttered, "That's a romantic notion, Blake, but I don't think that's what happened. Cameras just can't do that—take a spirit and move someone through time."

"Then how do you explain my presence in this time?"

It was Molly who responded. A long sigh passed through her lips before she spoke, shaking her head. "I don't know, I don't know. Come on, Carrie, Blake, no one's there. Let's go home and see what we can figure out, huh? Come on." Molly pulled them both back by their arms and moved them towards the car.

"I guess—I feel—I just feel—well, I just don't like someone manipulating my life, you know?" Carrie told them.

"Yes, Carrie, I know." Black Eagle's somber look brought home to the women that he was having a hard time with his appearance in the twenty-first century, a much harder time than Carrie. He had left a simpler, yet harsher world, where just being alone with the two White women would have gotten him in trouble, if not killed.

"Well, let's head home. I thought maybe a move. I don't know though, should we download one or would that—maybe we should rent a DVD, order a pizza and just relax and see what comes up for us, huh?"

"Great idea." Molly answered with a nod.

"Yes," he glanced around, clearly feeling lost, even in the small town. "Carrie, what are a D-V-D and a pit-za?"

"Oh. Um, well, the DVD is—ahhhh, it's probably not a

good idea."

"Why?"

"It's well. Ah, it's you know how you aren't too keen on photographs? Well, they are like moving photographs."

"But there is no camera?"

"No."

"Then I will only see other spirits trapped in a photo that moves, but mine will not be taken again?"

"They aren't trapped, they, well, the actors and actresses want to make the movies. You've seen a play, right?"

"A play?"

At this point, seeing that they were heading down a dead end with lots of locked doors to choose from, Molly broke in. "If I remember reading it correctly, the Indian tribes, when there was a celebration there was dancing and in the dancing you acted out what happened as part of the dance."

"Yes," he confirmed.

"Well, that's kind of what the video is. It's people who want to tell a story, but instead of just being able to say it to a small group, they do it on the videotape or a film so that lots of people can see it. No spirits are involved."

"I see. And the Pit-za?"

"Food. Really good food. Carrie and I eat pizza at least once a week."

"Then I will enjoy the pit-za. Thank you, Molly."

Dean hadn't heard the conversation, but it was clear that whatever they wanted to get from Arthur Merle or Treasures hadn't happened. "I can't believe how much Carrie likes going into that old junk store! Who would want someone else's old garbage when they could have something new? Antiques, my ass."

He couldn't decide whether to continue following the

threesome as they headed away, or checking to see why they hadn't gone into the junk shop. Figuring Napa wasn't that big, and he'd find Carrie's car again fairly quickly, he ran up to the store and saw from the sign that the old man was gone for a couple of weeks. He peered inside to see if there was anything interesting and seeing nothing, ran back to his car, in search of Carrie and her two friends.

I'll sure be glad when she realizes that being married to me is the only way to go. I can stop all this running around and all that stupid overtime. Just get my partnership and palm the work off on some schmuck law clerk or associate.

CHAPTER FOURTEEN

On the way home Carrie, Molly and Black Eagle stopped at the video store near the house. As they all started out, it occurred to Carrie that taking Black Eagle into the store probably wasn't the best idea. If he thought the camera had taken his spirit and sent him to the present, what would he think of the videos?

"Um, Molly, why don't you pick out something good? We'll wait out here in the car and . . ." Carrie stopped speaking, seeing Black Eagle's look of distress. "Black Eagle, please don't take offense—I only thought the store would make you uncomfortable."

"It is okay, Carrie. You have been kind, generous, but I think it best I go. I have no way to pay you for the clothing or food, but I will find a way. Perhaps I can find a pony for you and . . ."

"A pony? Huh?"

"What does he mean a pony?" Molly frowned at the tall, dark haired man."

Carrie nodded to herself, "I think it's like a gift or a thank you thing. Black Eagle, no. You don't owe me anything, and I want to help you. Really, I do."

"It is not right, Carrie. Not only are you not a member of my family, and you are not my *mitawin*. You are—White."

"So?"

"I am an Indian, you are White, a White woman. Are you not afraid of what people will think? What they will say?" he patiently explained.

"Oh dear, I hadn't thought—it didn't occur to me and it should have because I read all the westerns and I know what happens in them. Oh, man. Black Eagle, I've been so caught up in figuring out how you got here that I just didn't think about how you felt or how different all this is for you. I'm so sorry. Please, forgive me?"

"There is nothing to forgive, Carrie. You did not cause me to be here. Now it is best I find my own way. Thank you for your kindnesses." He turned to walk away, the look in his eyes so bleak it cut to her heart.

"Please, don't go."

"It is best, Carrie." He walked the opposite direction from their house, his head down.

"You gonna stop him?" Molly asked.

Carrie looked from her roommate to the retreating man. "Blake, Blake Eagleston..." She ran toward him, quickly catching up with him despite his long stride. Taking his arm, she pulled him to a stop, the look of despair in his dark eyes breaking her heart. "You can't leave—I, I, well I have the picture! It's at our house. Right, you can't leave because I have the photograph! I'm willing to bet you need the picture to go home and I don't want you to leave. Please, don't go."

"I must, Carrie. Don't you see, people will talk, they will call you names..."

"No, not anymore! Black Eagle, in today's world, men and women live together without marriage; they—well, roommates always share houses and don't have to be married. And race doesn't matter, or it isn't as big a deal in today's world, at least in California. In fact if you read the romance novels, it's the in thing to do. Wait, no, I didn't mean that, I meant that in books, well, never mind the books, in real life there are mixed couple relationships all over. Not that we're a couple. I didn't mean that, 'cause, well, you probably have a wife and kids or have someone you are in love with and that's why you want to go back. What I mean is that it doesn't matter now, in today's world, this time and even if it bothers you, Molly's with us, so if you're worried about appearances . . ."

The man stood staring at Carrie as if she had two heads. "May I speak honestly, Carrie?"

"Sure! Of course, please."

"In just the few hours I have been in this time, I have discovered that while you talk from idea to idea, it is endearing. It is, though, a bit hard to follow at times."

"Oh dear, sometimes I don't know when to shut up. I'm sorry, but please, come home with us. Please don't leave."

"For you, Carrie, only for you, I will stay, for a time anyway. At least until your Mr. Merle returns and can tell us what he knows. Will that please you?"

"Yes. Yes, it will." She took his hand and pulled him back to the car. "Do you want to try a video? If you don't like it or it makes you nervous we can stop it, but just in case, do you want to get one?"

"Do you speak while they are in use?"

"No. Well, um, ah, I guess sometimes someone says something or a comment or, you know, like watching a show . . ."

"I would like to try one. Not to bring silence to your lips, but to know your world."

"Comedian."

At his puzzled look she waved her other hand. "I'll tell you about it later."

Molly smiled at their approach. "So, you two work it out?"

"Yup. You wanna pick up a movie for us?"

"Sure." Molly disappeared into the store while Black Eagle looked around him, taking in the passing cars, the stores, streetlights, people walking by.

A few of the women that went by gave him long appraising looks, with one commenting, "nice buns" as she passed — which promptly earned her a dirty look from Carrie.

Rather than take offense at her apparent possessiveness, oddly, he seemed proud and secure. "Carrie?"

"Yes?"

"What are my buns?"

Carrie sputtered, obviously looking for the right words, stammering she finally managed, "Ah, you don't really want to know."

Fortunately, with that, Molly emerged from the store, movie in hand and they headed back to the car. "What did you get?"

"Sleepless in Seattle."

"Good one — Black Eagle, I think you'll like this one. It's about a widower, you know, a guy whose wife died, and his child and this woman who's engaged to a guy, but he's the wrong one and . . ." catching his look, the slight smile on his lips — lips she remembered kissing that morning and how good it felt. Carrie stopped her rambling. "Well I think you'll like it when you see it."

In a short time they were home. Carrie showed Black Eagle to the guest room. "I think you'll be comfortable in here — a little more private than — well, it has its own bath and plenty of room, okay?"

"Yes, Carrie Taylor. It is a good room. I will like it."

"Great, then let's get you unpacked."

"Hey, Car!" Molly yelled from down the hall.

"Yeah?"

"Pizza?"

Carrie looked at Black Eagle to see if he agreed. At his shrug, she realized despite their earlier comment about it and how good it was, he had no idea what pizza was. "Yeah, lots of meat on it and order some salad, too, okay?"

"Got it."

"And the pit-zah?"

"Total yum. It's like supposed to be Italian food, but they don't have it in Italy. It's got thick bread on the bottom, tomato sauce and lots of great stuff on top, like meat and cheese and, and you have no idea what I'm talking about. I'm sorry."

"Carrie Taylor, if you continue to be sorry for everything you say to me, I will never learn about you or your world."

"Okay, I just feel bad that I say things and forget you may not know."

"Please, do not feel bad. You did not plan for me to be here any more than I looked to come. I thank you for your kindness."

"And I thank you for your patience. We're going to be okay. I promise."

While Molly ordered dinner and took a short nap they put away Black Eagle's new clothing and shoes. "I'll give you a few minutes to unwind and settle in. Come on down to the living room when you're ready, 'kay?"

Black Eagle nodded and moved to sit on the bed to collect his thoughts. The last thing he remembered from his own time was wishing for a wife, a woman who was strong and kind and generous. A woman he could love and who would love him. Could Carrie Taylor be that woman? Did *Nagi Tanka* send him to her as an answer, rather than to mock him? From what he had seen, she was everything he wanted. She was warm, friendly, generous, could cook, kept a clean home and his man-root seemed to be hardened almost constantly since meeting her. Was that why he was sent here, to be with this woman? Could he live in this world? In this time? His mind said no, that he was a man of another time and place. His heart said Carrie was the one he waited a lifetime for.

The scent of freshly delivered pizza permeated down the hallway, but to Carrie's surprise their new house guest didn't respond to it in any way. "That's kind of weird, isn't it?

"What?" Molly shuffled into the living room, wiping the vestiges of her nap from her eyes.

"Black Eagle and the pizza. You'd expect a guy to head towards the smell of food even if he doesn't know what it is."

"I suppose so."

"And check it out, even Taister, Mr.-I'll-Have-Some-of-that-too-whateveritis, is nowhere in sight. I guess I'll give them a few."

When Black Eagle didn't show his face, Carrie headed down the hall. Stopping at the doorway, she took in Black Eagle. He sat on the bed, the look on his face the bleakest, most forlorn one she had ever seen, sadder than the kids she knew who didn't get what they wanted for Christmas. His new shirt hung open revealing a chest that wasn't just eye candy, it was a whole gourmet chocolate shop. He sat holding his loincloth in his hands. To her surprise, Taister lay by his side on his tummy, his front paws curled in front of him in what she called his meatloaf or cat curled position, staring straight ahead as if sharing the man's deepest thoughts. Black Eagle was clearly deep in thought. She knocked twice before entering and sitting beside him. When he still did not respond she put her hand on his shoulder.

"Black Eagle?"

He turned to face her and she found herself nearly lost in the depths of those dark brown eyes. She wanted to reach inside somehow and heal the pain the man clearly felt.

"Carrie, I have been thinking, trying to put together how I came to be here. I have also come to think that I will not be able to return to my home and I need to fit here in your world. I think the name you gave me, Blake Eagleston, is the one you should use from now on. I do not know how I will repay you, but will you please teach me to live in your world?"

"Of course, Black—Blake. Of course. This is your home now, here with Molly and me. We'll get you a key and help you fix up this room and we'll just make it your home. There are lots of 'guy' things you can do here when you're ready."

"And Tai-ster?"

"Sure. You really like the little guy, don't you?"

Black Eagle ruffled Taister's head. "Little panther seems to like me as well. I think he is pleased he has a man to tell his troubles to."

The little smile that came to his lips assured Carrie that somehow things would be all right. "So did you want to join us for dinner, or should I bring you a plate?"

"I would join you, Carrie. You won't mind?"

"Heck, no! And like I said before, if the movie bothers you, we won't watch it." She laid her hand on his arm to assure him. "Really, it's going to be okay. I promise."

Together they walked down the hall and Carrie found herself hard pressed not to laugh at his expression when he saw the pizza. He looked like he had been given manna from heaven, but then, that's what most of the guys she dated thought about it.

Over dinner, Molly and Carrie explained about pizza and just why they liked certain foods on it, like the black olives and pepperoni.

Taister had climbed on the chair beside Black Eagle and waited expectantly for a treat.

Seeing the question in his eyes, Carrie told him to go ahead and give Taister a bite. "You'll be his friend for life."

"I thought I already was," he joked.

Dinner finished, Carrie decided to broach the subject of the movie. "Okay, so I know you aren't so sure about it. I know you think your Mr. Merle took your spirit when he took your picture, but believe me, that's not what happened. And cameras have come a long way since back then. We even have pictures that move, and that's what this video is, and this is such a good movie and really, the people aren't trapped in the TV or the box, okay?"

He nodded. "This 'sleeping' movie, you like it a lot?"

"I do. *Sleepless in Seattle* is a wonderful love story where he, or actually first she goes all the way across the country to meet him and then his son goes to New York and they go to meet this woman and they fall in love."

"Much like how I came across time to be here."

Does he think he came to the future to be with me, or someone else? Is that possible?

"Well, yeah, sort of, I guess. Except in the movie he goes by an airplane, which I'll tell you about soon. There's so much to show you and tell you."

After Carrie popped in the DVD the threesome settled in to watch the movie. They were barely settled on the couch before Taister jumped up and made himself comfortable in Black Eagle's lap, casting a look at Carrie as if to say 'he's mine'. As the movie started, Carrie felt the man next to her tense, ever so slightly. She could see from his expression he was trying to believe her that all was well, that no one was going to be hurt by the video.

He marveled at Tom Hanks' houseboat, couldn't believe the airplane really flew in the sky like his brother the Eagle, and wanted to call out Meg Ryan's fiancé to fight. Halfway through Carrie stopped the movie, announcing she wanted ice cream. Carrie noticed that while Blake enjoyed the pizza, the ice cream totally put him over the top.

He clearly became more relaxed as he spooned the mint chocolate chip into his mouth, savoring each bite. "I like this ice cream. Do you eat it often?"

"Me, no, I have enough of a weight problem without eating it often, but you won't have that problem."

"I think you have a good body, Carrie Taylor."

They finished the movie with Blake more relaxed than when it had started. That was a good sign. At least it didn't scare him half as much as Carrie thought it would. Walking down the hall to his room with him, Carrie showed him how the lights worked and how to use the toothbrush and other items in the bathroom. "If you need anything tonight, anything at all, just come in. Don't worry about waking me. It's okay. I'd rather you tell me if something is wrong or you need something than for you to worry about it, okay?"

"I will, Carrie."

Her heart went out to the man, trapped in a time not of his choosing and all the obstacles and changes he was going to have to face. Could she take care of him, ensure his safety and help him to be comfortable here? Well, time would tell, time would tell.

Chapter Fifteen

Black Eagle watched the young woman leave the room she'd given him, glad the little panther had decided to stay by his side. The little black cat jumped up on the bed and made himself comfortable.

"It is good you are here with me, Taister. Let us look together at the wonderful things Carrie has given me. I will tell you this, little panther, this is not at all like my teepee at home. I think you would like it though. There is a warm fire and many furs to lay on. Home. Do you think my home still exists? That my people wonder where I have gone?"

The cat looked up at him, seeming to wait for his questions to end so he could respond in some way.

"Do my people exist anymore? What happened to them? Do they know I am gone? Did they look for me? Or have I ceased to exist?"

Taister chirped a little meow before sitting up and beginning to groom himself.

Black Eagle watched the cat go about his business. "Perhaps you are right. It is best to live each day as it is, and not worry about other things."

During the day Carrie and Molly mentioned they were in California. He knew of California. Many men from his time were headed here. Back then it was there, for gold. As if something material was worth more than family and friends. At one time, he thought it was all white men that took without giving back.

Today, spending time with Carrie and Molly, their

generosity had shown him differently. They were warm, caring, they had been kind to a stranger, compassionate about his fears. They gave him a home. They told him about many of the wondrous things he had seen both in his dreams and now in reality and, in turn, he answered Carrie's questions about life in his village. He was pleased she had such an interest in his home, his time. It seemed she already knew much of his world. She said it was from her books and while some of it was not accurate, there was much that was true. Perhaps, he thought, the reading she had done was *Nagi Tanka's* way of preparing her for a life with him. After all, why would Mr. Arthur Merle's box take his spirit to bring him here to her home if they were not meant to be together? Whether it be here in her time or back in his, if he could return, he did not know.

This Carrie Taylor, though, was one of a kind and in a short period of time, one he knew he wanted to be with. Yet, was it really that short a time?

"I will tell you this, Taister. From the day Mr. Arthur Merle took my photograph I have dreamed of Carrie."

In the dreams he saw many of the things he had since seen in her home. He had also seen Carrie and puzzled at some of the things she had done which, after speaking with her today, he learned could be her 'work'. In the dreams she did not seem to have a man to care for her and now, in her home, he knew for certain she was alone. There was no husband. Only Carrie, Molly and the little panther.

Again he looked over the room. Each item seemed to have been chosen with care. From what he had seen of Carrie and Molly, it seemed to reflect parts of both women. He guessed the gentler items, the quilt on the bed, the pictures with the soft shades of blues and pinks, the beige pitcher with the bowl—like the ones the women of his time liked—would be from Carrie. From his dreams, and what he had seen of her today, he could only credit these things to her.

The metal work things and things on the desk, they would be Molly's influence, he decided. Molly was clearly the more practical of the two.

He wandered over to the window, pulled the curtain aside and looked out into the dark night. The stars here seemed somehow smaller and not quite so bright. He would ask Carrie about this tomorrow. Resting his forehead on the cool window, he closed his eyes and sought to see his home in his mind. Had it only been last night he had been taken from it? Carried to this new place? Had it really been just last night he had looked up at the stars and thought again of finding a wife?

So much had happened in so short a time. He hoped the next day would hold fewer new things to see and understand. Not that they were bad, and he did not care to learn. It was that so much new had happened to him, in so short a time. Perhaps it would bring answers to his questions, especially the one as to how he came to this time. Somehow, he knew it would not.

Starting back over to the bed, he saw Taister already lying on one of the pillows, his black fur seeming even darker against the pale pink pillowcase. "Little panther, you know what is best in life, do you not?"

Taister glanced over at the tall man approaching the bed, his yellow eyes taking in every move the man made. As Black Eagle lay down on the bed, Taister extended one paw towards him and rested it on his arm. "Carrie says you are a cat for her house. That you will not grow into a mighty panther. I think she is wrong. I think you are as brave and cunning as the big cats. I have no doubt you have the heart and soul of a panther."

Taister looked up at him, meowed and laid his head down on the pillow, clearly ready for sleep. "Good night, little panther. Sleep well."

Black Eagle lay there a long while waiting for sleep to claim him. He was tired, so tired, but his mind would not still. Alone with his thoughts, he began to fear that the unknown forces would take him again, but not back to his home, or to someone as kind as Carrie.

The sliver of moonlight that peeked through the window cast a mosaic of patterns on the walls and floor, bringing his mind to the things he had seen not only in Carrie's home, but when they went, what she called shopping, today. He had immediately recognized the boxes in her kitchen, the shapes, but not the names until she and Molly had told him what the dishwasher, microwave and coffeemaker were. He wanted to ask them more about these wondrous things, but first there was Molly's entrance to the kitchen, then talk of the shopping and then their outing. As much as he wanted to know about the strange, yet apparently useful devices, he felt it would be rude to ask.

If he remained in this time, if the fates did not send him back to his time tonight, there would be time to ask. And if he were returned to his time, then they would not matter. They would be memories for him to hold, tales to tell around the fire. His mind drifted, near sleep, yet unable to cross the bridge to the world of dreams. Dreams and sleep evaded him as again and again he replayed events in his mind from when Mr. Merle took his photograph. The elderly man assured him the camera would not take his spirit, but there was a knowing glint in the old man's eye — one Black Eagle had chosen to ignore because he did not want to appear weak or afraid.

Thinking back on that day, he once again saw the events as they unfolded. He and several of the other warriors had left early that day to bring their women to town. There was word of new finery arriving and when the women heard, they wanted to see what the Whites had found so fascinating.

There were five men, including himself and three of the women. They brought some pelts and rich hides to trade. When they arrived, they went to the trading post and offered their wares. One of the men, Burt MacAfee, eagerly told them about the stranger who was visiting and his cam-er-a-a tin something he called it. Burt described how this cam-er-a would capture the likeness of a person.

Black Eagle and a few of his friends had heard of these before, and had heard that they would steal a man's spirit, forever encasing it in the box. He thought it best not even to see the strange box, but at Gray Wolf's prodding they went to see.

Gray Wolf and he had competed many times. There was no malice between them, just a healthy rivalry. His friend had quickly found a bride — once he decided it was time to take a wife he chose a woman from the village and swiftly came forth with the bride price. Already he and Runs Like A Deer were expecting their second child. Black Eagle often wondered why each woman he thought perhaps would make a good wife soon fell short of what he wanted for himself. All the women in his tribe were good women, strong, with a love of family. Yet not one spoke to his heart. His friend, White Elk, told him he was too picky, and if he continued on that path he would find himself with no one. But still Black Eagle found no one he wanted to share his hearth and furs with.

With his friends so interested in this Mr. Arthur Merle and his mysterious box, they all went to see the wondrous sight. At first glance, Mr. Arthur Merle could have been just another man. There was nothing special to him, nothing that would stand out. At first, anyway. As Black Eagle watched him, though, he saw there was much to the man. His snow white hair told him this was a man who had experienced much. Perhaps even a wise man. His twinkling blue eyes seemed timeless, yet at the same time they seemed to have seen more than the events of one lifetime. The blue was crystal clear, like that of a young man. It was the light in them that spoke of the ages.

Mr. Arthur Merle's shoulders were slightly stooped, as if he had depended on a cane or walking stick for part of his life. Yet his hands seemed to be those of a younger man. At first glance Black Eagle felt Mr. Merle to be a study in contrasts — so many contrasts that it would take many years to find out who the real man was.

When they approached the area where Mr. Merle was taking the photographs a line of people, white people, waited their turn, each eager to have their own photo taken. The normally playful children, dressed in their Sunday-go-to-meeting clothes, stood in awe as each family approached to have their moment before the camera.

Only now, thinking back on that day, did Black Eagle think it strange that Mr. Merle seemed to study him so closely. Yes, he and his friends had been watched before. Whenever new people came to the town and they rode in, those who had never seen a Lakota were curious. Black Eagle learned early on, it was best to smile and be friendly to these newcomers. It was obvious to him more and more of them would come and it was better to be genial and welcome them. But the way Mr. Merle watched him was different. It appeared Mr. Merle knew Black Eagle would be there, and that he wanted to meet him. There was good-natured ribbing about having his photograph taken and truly, he had no fear. For the most part, he believed that only *Nagi Tanka* could take his soul, yet now here he was, in another time, with only a woman he had seen in his dreams to help him.

Just before Mr. Merle took the photograph he made a strange sign with his hand, gliding his hand one way, with his palm down, and back the other with the palm up. It reminded him of the signs the medicine man made during a special ceremony. When the photograph was taken, he did not feel any different, nor did he feel odd afterward. Yet, as he thought back on it now, Mr. Merle had again made the sign with his hand and he did not make it with any other person. Did he? Black Eagle went back over each person whose photograph he had seen taken that day and no, only with Black Eagle's was the sign made. What did the sign mean? Would Carrie's Mr. Merle perhaps know?

Carrie knew many things. Perhaps she knew what it meant. What of his people? Did they know he was gone? Would they look for him? Or . . .

Had his friends also been transported to other times through their photographs? Had Mr. Merle captured all of their spirits? Would he see Gray Wolf on the street? Or Falling Leaf in one of the stores here in Napa?

If Carrie's Mr. Merle possessed the one that held Black Eagle's spirit, perhaps he had the rest. If that was so, then perhaps they were also here in this time. The thoughts whirling in his head refused to settle. Each question led not to answers, but to more questions. Ones he now longed to ask Carrie.

However, he was a guest in her home and would not disturb her sleep. Tomorrow would be soon enough to seek the answers. And since her Mr. Merle was gone for a time, they needed to wait for his return to see what he could tell them.

Carrie. She was good and kind and generous, yet he sensed there was more than goodness to her. She was a woman from another time, yet something about her spoke to his heart. Finally, unable to sleep, he rose and made his way to Carrie's room. He stood at the foot of the bed staring at the sleeping woman, not knowing that before she had fallen into the deep sleep, she had sat staring at the photograph.

After he held no doubt that she slept, he moved to the side of the bed. He glanced at the photograph, but only briefly and did not move to touch it. He did not know what would happen if he did, but the fear that it would send him back to his time was foremost in his mind. Black Eagle missed his home, yes, but for now he felt the need to stay. It was best he stay and learn the answers to his questions, than to return to his own time only to find himself once again waking in yet another time. Who knew what other secrets or travels Mr. Merle might have in store for him? No, it was better to remain in this time and learn what he could.

Lying down on the floor beside Carrie's bed, the sleep that eluded him earlier came quickly now, with dreams of his home and wondering if he would see it again.

CHAPTER SIXTEEN

Carrie heard a sound toward morning. From the creak of the floorboards, it sounded like someone walking across her floor.

She lay listening for a moment before turning and lifting her head to look. There was no one to be seen. "Must have been Taister," she muttered to herself. She punched the pillow and fell back asleep for a short time more.

On her way to the kitchen later, she stuck her head in Black Eagle's room. How quickly she came to think of it as his room? Was it really just yesterday he had landed in her life? She saw him sitting on the bed, talking softly to Taister. The little guy was looking up at him with complete adoration in those yellow eyes of his. Taister never really sat that long to listen to anyone, if he listened at all. Like all cats, it was all about his opinion, whether you wanted to hear it or not. Never mind telling him you didn't understand Cat-anese! In the morning he would be yowling for food before she was even half out of bed.

Yet, he totally adored this man from the past. Then again, Black Eagle was the first and only person who thought the little cat was a big brave panther. Her glance at the cat was short lived due to the view of the man sitting there, without a shirt and the top button of his jeans open. The man was pure walking eye candy. His long black hair begged for her fingers to thread themselves through it. His lips—oh man, just the thought of the slightest brush against them set her pulse racing. That first kiss, when she was sure he was a fantasy, filled her mind, making her wonder if it would feel that good if she kissed him not believing him a figment of her imagination? That first kiss was one heck of a steamy one and she wouldn't mind a steady diet of them.

And his chest. She sighed. Carrie knew guys who worked out in the gym two to three hours a day, five days a week, to try to come close to Black Eagle's. The smooth skin and well developed muscles were temptation incarnate.

She glanced at his belly. Talk about six-pack abs. Her fingers tingled in anticipation of running all over them. Then there were his hips and butt—the man had the tightest, most grabbable buns she'd ever seen. Of course, that butt of his couldn't be quite as delectable if it didn't rest upon those thighs that bunched and bulged just so absolutely perfectly. Yes, walking eye candy just begging to be . . .

"Good morning, Carrie Taylor."

"Uh, umm, morning. Ah, so, you two hungry?" She knew her face flamed totally red at being caught staring.

"Yes, Carrie Taylor, I am."

"Well, great, I'll get started on some breakfast for us." Oh gees, he didn't see me salivating just from looking at him, did he? Someone get me a sponge with a jaw strap, please!

He stood and reached for one of the tee shirts Carrie had bought him the day before, a slight grimace on his face.

"You know, if it's umm, uncomfortable, you could, well, I wouldn't mind if you—well, here in the house you can be comfortable and if you're cold I'll just turn the heat up a bit." *Oh no, I wouldn't mind at all. — .but if you leave that shirt off, fella, I don't know if I'll be able to control my hands.*

"No, I need to learn to live in your world. I will learn to wear the clothes of your time."

"Well, whatever works, or whenever you're ready."

As he pulled the shirt over his head, Carrie couldn't decide if she was relieved or agitated because she wouldn't see those magnificent pecs over breakfast. Oh, she could just see it now . . .

"Carrie?"

"Huh? What? Did I say something?" Oh my God, I didn't say anything aloud, did I? I so have to stop these fantasies.

"I asked if you were well. You seem to have sent your thoughts to another place."

"Ah, no, just thinking. You know, just — thinking."

While they walked to the kitchen Carrie's mind went to one of its favorite places — hot sex with a good-looking guy and today's male *du jour* was Black Eagle. *Wrong, wrong, wrong. He doesn't even know what a romance novel is, let alone that he's the walking, talking epitome of one. I'm sure my thoughts alone would send him back in time without the photograph.*

"Should we wake Molly?" he asked looking toward Molly's room.

"Um, no. She sleeps in on her days off. We'll see her later."

"What is the work she does?"

"She works for a police department. Sort of like for the sheriff in your time. Now, though, because we're more spread out they have what are called dispatchers to tell the sheriff type guys where to go. Her boss is a real piece of work. Molly'd leave if she could, but until something else comes along she's kind of stuck."

"It is good you let her rest. I will help you tend to your chores."

She started to laugh before she realized he was serious. *In all the excitement yesterday, he must have missed the no cows and chickens thing.* "No, people who live on farms do, but we town type people, we just buy stuff at the grocery store. I do appreciate the thought, though."

Seeing his confused look, she continued, "We'll go to a grocery store today and stock up on things you'll like. You'll see they're pretty cool."

"And we will buy more pizza?"

"Yeah, we can pick up a pizza, or see what else looks good

to you for dinner. They have some frozen ones we can buy, and you can heat them up while I'm at work."

"Your time is strange to see. In my time, Indian women work in the village—each person has their responsibility. Very few White women work, those that do, they are . . ." He shrugged, and gave her a small smile.

"I can assure you, that is not the kind of work I do." Although, I wouldn't mind pretending to with you, sweet cakes.

"I did not mean that of you, Carrie Taylor. I know you are not what the men of my time call a prostitute. You are a caring, kind and generous one. *Nagi Tanka* smiled on me when they sent me to your home."

"Oh sure, I know. I guess I just get kinda nervous, you know, I get worried you might not understand or I might say it wrong, or . . ."

Black Eagle put his fingers to her lips. His scent filled her and the shock that went right through to her groin was unlike anything she'd ever felt before. Oh yeah, she'd been horny and gotten turned on, but nothing like this. It took every bit of her will power not to launch herself into his arms and get him in a lip lock that he'd never forget. Then again, any woman instigating a lip lock with him would probably shock him onto that sweet butt of his.

No, no, no, Carrie, put a lid on it. You are now officially bawdy-brained and the poor man isn't here because of anything he did — fate played a cruel joke on him.

"So after breakfast, I thought maybe we could look up some information on your tribe and see if there's any record of you, or what may have happened. It seems to me that if we start there and work forward maybe we can figure some of this out, you know?"

"That seems a good idea. I also have some questions that maybe we can answer. Perhaps we can find other relatives of my Mr. Merle. Carrie, I am also concerned that if there were other photographs, that others from my time may be here somewhere. If so, I need to find them."

"Oh wow, yeah, I hadn't thought about that. I was just so focused on you and what's happening with you."

"I am flattered, Carrie."

"Thank you. I guess we need to look at those issues, as well."

"Yes, but how do we do this looking?"

"The Internet. Not to worry, I'll take care of the looking part. You, my friend, will be telling me what to look for."

While Carrie made breakfast, Black Eagle took care of Taister's meal.

The little cat seemed pleased that the man remembered how to open up the can of food, and actually ate almost all of the fishy smelling victuals rather than his usual two bites.

After breakfast, Carrie took Black Eagle into their library. "We, Molly and I, lucked out when we rented this four-bedroom house. Actually, it's Molly's great uncle's. When it became too much for him to maintain, we moved in and in exchange for low rent, agreed to take care of it and make whatever renovations needed to be done, painting and other upkeep. We've known each other since junior high, so in a lot of ways we're more like sisters than friends, you know?"

"Yes, I think I understand."

"We've gone through so much together. First dates. First breakups. First sex. First jobs. First vacations without the parents. Almost all our firsts. And now, well, now we have our first time traveler."

"Yes, that I am, and I am grateful you have given me a place to stay."

"I'm glad, too. You know, at one time we thought about getting a third roommate, but honestly we like the idea of having a library and guest room, just in case and the just in case happened with your arrival."

He wandered about the room, apparently awestruck by the

number of books. Carrie realized that even the richest people from his time wouldn't have nearly as many as she and Molly had amassed—or at least the ones that came with the house. And an Indian, well, she would be surprised if they would have any real use for books. Not from what she knew of how hard it was for them to even live off the land. "Do you like to read?"

"Read? No, Carrie, I do not read. But I would like to. You would teach me?"

"Yes. Of course. That's a great idea. We can start today."

Carrie moved to the desk where the computer was, sat down and turned it on.

When the monitor first lit up, Black Eagle jumped back, just for a brief second, before running to Carrie's side and taking her into his arms as he pulled her off the chair. They rolled to the floor with Black Eagle's arm cradling Carrie's head while he broke the fall with his body, yet at the same time rolling him under her. He lay there, holding her gently but firmly, protecting her, but Carrie couldn't begin to imagine from what.

Her hand pressed to his chest, she felt the slow, steady beat of his heart, while his hips lay nestled against hers, one of his muscular legs between hers, his knee comfortably close to her pelvis, causing the most wonderful little shocks to move through her. Without even trying, the man was just hot, incredibly hot. But what had frightened him?

"Black Eagle?" She looked up at him and into his eyes. He was staring straight ahead, his breathing slow and steady, but not deep enough to truly move his body. It was like he was staring at some sort of prey. "Black Eagle, talk to me, please?"

"Carrie, the light."

"What light?"

"Up there, on the desk. It almost captured us."

"No, Black Eagle, no, it's just the computer monitor,

nothing more. It just comes on so you can see what's there." Oh man, I blew it, I really blew it. The guy is afraid of cameras—simple box camera—I should have known or at least thought about what the computer would do to him. "I'm sorry. I should have thought. Black Eagle, I'm so sorry. I guess a lot of our gadgets and gizmos are confusing to you."

"What, Carrie?" He rolled slightly off to the side, still in a position that would protect her, but not quite so intimate.

She was sure it was not that he was looking to be intimate. The man tried so hard to protect her, and no one had ever done that before. Imagine an honest, decent, caring man wanting only to protect her. "The computer, the electrical things and all we have—I forgot about the camera you saw, the one from your time and your concerns about it. Cameras have come a long way since then, in fact, you barely even notice the flash anymore and computers are sorta kinda like a camera, but not really. Now people all over the world can talk to each other and share information almost as soon as it happens. But it needs something to make it happen and that was the light you saw."

She could see from the blank look on his face that he did not understand one thing she said and that she, herself, made no sense at all. "Tell you what. As much as I like laying here sort of underneath you, maybe we should sit up and talk?"

"You like my body on yours?" The amazement in his voice was clear.

Who wouldn't? "Well, umm, wel—to be honest—yeah, it's kinda nice. I don't normally just roll around on the floor with a guy and I don't have sex with just anyone, but well, it's nice being around you. I like the way you feel."

"I like the way you feel, too, Carrie Taylor. And I, too, do not have sex with any woman."

"Well, I'm glad we agree on that. And anytime you want to lie on . . ." She caught herself before she said something totally stupid. "Well, what do you say we sit down and I'll try to explain the computer?"

"And after you explain that, we will talk about lying beside each other?"

She sure did like it when he smiled like that. Heck when he smiled period she liked it. "Sure. Sure, that will be nice. Yeah, sure."

They rose and with Black Eagle moving his body between Carrie and the computer monitor, they went to the couch. Carrie saw the screen saver come up and wasn't sure if she should mention it and what it meant or not. She'd chosen it from one of her favorite romance novels, a futuristic called *Jason's Accord* that was about this totally hunky alpha male named Jason who marries this woman from another planet. The screen saver was a picture of the cover that was beyond hot. It slowly popped on and off the screen. Erring on the side of caution, she said nothing and as they sat, she positioned herself so he wouldn't need to see the desk, or the hot guy on the screen saver.

Over the next few hours Carrie explained, as best she could, the history of cameras. How they went from the daguerreotypes to the tintypes that Black Eagle had seen, to the Polaroid instant pictures, to disposables and digitals and now taking photos with phones. He sat and listened, at first concerned that so many spirits had been taken and then impressed with her knowledge of what could be done. When she pulled out her cell phone and showed him how it could also take a picture, he went from impressed, to awed, to wanting to know how he too could have one. He was quite fascinated by the fact that through the little box he could talk to someone on the other side of the world and sad to learn he could not call back to his own time.

Seeing how he became increasingly relaxed, at least with the knowledge of technology, Carrie told him, "See, there's not that much difference between you and modern man."

"Ah, Carrie Taylor, there is much difference between us."

She saw the smile peeking out from his so kissable lips. "And what is that difference?"

"The modern men only travel a few miles in the large metal boxes to be with you. I traveled many miles and through many years, did I not?"

"Yes, I suppose you did."

"And this impresses you, does it not?"

Carrie felt relief at his words. They told her he was feeling better about what had happened. That he was becoming more interested in the world he had ended up in. "*Yeah*, I suppose it does. Does it impress you?"

"It does, Carrie Taylor, it does. And you, woman, you impress me."

"Well, since we're telling each other what we think, you impress *and* interest me. I—ummm—to tell you the truth . . ."

"What? Carrie, tell me. There should be no secrets between us."

At first, Carrie thought that an odd thing to say to her. Like they were going to be more than just acquaintances, or that he felt he would be in her life for a long, long time. Then she thought about the little she knew about him, and his people, and what was important to them. "Well, I read a lot of umm, books about people who aren't real or are pretend, you know, stories?"

"Yes, I understand stories."

"Well, a lot of the ones I read about the old west—It wasn't old when *you* lived there—but it's old to me now and I always wanted to meet a real Indian warrior. And now I have, and you are so much better than the men in the books. I feel like now I can find out more about what life was really like."

"I would like to do that for you. It would be a good way to learn about each other."

"Great." Feeling a moment of unease, Carrie glanced about the room. "So, ummm, how about some coffee?"

"Yes, coffee would be nice."

"Good, I'm ready for some." They rose and headed into the kitchen. Glancing at the clock, she suggested some lunch. At Black Eagle's ready agreement, she pulled out the makings for sandwiches.

Over a meal of roast beef and cheddar cheese on warm sourdough bread, Carrie decided it would be a good time to introduce him to the computer and what could be done with it, hands on. After learning more about cameras, he was a bit more amenable to hearing about the computer. By the time they finished their sandwiches, he was more than ready to try the computer and see what they could learn.

The phone rang as they entered the library. Black Eagle followed closely after Carrie to the phone, eager to see how the device worked. "Hello?"

"Hey, babe."

"Dean." Her voice clearly filled with disgust, she continued, "I thought I told you to stay the hell out of my life."

"Come on, babe. Lighten up. I keep telling you, it was just sex with Jolene. Just plain ole sex. She wasn't even that good."

"I don't care what it was or wasn't. You broke my trust, you treated me like dirt and, well, you know what? I don't have to explain anything to you."

"Aw, babe, come on. You aren't really going to hold that simple screw session against me, are you?"

"I'm not holding anything against you, Dean, nothing at all, if you get my drift. And stop calling me. I've told you and told you, stay-away-from-me." With that she hung up the phone and turned to discover Black Eagle standing closely behind her, concern marking his handsome face.

"What has troubled you, Carrie?"

"No one important."

"If it was no one important, why did your face turn so pale and your shoulders tense so?"

"It's nothing, really."

"I thought we agreed for honesty. This does not seem honesty to me."

Carrie sighed. "You're right. It's not important, not anymore, but I'll tell you a little, okay?"

"Yes."

She led him back over to the couch and sat crosswise to him before beginning. "Well, you see, I haven't had the best of luck with men. Dean, the guy who just called, was the latest in a long line of losers. I wasn't looking for a husband, or anything like getting married. I like dating and meeting new people. Every once in awhile, though, you meet someone who you think is a forever kind of person, that they'll be in your life forever. I had started to think Dean was that guy. Turns out, if anything, he was my worst choice yet. At least I found out before things got too far, before I got my heart really involved."

"What is a phone? And he is your husband?"

"No. Thank goodness for that. The husband part. A phone, the phone, what I just talked to Dean on? Well, it's really called a telephone and it helps to talk to people who aren't right there with you."

"Then what was he to you, if not your husband?"

"I don't want to overload you with too much information, you know?"

"You will tell me, Carrie Taylor." Gently given, it was an order and it made Carrie bristle until she thought about it— Black Eagle was a man from another time and place, a time when men, at least men like him, were honest and caring and in charge, a man who was going to protect his family and Carrie was, by his standards, a part of his family. And what harm was there in telling him, just a little, about Dean?

"Okay. Today we—all of us—well, most of us date. We go out with different people before we get married. And we, a lot of us, will umm, well we, if we're dating and it looks like it might get serious, we may sleep with them. You know, have sex."

"You told me you do not sleep with just any man. You slept with that one?"

"No, not quite like that. I mean some women do. But Molly and I, with both of us, it's only been someone very special or someone we thought or think is special."

"So this Dean was someone special to you?"

Carrie thought she could have been mistaken, or maybe it was wishful thinking, but he seemed to look upset, like maybe he didn't want Dean, or any other man, to be special. *Okay, I'm being fanciful because at some point this guy is going to go back to his own time and you, Carrie-girl, will remain here with the slugs you always seem to meet.* "Like I said, I thought he might be the one, but I was wrong. I—I caught him in bed with this other woman from his work. This bitch, Jolene, was in bed with him."

"At his work? Who is this Jolene? How did you catch him in his bed? The one for what?"

Clearly, her explanation created more questions, than answers, for him. "No, actually that would have been funny, especially with how conservative his company is. No, I had a key to his apartment and stopped in one afternoon to surprise him, and it was me who got the surprise. He was in bed with this other woman from his work. I always knew she was a dirty sneak. She has something just smarmy about her. Her name is Jolene Crane and she's one of the newer associates in his office."

"Ass?"

"You got that right. A major ass. Oh, you were asking about Jolene being an associate. See, Dean's an attorney."

"Attorney?"

"A lawyer. You know, the guys who go before judges."

"Ah, yes, that I know."

"And now-a-days lawyers don't always work for themselves or by themselves. They work in groups, firms. Dean works for one of the biggest ones in the area and they often hire new lawyers to work there. Jolene was one of the ones they hired about a year ago. She's a total sleaze, and what really stinks is she's in charge of hiring and firing for secretaries, and stuff. I met her at the firm's holiday party, and she slithered up to every guy who let her, even in front of their wives."

"We have women like that in my time. They dress in clothing meant to make men look at them and accept money for time in their beds. Prostitutes," he spat.

Well, I don't think Jolene ever took money for sex, but she definitely did it to move up in the firm. She's moved up the ranks in a short period of time, and from what I hear, she's just mean. Manipulative and mean." Carrie nodded for emphasis. "I've heard stories about her from people who work at the firm about her — people I'm still in touch with. She's a piece of work, that's for sure. I just never thought she'd sleep with a guy she knew belonged to someone else. But it was pretty naïve of me, 'cause I knew her past, or at least heard it. Of course, you never know what Dean told her. He's a liar and a sneak. Then again, they're really perfect for each other."

"And what of her past, Carrie?"

"I knew she'd been married twice before and both times it was to men she stole from other women. And I heard these stories about her, from friends of mine, one of them who worked for her as a secretary. She makes it so she always wins. Like my friend Rose. Jolene had it in for her because Rose is smart and wouldn't take any crap from her. She twists things to make sure she's always right. Rose told me Jolene pads her billing, so she's basically stealing from her clients."

"No one has done anything about her and what she does?

They allow her to steal?"

"Well, by stole I don't mean she took something, like a crime. It's a phrase we use to say someone did something slimy—but when it comes to relationships, it's free will. Rose also told me twice before Jolene met men who were married and started affairs with them. They left their wives and married her."

"At the same time?"

"Oh, no. For as awful and trashy as she is, at least she was only married to one man at a time. No, the first time she met a guy, he was married and she enticed him into an affair. He left his wife and Jolene married him. Then when she was still married to the first guy, she met Joe Crane and figured his money was more important than her marriage, so she dumped her first husband and started an affair with Joe and Joe married her. She's still married to Joe—or at least I think she still is, I don't pay much attention to her—but she decided she wanted Dean and went after him, only I didn't know she set her sights on him until I dropped by to see him and found them in bed together. It hurt, it really hurt, at least when it happened."

Clearly interested in her story he asked, "What did you do?"

Carrie took a moment to drink in the care and compassion in his big brown eyes—his lashes seemed far too long for a man. "I ran out. I wasn't about to let her see me cry. I drove around for awhile and called Molly and we went out drinking. I got so roaring drunk it wasn't even funny, at least then. Now it is, because apparently I did some really dumb things."

"Like what?" His voice was soft, and doing things to Carrie's tummy that had never happened to her before. "Like I decided I wanted to go up to Reno and get even more drunk and do all kinds of crazy things for a week or two."

"And did you?"

"What? And leave Taister to fend for himself? Little panther may be good at getting you to do his bidding, but hunt for himself? I don't think so. If he even saw a mouse he'd probably run so fast my head would spin."

"So little panther is not the mighty hunter he has led me to believe he is?"

His eyes twinkled, while a smile spread across his mouth. She smiled in return. "It seems all he's captured lately is you."

"I am very good to catch." The look in his dark eyes, reminding her of liquid chocolate, spoke volumes more than the potent words coming from his so very kissable lips. Yes indeed, he would be a very good catch. Unfortunately, at any moment he could leave, disappear back in time, and Carrie would never see him again except in the photograph. If, and it was a very big if, the image returned there.

"You know, I think we've done a lot of thinking work today and it's really a gorgeous day out. I know you want to find your way home or back in time, but why don't we give our brains a rest and take a walk?"

"I am in no rush to return to my time, Carrie. Yes, I would like to return home, but I see there is more for me to learn about you, your time. I like the idea of a walk. Yes, let's go."

"Good. We'll do some grocery shopping and then hit the park."

"Hit the . . .Carrie, I do not wish to hit . . ."

"It's a figure of speech. It doesn't mean we're going to hit like actually touch or strike anyone—just that we're going to go there and hang out."

"You have strange ways of saying things in your time, Carrie Taylor. I will have to learn them all, especially the ones you have told me about Jolene Bitch."

Grabbing her jacket, she paused a moment before giving a quick nod of her head. "Yeah, I guess we do. I'll try to speak more plainly."

"I like the way you talk, Carrie. Very much."

"Thanks. So are you good about the grocery shopping? That makes sense, right?"

"We go to obtain food."

"Yup, that's it."

Carrie quickly disabused any notion that grocery shopping with Black Eagle would be a walk in the park.

The cart fascinated him and the rows of meat in packages quickly caught his attention. It took a bit of pulling and assurances that they had plenty, to get him moving to pick some vegetables and fruit. She contemplated steering him away from the frozen foods until it occurred to her the microwave would be fairly safe and she could teach him to use it, so down the frozen food aisle they went. Trying to pick out what he'd like seemed fairly easy until she saw he had gone right to the ice cream section. Even the promise of pretzels and chips couldn't lure him from the frozen treats.

The man may not be able to read, but he sure picked out the picture pretty darn fast. "I would like the one we had last night."

"Sure. Want to try anything else?"

"No. Just what we had last night."

"Okay. I'm going to get cherry for me. We also need to get some dinners for you while I'm at work."

"Dinners?"

"Um, yeah, frozen dinners. We used to call them TV dinners because you could stick them in the oven and then eat them in front of the TV. Now we just call them frozen."

"I see."

They went to the cat food aisle to choose some of Taister's favorites, and then to the personal care to get him guy type supplies.

Making a quick trip home to unload the groceries, Carrie grabbed a sweater and a few apples and stuck them in her fanny pack with her keys and some money. She caught Black Eagle's appraisal of the pack and ran to her room and returned with another one, along with some paper and a pen. "I know you can take care of yourself, not a problem, but, well, just in case, let me write down our address and phone number. If we get separated for some reason I want to know you can find your way back home — here — home here — well, you know . . ."

"I know, Carrie." The smile in his voice was evident to her. "I understand what you mean, Carrie, and it gives me happiness to know you wish this to be my home. Yes, I want to return to my time, but until we know how I can do so I am happy to be here with you."

"Thanks. Sometimes I kind of run away with my thoughts, my words get jumbled and I don't say things well."

"I have seen this."

"Yeah?"

"Ye-ah, and it is part of what makes you a desirable woman."

Desirable! He thought she was desirable! Well, total coolness. This gorgeous man found her des . . .oh — wait — what he meant by desirable probably wasn't what she meant by desirable. It probably meant something very different to him, his people and the people from his time. It probably didn't mean he wanted to get naked with her and do the horizontal mambo. No, probably not that at all. *Darn!* Getting naked with him would be . . .

"Carrie . . .Carrie, are you well?"

"Huh?" She mentally shook herself. "Yeah, sure, I'm great. Here." She handed him the paper with his name on it, their address and phone number. Realizing she was treating him like a child, she apologized, "I'm sorry. This is wrong, so wrong. I know you know your name, but I figure if I put your name on it, someone might think that maybe you meant to give it to someone you met in a club or something, not that you don't know the name we're calling you."

"You mean Blake Eagleston?"

"Yes."

"It is a good thing, Carrie. And I will remember my White name." There was sadness in his voice as he reached out and placed his hand on Carrie's arm.

They walked up to a nearby park and Carrie explained to him about the money she had given him, the denominations. After considering it a moment, she also went on to tell him how he couldn't take it back in time with him because of what happened in one of her favorite movies of all time, *Somewhere in Time*, which led her to consider: "You know you can't talk about being here if and when you get back in time?"

"No?"

"I don't think it would be a good idea. First, people might think you are crazy, think about it—how did you feel when you saw the first cars and the microwave? You saw them and I know you were a little nervous about them. Think about how people would feel if you told them about this time and you couldn't prove it? And history could change if you talk about it. Gees, history may have already changed because you are here now. So, no talking about traveling through time. That would get you into the loony bin faster than you can say pizza."

"Looney? You use more words and phrases than I have heard at one time. How do you think my being here has changed time?"

"Well. Did you have a wife or children?"

"No."

"A girlfriend, um, you know, a special lady?"

"I . . ."

She saw the confusion crossing his features and wondered if he was searching for an answer that would not upset her.

She remembered Mr. Merle said he didn't have a girlfriend or wife, but things could have changed after the old gent's ancestor left the area. Who knows, maybe he met someone the very next day. "Look, if there was a Mrs. Eagle or an intended Mrs. Eagle, I'm cool with it, and I'm totally behind you getting back to her."

"There was no woman in my time. I wished for one. I hoped *Nagi Tanka* would send me one, but it was not to be, at least not before I came here."

"Well, that could be one way time got changed. It might have been that you were going to meet her in a few days or weeks or years. So, there might be this woman who you are supposed to marry and be with and now you won't meet her because you are here."

"I do not see the problem with that."

"You don't?"

"No. I like you, Carrie. I like being with you."

"You do?" She hated that her voice squeaked and she sounded so surprised that someone would actually like being with her. He probably meant as a friend. A guy like Black Eagle couldn't possibly be interested in her romantically, right? Besides, they had just met. He couldn't have feelings for her, right?

"Yes, I like being with you. You are unlike any person I have ever met."

Oh great, he thinks I'm a freak. "Um, and you aren't like anyone I've ever met. In real life, anyway."

"I hope that is good, Carrie."

"Oh yeah, but see, there could be a problem. What if you and the woman you were supposed to marry were supposed to have a child, who was supposed to be someone famous?"

"I *suppose* that will not happen now."

Carrie laughed, "Yeah, well *I suppose* I need to speak a little more clearly. So, um, what I was trying to say is that maybe either a child you are going to have, or would have had, or their child, would be someone famous or special. Now it might not happen, because you are here."

"I understand your concern about duty, Carrie, but I am here through no doing by you or me. So we must live with what we have, yes?"

"I guess, but what if we do something now to make some sort of change that wasn't—"

"Carrie, what is, is. I am here with you. For whatever reason, powers stronger than us have sent me here with you. Yes, I would like to know how this came to be, because if suddenly I am back in my own time, I would want to know what I need to do to remain in my time."

"I understand." Sadness crossed her features and settled in her gaze. "You know, I should have thought about this earlier ... yesterday, even. I haven't even asked you how you felt, you know, physically, when you came through time. I'm sorry."

"There is no reason to be sorry."

"No, there is. I never stopped thinking about, well, I got so caught up first in thinking someone was playing a joke on me and then just trying to get a grip on the fact that you are here, that you really are here. I was at a loss of what to do, and I never thought about what it felt like for you. Can you tell me? Will you tell me?"

"There was nothing to feel. One moment I stood in my time. Then I woke here in yours."

"So you didn't feel anything, not like your body changed or anything? You didn't get a head ache or upset stomach or dizzy?"

"No, nothing that I remember feeling. I could not sleep and went to the river. There I looked to the sky and watched a star fall. I remember nothing until I woke up beside you."

"Oh."

"You sound disappointed, Carrie."

"I guess. I know I shouldn't. It's not like anyone I know has ever met a real time traveler. I never thought about what to expect."

"It is not anything I ever thought to happen to me either. So how do we know if my being here has changed time?"

"I don't know. I was thinking about it and unless you were a key player for some big battle or event, what are the chances you were even written about? I don't mean you aren't important, just that news didn't travel as fast then and your average person didn't have much written about them, you know?"

"I do not think much good was written about the Lakoka or my tribe, the *Sihásapa*."

"It would be good to change that. I sure would like changing it."

"Maybe we can, who is to say? So, Carrie, tell me about this movie *Somewhere*.

"Ohhh, it is one of the most romantic movies of all time."

"More than the Seattle one?"

"Different. Romantic in a different way. In *Somewhere in Time*, the main character gets caught up in learning about this actress who lived decades before. He goes back in time to meet her, and to prepare, he does everything to dress and be like her time. He uses hypnosis, I think, to go to her time and they meet and fall in love. One day, they are sitting talking and he pulls out a coin from his time and he ends up back in the future or his time. It messes things up for them." She shook her head. "It was so sad. See, the movie doesn't talk about how he being back there messes things up, just how he messes himself up when he forgot about a present-day thing. That jolts him back into the present. At the end of the movie, it's so sad 'cause they show him in bed, but either in a dream or he's dead he sees her and she's young again. It's all about love transcending time."

Carrie couldn't help but feel wistful, and a little sad at this story about two people who loved each other so much, they moved through time to be together.

Black Eagle seemed a little at a loss what to do with Carrie's memory of the movie. Instead of asking her about it, he pointed to the children at play and commented, "Children are the same no matter what time."

"I guess so. They're doing the same things I did as a kid." They watched in companionable silence, eating their apples, until Carrie saw the ice cream vendor.

CHAPTER SEVENTEEN

"Be right back!"

She took off running towards the vendor, Black Eagle unsure whether or not to follow. If she was in danger, she would need him to protect her. If the man was her lover — well, he didn't want her to have a lover. Black Eagle recognized the feelings in his chest as the ones of longing for a woman, only with more. They were the feelings of having found his woman and knowing it was not meant to be. So he stayed standing by the bench.

When Carrie returned a few minutes later, she held two oddly shaped pieces of a bread-like substance, hard looking bread, one with a white swirl on top. She handed one to him. "I got us ice cream cones. A vanilla and a strawberry, so if you didn't like one, you might like the other."

He watched her lick the side of what she had called the 'ice cream cone,' and the look of utter pleasure on her face made him decide he would try it as well. What he really wanted to try was to have her lick him in a similar fashion, on his lips, his chest and yes, even his manhood. Carrie Taylor gave him thoughts he never expected to have. She was a woman he never thought to have for himself. But some unknown force had brought him to her, and he would find a way to win her. He liked her chatter as she tried to say something, but didn't want to hurt someone's feelings, while at the same time trying to figure out what she herself wanted and felt.

She had the kind of body a man could easily be lost in. Her long brown hair begged to have a man entwine his fingers in the lush locks, holding her head firmly while he captured her mouth with his. Her breasts — full, plump — left his mouth watering at the thought of taking them into his mouth, having his tongue tease those tempting nipples to life. She had a body to hold on to, not like the skinny women he had seen in this time. For all their wealth, they seemed poor when he looked at their bodies.

His man-root responded quickly to his thoughts — something that had happened to him often since landing in this time and seeing this woman. He told himself to stop these thoughts, lest he frighten her. That was the last thing he wanted to do. A part of him knew she wouldn't abandon him, but it wasn't abandonment he worried about — it was losing the woman he knew the fates had sent him to be with. He wasn't sure if it was meant to be in this time or his, only that they were meant to be.

They sat convivially licking their ice cream cones, Black Eagle enjoying the sight of her taking pleasure in the food.

The peaceful silence was broken by a male voice coming up behind them, the slight twang to it harsh on the ears. "Carrie, what are you doing? Don't you know you'll never lose weight eating ice cream?"

Carrie almost dropped her cone with how abruptly she turned to the voice. "Dean." Her whispered response held a thread of disgust, along with . . .fear?

"I thought I'd find you here when you weren't home." The short, dark haired man, who seemed to have come from nowhere, reached for Carrie and tried to pull her up and into an embrace.

Carrie moved to rise and before Black Eagle could respond in kind. He saw a glint enter her emerald green eyes as they both looked down at the strange man's foot. She stood up and her foot landed on top of the man called Dean, before she seemed to stumble into him, while at the same time pushing the ice cream cone into his face.

"Oh Dean, I'm so sorry. Oh dear, you better go right home and get that cow Jolene to wipe your face, you stupid ass." She stepped away from him, but not before she took a moment to 'accidentally' grind her foot into his.

Black Eagle felt a little sorry for the man, as he saw the wince of pain enter his eyes.

"Carrie, that's no way to talk," the short man told her. "Come on, sweetheart. I told you Jules didn't mean anything to me. She was just a cheap lay. A stupid, dull, cheap lay." He reached for her again and once again, before Black Eagle could step in to help her, she pushed away from the strange man.

"And I told you to stay the hell away from me, and keep your stupid ass out of my life."

"No way to talk in public, babe."

"I'm not your 'babe.' Dean, just get over it. You blew it. I have no interest in you and could care less if I see you again."

"Ahhhh, Carrie. Anyway, who's your friend here?" The short man turned to look more fully at Black Eagle, "Listen, Bud, whatever she paid you to act like the smitten lover, it worked. Take off. I'll take care of my girl from here on."

"I didn't—"

"Carrie is my *nimitawa ktelo*. We plan to marry in a short time."

Black Eagle wasn't sure which one was more surprised, Dean—who sneered at Carrie—or Carrie as she stood there, her lovely mouth stuck in an 'o'. Experience in battle, and on the hunt, taught him not to lose any ground once gained and in this time, this was a battle and he was on the hunt to win Carrie's heart.

"Nimi tele-a-what? What the hell kind of talk is that?" Dean snorted. "Did you manage to find a way to bring a character from one of those stupid books of yours to life? Nimnut-

134

tell shit. Gees."

"Yes, before the next moon we are to be wed. I will thank you to stay away from my woman, or the price you will pay will be great." Black Eagle glared at Dean.

"Next moon? Price will be great? Carrie, you haven't taken up with those witches, have you? And what's with the weird language, bud?"

"My name is Blake, not bud. But you, little man, will address me as Mr. Eagleston. Where I come from we use the moon to guide our path, our decisions."

"Carrie, you hooked up with a loon! Come on, babe, just walk away with me now and leave this loser behind."

Black Eagle stepped forward and picked Dean up by the shoulders, holding him fairly high above the ground. "Carrie will not walk away with you. I assure you, in my home I am an accomplished warrior and of importance in my village. Go away now, little man and we will not pursue you."

"Yes, Dean." Carrie pushed forward. "Just go away. You don't want Blake to call in his bodyguards, or the authorities, because you won't stop harassing me."

Black Eagle lowered the man so his feet touched the ground.

Dean stepped back, straightening his shirt, which now had not only Carrie's ice cream dripping down it, but Black Eagle's as well. "Carrie, how many times can I say it? I'm sorry. Look, I promise not to pick on you about your weight ever again, okay? Or sleep with anyone else. I'll do anything you want, just come with me now. I'll make it up to you. All of it. How about that?"

She raised her hand and slapped Dean's face. "Get the hell out of my life and stay out, asshole."

Fingering the red mark on his face, he stepped back, not taking his eyes off Carrie and Black Eagle.

"And don't expect an invitation to the wedding, either,

dumb ass," Carrie spat.

"I wouldn't come if you paid me. You'll be sorry, Carrie, I promise you, you will be sorry. You'll wish you married me, you'll see."

Watching him walk away, Carrie shook her head. "I'm sorry you had to see that. You must think I'm just awful and have absolutely no manners."

"There is no reason to be sorry, Carrie. I don't think you are awful. I think you very brave. I applaud you for fighting that man. He tried to force you, and I think he would have hurt you if he could. There is much to be said for a woman who fights for her virtue."

"Really?"

"Yes, really. So that was the ex-boyfriend you had?"

"Yeah, pretty pathetic, isn't he? Kinda makes you wonder what was wrong with me to even bother with him, doesn't it?"

"No. It is our nature to do something stupid so that we can appreciate that which is good in our lives. Do you know why he acts as he does?"

"I think so. He's got what in this time we call 'short man syndrome'."

"Short . . ."

"Short man syndrome. Or what they call a Napoleon Complex. They get all hung up on what they look like, or their height, and think that everyone thinks they are less than adequate because they are so small. It's like they have to do something big to prove themselves, you know, like pick a fight or pick on someone bigger than they are. Dean was never happy with anything he had. He always had to have more and I think it was to compensate for his size. And really, he's not *that* short. He's a lot smaller in other places that guys seem to think count, at least in this time. But if you know how to use it, it's . . ."

Carrie felt her face heat. She turned away, sure she was beet red, and unsure whether she should laugh, hope the comment just blew by Black Eagle, or go on.

"I understand, I think."

"You do?"

"Yes. Because he does not have a great height he thinks he must be big in other ways. So he does things that are not kind."

"Exactly. I'm so glad you understand. And you know, I met his family and they are all normal. His sister told me once that growing up, he'd act like the big peacemaker, but in reality he was the one who started things. He'd start trouble just so he could rush in at the end and smooth things over. Even in his job, he does things like that and he doesn't need to. I found out from a friend of mine who knows someone in his company that he'll mess up other attorneys' files. A few times he has come close to costing them their cases. Just to be mean. Then he goes in and acts like he's got everything under control, and can fix whatever's wrong. I don't understand why no one has caught on to him, or tried to stop him."

"Well, it appears that you are better off without him."

"Yeah, I think you're right about that. Well, we lost our ice cream, but it was worth the sacrifice to see it all over him, wasn't it?"

"Yes. Carrie, I would ask you a question."

"Sure, go ahead."

"Why did he wish you to deny yourself the ice cream? There is nothing wrong with your body. I find it most pleasing."

"Well, I'll tell you, I find *your* body pretty pleasing myself."

Black Eagle considered her statement and between that and the fact she had not disputed they would marry, he

137

considered the matter settled. It seemed that Carrie, too, knew she was his *nimitawa ktelo*. If that was so, then perhaps the matter of marriage had not greatly changed with the passing of the years. Then again, the man, Dean, seemed to want to marry Carrie, but she refused him. She did not, however, re-fuse Black Eagle. The question settled in his mind, he now needed to find a way to show her he could provide for her.

The question was how in this time he could do so. He could not read or write, though the machines seemed easy enough to learn, and she had promised to teach him. The forces that brought him here had made things easy so far. There was no reason to doubt they would continue to help. When Carrie told him she felt they had had enough excitement for one day, the twosome headed back home.

"Maybe, this time Dean had gotten the message. I sure hope so," she muttered as they headed up the street.

Dean watched from further up the street, his burning glare an ominous sight to anyone passing by. He'd lost out too many times in his life. Despite the number of times his parents and teachers told him that he'd been treated fairly, he knew he wasn't. His parents never seemed to understand that he wanted to be tall. Not that there was a way for anyone to help him grow. PE was the worst because the other guys knew that he didn't measure up where it really counted. It just wasn't fair.

Dean clenched his fists so hard his bitten nails cut into his palms while he thought back on the years of being treated less than everyone else. No matter how the coaches told him it wasn't his height that kept him from being picked for sports, he was sure it was his lack of stature. He kicked at a rock, thinking about the one who told him he didn't exhibit good sportsmanship.

"Good sportsmanship, my ass. What does good sportsmanship have to do with winning?" He asked the question then, and asked it again now, and smiled at just how he'd shown that coach good sportsmanship—four slashed tires.

Behaving right, doing good things, acting nice, never got him anything. Everything he'd gotten, from his college scholarships to his law degree, to his job at Turnberg & Jeffers, he'd gotten on his own cunning. Well that and pretending to buy into that whole win/win bullshit. He watched until Carrie and that man she was with walked out of sight. He vowed he would not only get Carrie back, but he would bring down the man she planned to marry. Carrie was his and his alone. He needed her so he could make partner and damn it, she'd be his wife. She wasn't model gorgeous, but she had what he wanted—she was smart, really smart and she would get him where he wanted to go.

"Oh yes, Carrie, I'm going to get you back and then I'm going to make you pay."

CHAPTER EIGHTEEN

Molly returned home from spending the day hanging out with Vincent on Sunday evening, just as Carrie and Black Eagle were clearing up the remains of a spaghetti and meatball dinner.

"If there's one thing Black Eagle is enjoying in this time, besides us I mean, it's the food," Carrie told her with a smile. She noted he'd been excited about all the different kinds and flavors. Carrie told Molly that he said he would miss the foods when he returned to his time. That was quickly becoming the one thing Carrie didn't want to think about. Black Eagle had only been in her life a little over a day, but it felt like he'd been a part of her life forever. "So hey, you and Vincent have a good time today?"

"Yup. He's such a sweetie. Maybe next weekend we can double or something, if Black Eagle is here . . ." her voice trailed off.

"Do not be sad, Molly," he told her. "I do not think we will find the way for me to return so soon. We need to wait for your Mr. Arthur Merle to return, yes?"

"You sound okay with that." Carrie tried not to sound hopeful about it. It wasn't just that he was one of her characters that had come to life. He was a real living, breathing man who had all the qualities she could ever want in a forever kind of man.

"I am. I have already learned much, and know there is more to learn."

"So what did you guys do today?" Molly asked, grabbing

a handful of the M&Ms that sat on the coffee table in the living room.

Taister, with a look at Carrie that seemed to convey staking rights, quickly claimed Black Eagle's lap on the couch.

"Well, this morning we were going to go on the 'net to see if we could find any trace of Black Eagle's tribe the *Sihásapa* and, well . . ."

"The computer's light concerned me. I thought it would trap Carrie's spirit or take her to another time."

"I see. So?"

"We talked about cameras and then went grocery shopping, and off to the park for awhile, and had ice cream. Dean happened by."

"Oh, Mr. Congeniality. What did you think of him, Black Eagle?"

"Mr. Con — I thought his name was asshole."

The women laughed. "It's a nickname. Like I call Molly 'Mol', and she'll call me 'Carr' . . . and Dean is asshole, jerkoff, Sir D, like in dickless . . . anything unflattering."

"Dick . . ." He paused. "I see. He's not a very nice man, for your time or mine. In my time he would not be such a problem, at least after a good person learned about him."

"Maybe we can send *him* back in time." Molly's chortling caused the others to break into a hearty laugh. Their laughter mellowing down, Molly continued, "So, now what?"

"Well, from what I've thought and figured out about it, I think if we can find a record of Black Eagle or his people, we might be able to find out what happened to him. Problem is, they didn't really have people chronicling what happened to individual Indians back then, like if they just disappeared. But . . . if someone saw him, like, fade or something when the picture was taken, then maybe it would be somewhere."

"I do not think so, Carrie."

"No?"

"No. As I said today, I returned to my village after the photo was taken and spent several nights there. I do not think anyone followed me to the river; it is not the way of my people to do that."

"Well, if that doesn't work or we don't find anything, I guess we have to wait until Mr. Merle gets back and see if maybe he has some notes or documents from his ancestor we can look at."

"Not that we have to decide now, but have you thought about what we do for the next two weeks?" Molly looked from one to the other.

Carrie nodded, "We take one day at a time. Black Eagle wants to learn to read and write, so we'll do that and teach him about living in today's world. And I've always had a fascination with the old west, so he'll teach me about that."

Molly almost spit back into her cup her swallow of coffee at Carrie's last statement. "Carrie, ah, your fascination with the old west is more like with the heroes from the romance novels you read. However, to give you credit, you *do* have one of those romance heroes alive and living here with us. And, well Black Eagle, you *are* one hell of a good-looking guy. So, it all sounds good. Sounds like a plan. So what are you going to do while Carrie's at work tomorrow?"

Black Eagle looked at Carrie, the question evident in his eyes.

Carrie responded, "I don't know. Actually I was thinking maybe I need to take a few days off, just to be sure Black Eagle is comfortable with everything here in the house, you know?"

"I will provide for you, Carrie. Somehow, I will do this."

Carrie wasn't sure how to respond. Except for her parents she'd always taken care of herself. No guy she'd ever dated talked about taking care of her, of supporting her.

Fortunately, it was Molly who answered. "Yup. And besides, if you don't go to work, and ole Deanster calls to see if you are in and you aren't, he'll have a hissy and give up on you. Ya think?"

"It would be nice."

Molly headed off to her room a few minutes later, and for a while Carrie and Black Eagle sat and talked before they turned in as well. At Carrie's door Black Eagle turned to thank her for the day, his gaze lingering on her lips. He debated kissing her, and thought better of it. He would wait another day or so. And then, then it would be a prelude to what they would share in their marriage bed. While his people accepted marriage to someone they did not know well, he knew the Whites of his time courted. So, he decided, he would court Carrie.

"Good night, Carrie Taylor, sleep well."

He turned to head towards his room. Taister walked quickly beside him, his little face turned up in adoration. Black Eagle brushed his teeth the way Carrie had shown him, and looked at his long black hair. He had looked at the other men he had seen yesterday and today on the street and in the tele-vision and most had shorter hair than his. He determined he would ask Carrie in the morning if he should cut his. It was important that his looks please her. He went to stand at the window, breathing in the cool night air and studied the stars. None seemed to fall tonight—they seemed so far away. He waited until the sounds of the house settled and then slowly made his way to her room.

As the night before, he stood at the foot of Carrie's bed watching her, drinking in her beauty. He glanced down to see Taister standing beside him, his little face upturned, glancing quickly towards the bed as if to tell him that they should be lying there beside Carrie, not standing there in the chill of the night. His manhood hardened at the sight of her lush body . . . but he would wait. He'd waited already a long time for her. Till they were married, he could wait.

Shaking his head at Taister, letting him know that he at least would not join Carrie in the bed, he dropped to the floor. Taister glanced up at the bed one more time before climbing up on top of Black Eagle, curled into a ball and the two quickly fell into a deep sleep.

Despite how deeply he slept, he was not without dreams. Through the night, images of his home and friends filtered into his dreams. In each one he saw Mr. Merle and his camera, taking more photographs of him. It wasn't so much that Mr. Merle took his photograph. It was his smile. It was benign enough, yet something mysterious lurked behind the kindly expression. More than the smile, he saw the twinkle in Mr. Merle's blue eyes, eyes of a much younger man.

And his hands. They too seemed somehow younger than the wrinkles on his face would show. Each time he saw Mr. Merle's hands, he tried to focus on what the man did, how he did it, but the scene in the dream would shift. What caught his attention more were the different costumes Mr. Merle wore. Sometimes it was the suit Black Eagle saw the day his photograph was taken, other times he wore what Carrie called jeans, a robe and other strange garments. Each time Black Eagle tried to approach him, Mr. Merle managed to evade him and would fade away to nothingness.

Chapter Nineteen

As with the night before, Carrie determined she would not look at the photograph before going to sleep. Instead of one of her sexy night gowns she once again pulled on an extra long t-shirt. She told herself it wasn't that she was embarrassed by the sheer gowns she'd bought at Victoria's Secret. No, she thought, it was in case Black Eagle needed something during the night she didn't want him to get the wrong idea. As to the photograph, once again she found she could not resist. There was still no change. There was no sign Black Eagle had never been in the picture at all, and after spending a few days with him on a constant basis, she wondered if he had been in the photo in the first place. Maybe she'd only imagined him there and in reality he was a modern guy who happened to arrive dressed in a loin cloth.

Seeing nothing different in the photograph, she carefully placed it on the nightstand, turned out the light and lay there in the dark, thinking over the past few hours. She finally fell into a deep sleep, noting as she drifted off that for the first time in years her mind didn't venture into the imaginary and have her starring in her latest romance novel. In fact, she hadn't even thought about picking up one of her romance novels in the past forty-eight hours, something she hadn't done since she was in high school. A dedicated book-a-holic, even when she was dating someone and they spent the night, she read a chapter or two before falling asleep. It wasn't hard when her partners would roll over to their sides after making love and conk out without a care in the world.

Since Black Eagle arrived, however, she hadn't even thought about picking up a book just to read. To show him something, yes, but not to escape into a story.

Once again the next morning Carrie thought she heard someone moving about in her room, but when she rolled over, she saw she was alone. "Must have been Taister up early trying to cover up where he spent the night. Little traitor probably slept with Black Eagle again."

She reached for the bedside phone and called in to work. She told him she needed to take the next few days off because of a personal emergency, and got up to start breakfast.

Molly breezed into the kitchen to say hello before taking off for her shift. "I'll be so glad when I'm off days. I'll never get people who think working in the day time is a good thing."

"Have a good shift." Carrier told her. "Just keep in mind it will soon be over."

"You're right." She stopped at the door, "Oh, don't go doing anything I wouldn't do today."

"Giving me lots of leeway there, Mol."

"Uh huh, just be good."

"How does careful work?" Carrie asked her with a smile.

"Careful works. Enjoy him, being with him. He's a nice guy, a really nice guy."

"Isn't he? It makes me a little sad that I know he'll leave, or that he might have to, you know?"

"Yeah. You finally meet someone decent and it turns out he's not even from this time. At least you know Dean didn't set this up—if his reaction from yesterday is any clue."

"That's true. Molly, it's crazy, but I really am starting to believe he's from the 1800's and somehow came through time to be here."

"I believe it, too. And that's saying something, you know?"

"Well, we'll see what Mr. Merle says when he's back from

vacation. I'm betting he knows something, or will at least know where to look. There were a ton of other papers in the trunk where I found the photograph. Maybe there's something in there that will tell us how this happened."

"Maybe. See you later." With that Molly breezed off to work. "Hey, Black Eagle. Have a good day."

"You, too, Molly. Good morning, Carrie. Did you sleep well?"

"Yeah, I did. Really good. How about you?"

An indignant meow sounded in the room, and two pairs of eyes looked over to Taister standing at his bowl, clearly chagrined that the conversation was keeping his breakfast from him.

"Sorry, little man," Carrie told him as she reached for a can of his food.

His meows continued, clearly telling her that one day of this chit chat with his new human was forgivable, but it was time to get back to business — the business of his food.

"He seems to have a great complaint this morning." Black Eagle chuckled.

"Yeah, Taister has this firm belief that if he has to wait more than ninety-three seconds after entering the kitchen for his breakfast, the world as we know it will end. "Carrie looked up at him, a startled look on her face.

"Carrie?"

She just continued to stare at him.

"Carrie, what is it?"

"Taister, oh Black Eagle, you don't think . . ."

"Think what? What about Taister? Do you think him unwell?"

"No, just that, well, he's always demanded his breakfast first thing. Even as a kitten when I first adopted him, from day one he would carry on till I fed him. I'd often tell him that the world wasn't going to come to an end if he waited a minute for his breakfast. On Friday, I told him that and it took me a little more time to feed him and — the world, *your* world — changed."

"Carrie, I do not think little panther had anything to do with . . ."

Taister practically howled his complaint.

Looking over at the little furfaced being, Carrie almost laughed. Taister's little face showed that he was contemplating shredding something important if he didn't get his breakfast that very second.

He meowed again, even louder.

"Talk about loud. Here you go, baby boy. Here you go."

True to form, he ate two bites and started to saunter out of the room.

"Just a minute, little panther." Black Eagle softly called to him.

Taister stopped in his tracks and looked up at the big man.

"Your momma made you a meal. You insult her if you do not eat it."

The cat seemed to ponder the man's words. Then he turned and walked back to his dish and ate a little more, glancing over his shoulder a couple of times to make sure Black Eagle saw that he ate the food.

"As I was saying, Carrie, I do not think little panther brought me here or that his lack of food did. Something greater than you and me brought me here, and that is what it will take to return me, if I am to return to my own time. For now, I wish to stay here, with you and learn of your world. I wish to learn to read and write and be a part of your world."

"Yeah, I know, it was just kinda weird that I said that to him the other morning and that night you showed up."

They ate breakfast, and then spent a few hours teaching Black Eagle how to read and write some of the letters. The man certainly was not stupid, and Carrie wondered just how far he could have gone had he been born in this time. At least he would bring some of the knowledge back with him and maybe even memories of her. If he could go back, that is and that was something Carrie didn't want to consider.

After lunch Carrie booted up the computer and by asking Black Eagle questions about his home, narrowed down the location he came from to James River, South Dakota, or what would be that town today.

"You mean we are in a different place, not only time, but place?"

"'Fraid so, sweetie." She pulled up a map and showed him. "This is South Dakota and we're here, in California."

"Carrie, maybe I am still in my own time, but just in California. This is what the gold seekers have built."

"No, no . . . not unless you were alive in 2020 in South Dakota. Were you? Is this a joke?" She shifted away from him, suspicion in her eyes. "Dean did send you, didn't he? You really are from California and this is a joke and you're here because . . ."

"I would not deceive you, Carrie. We do not have the metal boxes that move where I come from or the *me-crow-whav* or big white box for food. And I do not like that Dean. Does your South Dakota have these things?"

"Yes, yes, today they do. Well, not Dean. We're the unlucky winners there. I'm sorry. I guess I just . . .never mind."

"What, Carrie?"

"Nothing. My mind is just wandering again, that's all."

He nodded in understanding and then, to distract her, asked, "What is this blue?"

"That's the ocean."

"The ocean. I have heard of this. We are close to it?"

"Yeah, about an hour's drive."

"I would like to see it. Can you take me?"

"Sure! Hey, I think that would be a great idea. Tomorrow

it might be fun to go on an outing. Do the whole picnic lunch thing, and go. We can take the book and paper with us, and we can work on your reading and writing out on the coast, okay?"

"Yes, I'd like that." He thought for a moment before speaking again. "Carrie, you understand my problem? I am caught in two worlds. If I can return to my home, I will not need all the things your world offers. There is no place for them. I will miss pizza and ice cream, but we have other treats that I will miss if I must stay here. If I must stay here, knowing how to hunt buffalo will not be important. It will become a memory. But I will need to know how to read and write. If I can see things of your world that are beautiful, that are fun, these things I can remember if I return to my home."

"I understand. Really I do. I've read enough time travels to understand how you feel."

"Time travels? You have read about traveling through time? And you did not tell me?" He looked both hurt and confused, and perhaps betrayed.

"They're stories, Black Eagle. Only stories, like the movies we watched. You're here for real."

"But the stories, Carrie, in my time stories *are* from real life. When we tell a *kapi*, it is because some thing happened that made the story. The movies I see are make believe, an imaginary thing. But to be in the books, there will be answers. Do you still have these time travels?"

"Yes, of course. I keep all my books. I never know if I'm going to want to read one again. I don't always have the time, but they are right in here." She stood and walked over to a section on the bookshelves and pointed out several. "All my books are broken down by category, see. Time travel, ghosts, regency, and so on. Then alphabetical by author from A-to-Z. Then, if they have more than one time travel or kind of book, the books are in chronological order for each author."

His look told her he clearly had no clue what she was talking about.

"Well, you know I have tons of books, right?"

At his nod she continued. "Okay, so because I have so many, I break them down by type and these are the time travels, my absolute favorite. And because I have so many and a few of my favorite authors write a lot of them, I break them down by author and then the order they wrote them. See, here, these are the Ds, and this is my all time favorite author, either time travel or regular romance, Jude Deveraux, okay? And then we have my other favorite, Sherry Derr-Wille. Then here is another top auto-buy of mine, 'H' for Hannah. Okay, so then I break them down by when they were written — that way when I see a new book I will know if I have it or not."

"Carrie, that is very interesting and I will keep it in mind if I am to stay here, but for now, can you tell me the ways it happens in the books?"

"I'm sorry. I think I'm rattling on because, well, I know you want to go home, but I, well, I have to be honest . . ."

"You do not want me to leave." He didn't sound angry or sad. It was a matter of fact statement.

"No, I don't. I'm sorry, but I like you and I know I'll miss you when you go."

"I like you, too, Carrie and we do not know yet what will happen. If I am to stay here I hope we will remain friends, if not more."

"But don't you think we should talk about it?"

"We will, but tell me what happens in the books."

"Okay." She took his hand, enjoying how small hers felt in the warmth of his larger one and led him to the couch. "In most of them, the woman ends up going back in time. I don't think I can think of one where the main part was where the man went back, well, except in *Somewhere In Time*, the movie we were talking about. But in the books, it's usually the woman who travels to another time. In this one," Carrie picked up one of the books, "she goes back in the middle of a really bad thunderstorm. In this one, she gets knocked out and wakes up in another time. A plane crash. A mirror. In one of the earliest I read this sword brought her back."

"A sword?"

"Yeah. Sherry Derr-Wille has a whole series that has the heroine in love with an Indian, like I—" She stopped her rambling and looked out the window a brief second collecting her thoughts before continuing, "Well, um, this one, *Birdsinger's Woman*, is the first in the series and it's so good. This woman, Kit, is totally in love with Carter who is a Native American and . . ."

"A what?"

"Native American . . .oh sorry, it's the politically correct way we say Indian now."

"Polit—"

Waving her hand like she was shooing a fly, she told him, "Never mind." He gestured for her to go on. "Okay—so anyway, Kit's in love with Carter who is an Indian and they go to a Pow Wow and—"

"They—"

"Black Eagle, I will happily tell you all these things, but don't you want to hear about the story?"

"Yes, Carrie, I do want to hear. I will remember my questions and ask you when you are done with your story."

"I'm sorry, that was mean and rude of me."

Black Eagle looked at her hand as she rested it on his arm and put his own over it. "No, Carrie, it is your excitement. It is how you enjoy life and the things in your life. I like watching your excitement."

Her lips parted as she thought about what a sweet, really kind man he was. The things he said were so non-judgmental. He so clearly took pleasure in her being just who she was.

Aside from her parents and Molly, he was the only person who had ever accepted her for who she was, just as she was.

"So," he prodded, "tell me about this Kit."

"Ah, okay, Kit. Well, Kit is in love with Carter and she waited just forever for him to sit up and take notice, so they are going to this Pow Wow and she's decided that this is it. She's going to tell him how she feels. But before she can, she ends up falling back in time and ends up with this total hunkola, ummm, a really good looking guy, Atiko, who looks a lot like Carter and she gets it that she's back in time and finds herself falling in love with Atiko. They have these amazing adventures back in time, and in the end she knows that she belongs there with him. Oh, Black Eagle, it is *so* romantic."

"So, if we went to this place where Kit went back in time we could, I could, go back to my home?"

Carrie thought about it. On the one hand, she knew it was a story, but on the other, maybe . . . just maybe . . .

"I don't know, Black Eagle. In *Birdsinger's Woman*, it's a modern woman who goes back in time to be with the Indian warrior. It's the opposite of what happened to us. You came forward to be with me. Even if it *was* real, I don't think it would help. I don't know if we could go somewhere and go back to your time. I mean, well, if you could go back. That is — well I'm not sure it would work."

Carrie sat and thought for a few minutes before starting to go through the books again. "I'm trying to think of a situation like what you and I have here. Hmmm, well, *Traveling Bride* . . . no, in that one she goes back in time through a super-secret device. He finds it and hides it so she can't go home. Then she finds it and is royally pissed at him and comes back to the future, but he stays back there. Then, like in this one, the heroine has gone through this really bad break-up. That happens a lot in time travel novels; either the heroine has broken up with a boyfriend or she's just really lonely. She's always this really nice, sweet, woman who has just been kicked to the curb and either hasn't met a guy or has been with a jerk."

"Like you, Carrie. You are a sweet and kind woman and Dean was cruel to you."

"I guess, yeah. I guess. Anyway, in this one," Carrie held up a book with a tall man with a massive chest and long blond hair flowing wildly behind him, an upright sword in one hand and a woman held in a loving embrace with the other, "she gets into a fight with a boyfriend and breaks up with him and is driving home and her car goes out of control. She thinks she's going to hit a tree, but instead ends up back in time during the Viking era and meets this guy, Thor. A lot of the Viking stories have a Thor guy. I mean, you know, the kind of guy you want to meet. Well, not that *you* would want to meet them. Anyway, in most of the stories the couple falls in love and one of them has to decide whether or not to stay in the new time. I'm not so sure if I ended up back in time if I'd want to stay or not, you know?"

She stopped and saw a look she was sure was hurt cross Black Eagle's face. *Could he have feelings for me or am I rambling out of control again?*

"I think I understand. Someone, like your Dean, mistreats his woman. She is sad and a man from another time makes her life be as it should."

"In a book, anyway. In real life I'm looking for someone much more different. In real life, I like guys with dark hair. Guys who are smart and resilient and like, well, a guy like you, you know?"

"Someone like me?"

"Exactly. Thor and those are characters aren't real. They're wonderful in the story and you get into them—"

"So tell me, Carrie, does the woman stay with this Thor in the story?"

"She stays with—wait a minute! I have a great idea! We can

read this one together, how about that?"

He hesitated a moment, "Yes, that would be good, but unless you dreamt of me, it does not sound like that book has any answers for me."

"No, I didn't dream about you. I've dreamt about characters, but, I'm sorry, I didn't dream about you till I met you."

"So what about the others?"

"Now see I was thinking that maybe this one, *My Twin in the Mirror* might be kinda close, but I'm not sure. In this one it's a mirror that makes it happen. But the mirror controls it. I guess that might be like a photograph, but it's different."

"How does it work in that one?"

"Candace, the woman in the story, is restoring this great old house and there's this mirror and it's like she's sucked into it and ends up in the past and there's this guy, Kyle. They meet and fall in love, but, well, that one's different because they both decide they want to live in the future. But it's different, Black Eagle. It's just not the same. They end up separated. I'm not sure it's even alike."

"But these women, these Jude and Tami and Sherry persons, they know these things? Surely if they write of time travel they know how it works. Can you ask them?"

"Well, yes and no. They write really good time travels, but I don't think they know *how* to time travel, not the mechanism to make it happen. Especially since they write different ways to travel through time. And they are authors who live someplace else, away from here. I wouldn't even know how to find them to ask. I mean, we could go to their websites and see if there is a contact button and maybe they would answer. I'm not sure, though, that asking them how you travel through time would get a real answer. I can tell you this, though, in all the stories the right people end up together. Even through time and space they make it magical."

"What else? Do any other authors know the answer? I think

they might. Are you sure there is no way to talk to them to find out? Can't we try your magic box? Your website?"

"They are all stories, stories that these authors wrote. They didn't really happen. In them, well, once the woman is back there, she usually meets this guy who at first she fights against. Not like a fist fight, but he's usually pretty domineering and bossy and she's a modern woman and doesn't much care for it, you know? No, I guess you wouldn't know and say . . ."

He raised a brow, leading Carrie to believe he knew it was going to be one of her tangents.

"Like in the westerns, the Indian is *always* this macho, super brave guy who is real bossy and doesn't take no for an answer and he's always all hot over the female, but doesn't tell her, but doesn't waste any time in—well, you know . . ." She blushed such a deep red that even if he didn't know what she meant from her words, she knew he gathered it from the blush.

"He doesn't waste time in what, Carrie? And if these are stories, what about me? Why am I here? I am not one of your stories. I am a real man, here in your time. Are you sure none of these authors knew someone who traveled through time?"

"Black Eagle, even if they are real, no one is going to admit it. People would think they were crazy and lock them up. Everyone wants concrete—real—facts. We don't have a lot of imagination anymore. Everything is rush, rush, rush. We don't send mail. We don't even send email anymore. Now it's a hundred and forty character tweet and that's all she wrote. Seriously, if you or I were to go out and say you traveled through time, we'd be treated like we were crazy. At best, people would laugh at us."

"So talking to these others, it would not help?"

"No. I really don't think so. Black Eagle, I want to help you. I really do. But I don't think letting it out that you come from another time will help."

"Then I do not think we have wasted any time. Our time here is precious, yes?"

From the tone of his voice, and look in his eyes, Carrie had a pretty good idea he knew what kind of time wasn't being wasted and as much as she liked his body and wanted to touch him all over, it was wrong. He was a stranger in a strange time with strange people. Going to bed with him would only make it harder for him to cope with being here in the present. Looking to move the subject off sleeping together, Carrie answered, "Well, anyway, they are also so macho and don't take no for an answer and are real possessive. You aren't that way. So, do the books have it wrong?"

"No. I don't understand this macho, but in my tribe few say no to me and I am protective of what is mine. I will hold on to what is mine, Carrie. Closely, tightly, but I will also give her the freedom to be herself."

Carrie nodded. She knew there was something more to what he said, but she wasn't sure what. And, there was that feeling between her legs again. Not that it was ever far from happening around him, but while most of the time that sweet tension between her legs tugged at her, there were moments, like now, when she was sure he knew what was happening and she didn't know if she should be thrilled or embarrassed.

Guys had turned her on before, and this was definitely different. This was just like what the authors in her books described when their characters knew they had met their one and only true love. "Well, that's good to know—that you are—that you take care of—Well, anyway, the woman gets back there and isn't too keen on this bossy guy, but the guy is always gorgeous and the woman starts to realize that he's a decent guy and then she falls in love with him. Sometimes I think it's bogus, 'cause she falls in love in, like, a day. But, then again . . ."

Carrie realized she was looking into space. Was she falling in love with Black Eagle? In just a day or two? Did he know? Or was it just because her fantasy character suddenly had appeared in her life? It was all so confusing.

"Then what happens, Carrie?"

"Well, once she's in love with him, she tries to get him to fall in love with her, but he already is. They get into this really great tension thing about not wanting to tell the other they are in love, and finally they do, and then usually she stays back in time with him. Or in one story, she's all ready to stay back with him and she ends up being sent to the future, but he gets to come back as another person, but remembers her and finds her again — isn't that romantic?"

"So, it is for people who are in love?"

"Mostly, but there are stories out there where, like, a whole town goes back in time. That was a pretty good story, too, but not a lot of romance, which is mostly why I read them. To read about the romance."

"And what happened to me — a man coming forward — is not usual?"

"Not in the stories. And I can't think of any — well let's see, in *Time Mover*, but well, no. In that one he had a device with him for part of it, but the way I think you came, in or through a photograph, I don't think I've read one — "

"And for us, romance?"

She thought for a moment, and didn't quite know how to answer his question. She *wanted* to tell him that yes, he came forward to be with her, but she didn't know that, not for sure. If he went back in time, then what? So instead she went to what felt safe. Granted, she'd asked before, but it was safe ground, "Black Eagle, do you remember what you were doing right before you came here?"

"As I told you, Carrie, I could not sleep and went out to the river. I was sitting on a rock that is by the river near my village, looking at the stars. I saw one fall."

"How long after the photograph was taken did you see it?"

"Several days, maybe a little more than a week."

"And did you wish for anything?"

He grew silent and gazed out the window, deep in thought. Honoring his need for some silence to think, Carrie rose and went back to the bookshelf to look at the books, fingering them as if looking for something in particular: "Do I have a story where it's with a photo? I don't think so, I don't think I've seen it, but here you are."

"Yes, here I am. Carrie, I am not a story. I am a real man and I did wish for something. I wished for a wife."

He'd moved behind her and the feel of his body so close to hers rippled through her. She felt her nipples tighten and was glad she had on a loose sweatshirt, because she didn't want him to know just how much he turned her on. She felt his words, "*I am a real man*", to her very core. Oh yes, he was a real man, not the stuff of fantasy and make believe. A real man she wanted very much.

"A real man with real desires," he whispered in her ear.

Carrie turned ever so slightly just as his arms came around to hold her, his lips came down to meet hers. At first he gave her just a light kiss, the barest touching of his lips to hers, waiting for her permission to continue. She leaned into him, moving her hands towards his chest. She longed to touch him, to feel that incredible chest of his, to assure herself that he was all the steel and satin she imagined. She'd waited since she first opened her eyes and found him in her bed for him to kiss her again and he was finally doing it and it felt so good. Better than good. It was like heaven.

She parted her lips to welcome his tongue into her mouth. She moaned at the contact and caressed his tongue with hers. His arms took her in a firm grip, holding her as if he thought if he let her go he'd lose her forever. Carrie wrapped her arms round him, one hand entangling itself in his hair, her hips moving towards his, an erotic brush against him. The feel of his swollen member turned her on like no man had ever done before.

It was Black Eagle who moved to break the kiss. "Carrie, do you still think they fall in love too quickly?"

Collecting her thoughts, she drew in an unsteady breath. "N-n-no, I'm not so sure. I do think some people are just meant to be together."

"I do not think it too fast, either. And I, too, think that some people are meant to be together and that time and space cannot keep them a part."

"Th-that's good to know."

"So, in the books, they, the man and woman who love each other, find a way to be together? Always?"

"Yes, yes they do. Always. It wouldn't be a romance if they didn't."

"Let me ask you this then, Carrie . . . if you were to find you care for me, if I could not stay, would you go back with me?"

CHAPTER TWENTY

Carrie stood stock still, staring at Black Eagle's chest. Well almost, her mouth was watering at just the sight of that magnificent expanse. She twirled her tongue around inside her mouth and along the inside of her teeth, wishing it was one of his nipples. *Did he really just ask me to go back in time with him? After that kiss could he doubt it? Would I? Would I really leave my home here?*

"I—"

"I understand, Carrie, we are different. Not just from different times, but different worlds."

"It's not that, Black Eagle. You just caught me by surprise. Wouldn't you like to stay here in this time? I know some of our things are, well, odd or different. Still, we have some really cool things like cars and pizza, right?"

"I don't know, Carrie. Sometimes I miss my home, how simple life was. I think I would need first to have answers, answers about how I got here, who or what caused this to happen. Until I know how I came here, I will not know if I can stay. And, until we speak to your Mr. Merle, we do not know if others who his ancestor photographed that day have also come to this time."

"You're right. I hadn't thought about that. It was not fair for me to ask you that, either. I'm sorry." She reached to cup his cheek.

"No reason to be sorry, none at all. It seems then, from your books, that no one knows for certain how to make this travel happen."

"No, there aren't any rules. No rules we know of, anyway."

"So, we are back again to relying on the Mr. Merle of your time."

"Yeah, seems so." They stood awkwardly for a moment before Carrie suggested some lunch.

Black Eagle readily agreed and was totally entranced with the peanut butter and jelly sandwiches she made.

Carrie told him that the peanut butter was comfort food.

Black Eagle told her it was good they ate them so that they would have comfort through the day.

After lunch they worked a bit more on teaching Black Eagle to read, and then went for a walk. Thoughts of Dean's nasty comments the day before fresh in her mind, Carrie steered them in the opposite direction than the park.

The next day the couple headed out to Point Reyes so she could show Black Eagle the ocean. They'd dressed, at his insistence, in matching white fishermen knit sweaters and blue jeans. He was a lot more relaxed in the car this time, although she did keep the speed down, especially on the curves. Fortunately the scenery kept his attention on anything but the road itself. Carrie packed a big lunch of fried chicken, salad, apples and a pie she'd picked up at the store during their shopping trip. Before they left, she also grabbed one of the time travels so they could read it and off they went.

Instead of taking the faster route down the freeway, she headed up through the redwoods. She was relieved Black Eagle was more relaxed in the car this time, and enjoyed watching him look out at the forest.

"We do not have such big trees in my time," he told her with awe in his voice.

"No, I don't guess there would be—they were still growing. They're beautiful, aren't they?"

He looked over at her, "Yes, beautiful. The most beautiful I have ever seen."

If the trees thrilled him, it was nothing compared to the utter amazement on his face when he first saw the ocean. It gave Carrie a whole new perspective; a sense of how small she really was, seeing the ocean through his eyes. Even from the car she could feel its power, its beauty magnificent beyond mere words.

She parked the car, and when they exited, she reached for his hand as if it was the most natural thing in the world to do. They walked side by side toward the water. The salt spray bathed them ever so lightly while the salty scent revitalized them.

A fishing boat bobbed up and down out in the distance. For a long while they stood in silence, hands entwined, drinking in the raw beauty before them. The smell of the salt air a reminder that there were still parts of California that were, in their own way, untamed.

It was Black Eagle who finally spoke. "I know this water, this ocean, existed in my time. The scouts who came west with the miners spoke of it when they returned. Their words did not begin to describe its majesty, its greatness. Carrie, this is a memory I will have with me always."

She nodded. "I always tend to forget just how beautiful it is, how much energy it gives me when I'm away from it. Then I come back and remember, but it has never meant as much to me as today."

She looked up at him to see the expression of wonder in his eyes. Just like her books said, it was for the woman standing before him. Slowly, barely perceptibly, his head lowered towards hers. Carrie was barely aware of drawing breath as her eyes met his.

His lips met hers, the softest brush before he took her firmly in his arms and took her in the hottest kiss Carrie had ever had. Even her imagination or the descriptions of kisses in her books came nowhere close to the power of this one. It seemed each one got better and better. So immersed in the kiss, it was long moments before they felt the ocean's water caressing their legs.

As they backed away from the water, still in each other's embrace, their tongues still entwined, Carrie couldn't decide if the roar in her ears was the ocean or the desire Black Eagle sparked in her. She felt like molten liquid in his embrace and wanted this man, truly wanted him. And it wasn't just sex, it wasn't just that he had a body that would turn on any woman. It was him, the man he was, the man she already felt so attached to and so afraid of losing. Thinking back on his comment about sometimes getting homesick for his home, she wondered if she ended up in another time if she would miss her home here. Yes, she lived in the here and now. Did all the things that were expected of an upstanding citizen—went to work, paid her bills, cleaned the house and went grocery shopping. And she dated.

Oh yeah, she dated. Sometimes she wondered why she bothered, because she'd be so bored. It was like she was a vehicle for them to look good with, instead of enjoying being with her because she was a fun person. Dean was probably the worst of them. He acted like he was interested in her opinion, but in fact he was pumping her for information to look better to his bosses. How he managed to graduate from law school was beyond her, although knowing him, he probably dated some poor woman whom he pumped for information and got to take his tests for him.

Admittedly she spent a lot of time, well—back in time—at least in her imagination. The men she'd meet in her romance novels—'smut books' as Molly called them—they were amazing. They were smart, caring, and considerate, always in shape, always like about thirty. Of course they were *always* in shape and around thirty. They were frozen in time in the books. Were they different? Not the guys in her books, but men from back then? If they were anything like Black Eagle, they were. When they had talked about it one time, was it really just a few weeks ago?

That one time they talked about it, Molly said she wouldn't want to give up microwaves and cars and things. So Carrie wondered, could she cook from scratch? Really cook from scratch? Like pulling off chicken feathers and milking a cow? Not just pull a can off the shelf or a frozen vegetable out of the freezer? Or . . . really prepare the meat? But the other parts . . .it was a simpler life. That was for sure.

Could I live back then? What am I thinking? He hasn't really said anything to me about going back with him. Well he asked, but did he mean it? Would he really want me to go back to his time with him? What if we got there and he changed his mind and I couldn't come home? Was he just being nice or would he really want me there with him? How would I get back here? Oh but . . . oh yeah, he sure can kiss.

Carrie gave in to the feelings that coursed through her and rubbed up against him. Her nipples grew hard, so hard she knew he felt them through both their shirts by his sharp intake of breath. She responded to the hardness of his manhood. *How do I tell him how much I want him, the whole of him, not just sex, without seeming too forward? How do I tell him I want him to stay? And if he can't that I'd go with him in a heartbeat?*

"I like kissing you, Carrie Taylor."

"I like kissing you too, Black Eagle."

"Blake Eagleston."

"What?" Dazed, she stood there staring at him. Well, staring at his lips, too enamored of how they moved to actually form any thought of how much she wanted to kiss him.

"My name in your time. Blake Eagleston."

"Oh! Oh yeah! I'm so sorry. I forgot. I just—sometimes I feel like I'm living one of my romance novels."

"This is good, Carrie? Living your romance novels?"

"Definitely. Not living a novel but like living it. It's better than good. Being with you is like a dream come true. I'm not making sense, am I?"

"I will say this to you, Carrie Taylor, you are my dreams come true. Many nights before we met, I dreamt of you. I know you said you did not dream of me, but after Mr. Merle took the photograph of me, I dreamt of you. I hope not to wake from this dream."

The couple walked along the beach, dodging the waves that lapped the shore, laughing and enjoying each other's company. Every several paces they would stop and kiss or hug and more than once ended up in an embrace that led to a searing hot kiss and hug. Carrie knew she was falling in love with Black Eagle, and didn't know how to stop it, even if she wanted to. It saddened her, because she knew one day he would leave and return to his own time. He was nothing like the other men she had dated. They left because they were self-centered, with no substance, like Dean. No, he would leave because somehow he would be pulled back through time and she would be left with only a memory.

"Black—Blake, when we get home tonight, we need to make sure the photograph is safe. We need to put it where nothing can happen to it." Carrie couldn't keep a tremor out of her voice.

"Why?"

"Because if you ever do decide to go back, or if you are going to be called back, you are going to need it and to have it the way it is, or was, or . . ."

"Just safe, I think, Carrie."

"Yeah. Just safe." She whispered, the words conveying more than just wishing the photograph to be safe. In those few words, she affirmed to herself she felt safe with him. They stopped in a small café not far from the coast for dinner, and demolished several platters of fresh seafood. To Carrie's relief, Black Eagle enjoyed the seafood, particularly the clams and shrimp, as much as he enjoyed all the other foods they'd eaten so far. He had said they didn't eat that kind of fish in his village, but he clearly enjoyed their dinner. He ate not only his hot fudge sundae for dessert, but quickly dove into her tiramisu, indulging his sweet tooth and then some.

The drive home along the coast gifted them with a sunset in an array of colors to rival an artist's palette. The pinks turned to purples and then to deep blues just before a few stars peeked out of the velvety blackness creating a visual delight. Arriving home, they were so wrapped up in each other that neither noticed the silver car parked across the street, let alone the man with a grimace that would scare little children watching them.

CHAPTER TWENTY-ONE

Dean skulked in his car amidst old burger bags and milk shake cups and watched the couple walk to the house. So intent on the dark haired woman and her man he no longer noticed the stench of old food and spilled beverages in the vehicle. His anger at Carrie's break up with him seemed to reach a more intense level than ever before. It wasn't that he loved her. He crunched up a bag of half eaten garlic fries and tossed it on the floor. Sometimes he didn't even really like her, but no one left him.

Okay, that wasn't exactly true. He did like her. Sort of. Admittedly he liked what she could bring him.

And he would have eventually married her. After all, that was what the honchos at work wanted, and if that was what it took to make partner, so be it. It didn't mean he had to be faithful once they said "I do," right?

He sighed. Just once in his life he wanted something to go his way without having to manipulate it to make it happen. It seemed he always had to struggle to get what he wanted and it never seemed to be enough. It was such a drag to have to pretend he bought into the whole win/win thing or that everyone could come out with something they wanted. He hated reading the books from all those relationship and whoo whoo business gurus. Heck, he'd even read one by the blonde psychic woman one time because one of the mucky mucks in his company mentioned it. Talk about a stupid move. The managing partner had mentioned his wife read the woman's books and really liked them. That prompted Dean to say he was a huge fan himself and vented about how bummed he was when he couldn't get tickets to one of her lectures. When the wife called a few days later and asked which his favorite books was, he struggled to remember the title of one. While doing a verbal song and dance he looked one up on the online book site so he could to name one. Turned out to be a stroke of luck because it was also the same one she liked best.

Then, to make it worse, she happened to have an extra ticket for the woman's talk the next weekend and invited Dean. Not one to miss schmoozing with the boss or someone with an in with the boss, he said he was just thrilled to go. Kicking himself for opening his big mouth he had to rush out and buy a copy of the damn book, read it and then try to find a way to make it look like he'd read it over and over because he liked it so much. By time he'd creased the pages and frayed part of the binding so it looked used, he wouldn't be able to re-sell it, even with an autograph. Consummate brown-noser that he was he made up some index cards of certain portions and memorized them so that he could add something to the inevitable conversation. Dumb luck when the partner's wife wrangled an invitation to meet personally with the purported psychic.

Yeah, he had it down and got better and better at it, until Carrie. Damn if she didn't see through him. When he was a kid, his parents and teachers said he did average in his classes. But they didn't like him. He wanted them to like him. He wanted to be the big man on campus, the good looking quarterback or the valedictorian, but he wasn't. The teachers said if he applied himself he would do even better, but he didn't want to do better. He wanted something, anything, just handed to him. Just once couldn't he get what he wanted without having to manipulate it into happening?

That was why Carrie had seemed like a good choice. She was friendly, a little naïve and should have been grateful for

169

his attention. He had to admit she was cute, smart, and industrious and would have been just what he needed on his arm to climb the ranks in his company. Turnberg & Jeffers was one of Napa's premier law firms, one Dean was lucky to get a job with, especially with his poor grades in law school. Well, poor grades, until he got them 'fixed'. Not that they knew about the grades. He'd managed to fake the transcript they had looked at when he applied.

There were two things standing in his way to making partner. And they were two very big things. Marriage and two point five kids. Even more important, they were big on brains. Dean knew he wasn't the sharpest knife in the drawer, but he was smart enough to know how to hook up with someone who was and that was Carrie.

She was smart, really knew how to work her way around research and writing, even though her own company didn't have her doing any of that work, and she was good marriage material. Carrie was exactly the kind of woman management at Turnberg & Jeffers wanted their executives to be married to. One way or the other, she was going to marry him. He knew Carrie had thought her relationship with him was going along pretty well, until she decided to surprise him by coming by that day.

Unfortunately, she'd ended up with the surprise instead, and Dean got screwed in more ways than one. He'd continued to play the field, pretty widely in fact, throughout the whole time they dated. As long as he was basically on time for their dates, took her to half way decent places and didn't push going to bed too strongly, she was pretty manageable. Dean supposed he should have been offended that she preferred reading those stupid trashy books to time with him, but in truth, it didn't bother him at all. If it gave her ideas of things they could do in bed once they got married — she was a bit reticent about doing much of anything special in bed. She was pretty much what he heard some folks call 'vanilla' about sex.

That could change, though. Dean figured she'd get over walking in on him and Jolene in a couple of weeks, but then that big guy with the long black hair had showed up. He seemed to be new in town and very protective of Carrie. He looked like those guys on the covers of Carrie's books, with the enormous, hairless chests in ripped shirts. In fact, he looked like he had just walked off one of them. And the guy sure seemed devoted to Carrie. So now — how to break them up and get Carrie back . . .

Looking at the date on his watch, he growled to himself, "Two weeks till the big firm dinner, the one where I planned on announcing my engagement to Carrie. Damn." The dinner was one of the annual events, held a few weeks before bonuses and promotions were announced. Dean had no doubt that if he was engaged he'd be a shoo-in for one of the promotions. "So how do I get rid of Mr. Hunk?"

"Molly? Molly, you home?" Carrie called out as they entered.

Black Eagle watched her peek into the kitchen and den before padding back into the living room to tell him it seemed Molly was out for the evening. He smiled as she moved around the house, lighting a few lamps and settling in for the evening.

When he walked into the kitchen, without the little cat having to ask, he pulled out one of the cans of Taister's food. As he popped the lid, the black cat ran around the corner into the room with a loud meow. "Did you think we would forget you, little panther?"

The cat rubbed up against Black Eagle's jean clad leg as he dished out the food and placed it on the floor.

Having changed into her sweats, Carrie strolled into the kitchen a few minutes later. "So, what do you want to do tonight? Some TV, do a little reading, maybe a little more research on the computer?"

What he wanted to do was take the woman he saw as his wife to bed and make love to her till morning. But since she did not yet know he thought of them as husband and wife, he only asked, "What do you want to do?"

"Ummm, how about we see what's on the movie channel and curl up on the couch and watch?"

"That would please me if it pleases you." He smiled to himself, remembering the *Sleepless* movie and with how much Carrie liked romance. She may pick one that would give her ideas about him.

Carrie flipped through channels. "You know, I wasn't so sure when Molly wanted to order the super duper cable package, but this sure can beat waiting for the tapes and DVDs to come out."

"Super duper?"

"Oh. I did it again, didn't I?"

"It is no worry Carrie. It is important I know how to speak while I am here. Yes?"

She considered that a moment. "Yeah. You're right. So super duper means it's like the total best. The top of the line. Oh!" She stopped flipping through the channels. "This is a favorite of mine! *A Connecticut Yankee in King Arthur's Court*."

"Let me guess. This Yankee travels through time to the place of a King named Arthur."

She blushed despite the big grin she saw creasing his lips. "I can't help it. I love time travels and King Arthur . . . the Knights of the Round Table and all that. I did it again, didn't I?"

"Carrie. You must stop stopping yourself." He sat down on the couch and put his arm out towards her. "Let me see this King Arthur for myself."

When the movie over, Black Eagle walked with Carrie to

her room where she asked him, "So what did you think?"

"I enjoyed it very much. It is curious, though."

"What is?"

"The Merlin character. He reminds me of my Mr. Arthur Merle, sneaky and devious except with dark hair."

Carrie considered that, a look of surprise crossing her face, "You're right! He reminded me of my Mr. Merle, too. But not the devious part. Just that he wanted to be sure Arthur was okay and all. Isn't that interesting?"

Black Eagle said nothing. Instead, he reached for Carrie and pulled her into his arms. Unable to help herself she leaned into him, feeling his hard cock through the cotton of her sweats. With great effort she pulled away from him, not that he held her too tight or too close, but because she didn't want to let go of him. She had to, or she'd end up dragging him to her bed.

Not that that would have been bad. She just didn't want to shock him by behaving so forwardly. The things he said sure sounded like he was falling in love, or at least wanted her. But it was up to him to make the move to sharing her bed. Even though she was tired from the long day and the fresh air, Carrie tossed and turned for the better part of night. While she never really relived any kisses she'd shared with her former boyfriends, she certainly had done so with her imaginary lovers from her romance novels.

Not that she had actually kissed them, but some of those authors wrote such great descriptions of kisses and what followed that it was real easy to imagine what they felt like. The ones she had shared with her boyfriends never came close to what the heroines in the stories felt. That was why she mostly imagined kisses from the heroes in the books. Until now . . .

Standing at her bedroom window, looking out at the night sky with its bright stars shining like diamonds, she thought about the man down the hall. Black Eagle's kisses were the stuff of those books and then some. When he kissed her, Carrie's toes really did curl, she *did* feel that now popular—yet possibly slightly over the top—phrase of 'liquid pooling' between her legs. It really did feel like her heart was pounding so loud he could hear it and now, afterwards, she could *still* feel his lips on hers. And that was an incredible feeling, one she wanted to feel again and again.

"I am falling in love with him. Oh, please, please don't let this be a dream. Please don't let him disappear. Please, let him stay here in this time with me."

Not long after Carrie rolled over and punched her pillow yet again. For all the guys she had dated, marriage had never been her ultimate goal. She enjoyed dating, going out, doing different things, but unlike a number of the women she knew, marriage wasn't the ultimate be all and end all goal. She wanted someone who was special for her and figured he'd come along when he was ready. At first, Dean seemed like he'd be the one, but that didn't last long. Nope, not at all. Black Eagle . . .just being with him did things to her heart and mind she wanted to believe in, just 'cause the books said they did exist, but she never really thought they would happen. Now, at 2:00 a.m. she couldn't get the feel of his lips on hers out of her mind, or the thrill of her tongue tangoing with his and how that simple dance sent luscious shockwaves of pleasure down to her tummy and beyond. *I can only imagine what it would be like to make love to him. But, I can't. I can't because it wouldn't be fair to him and . . . and . . .*To Carrie's own surprise a little cry broke from her lips . . .*he could disappear again tomorrow . . .*

It wasn't an hour later when Carrie woke again. About ready to give up on trying to sleep, she sat up in bed. Maybe some warm milk would help. To say she was startled when her foot came in contact with a rock hard, yet silky soft and warm abdomen would be an understatement. *"Black Eagle?"*

He woke quickly to her startled cry. "It is me, Carrie. I am sorry to have surprised you."

"Wha—what are you doing there on the floor?" She'd sat up and moved to make room for him beside her on the bed. Patting the space, she asked, "What's wrong? Are you all right? Do you feel sick?"

"I am well, Carrie. I, I needed to be beside you. If this is wrong I will go now and find another place—"

"Oh, no! Don't go. Don't even think about it. Please. Promise me you will stay?"

"I do not want to leave you, Carrie Taylor. Not ever. I will stay."

"I'm glad." She placed her hand on his thigh and unconsciously kneaded it. Suddenly realizing what she was doing, Carrie's hand tensed, but before she could remove it Black Eagle put his hand over hers. "It is pleasant what you do, Carrie."

"Black Eagle, have you bee—did you—the past few nights . . ."

"I have slept beside you each night since I came to be here with you, Carrie."

"On the floor?"

"Yes."

"But why?"

"Why on the floor, or why did I sleep beside you?"

"Both."

As he shifted so he could face her, still keeping her hand on his thigh, Carrie realized for the first time he was naked, except for the loincloth he wore when he arrived. Naked and aroused, very aroused. And yet he was so natural about it. As if this was something that happened to him on a regular basis. It was really nice to be with someone who was comfortable with his own body.

"At first I came to sleep beside you because I felt safer near to you and the photograph. If I was to be called back in time,

I felt I would need to be near it and also to be able to say good-bye to you. And I was unsure in this time. Then, I continued to come to you each night, because I wanted — want to be with you. It may be wrong, I may offend you with my words, Carrie Taylor, but I love you."

Unconsciously she brought her other hand to her lips, still feeling him there. "You love me?"

"I do, Carrie, with all my heart. I long wished for the woman who would share my life, I despaired she lived. She did liv — she lives in 2021. If you wish me to leave now, I will."

At his talk of leaving, she grabbed his shoulders. "No! Don't even think about it. Please, don't talk anymore about leaving, promise?"

"I promise, Carrie. I promise I will not speak again of leaving, but Carrie, I am a man, with a man's needs and desires."

Carrie swallowed. She'd read thousands of romantic declarations, all in books, but never thought she'd hear one meant for her. She wanted this man. Physically, mentally and emotionally she wanted this man. "I don't want that promise. I want you to promise you will kiss me, again and again. Will you kiss me, Black Eagle? Now?"

He searched her eyes a long moment. As he lowered his head towards hers, she tilted hers upward, ever so slightly, to meet him halfway. Of almost their own volition her hands moved up his shoulders, feeling the strength of the man.

Giving in to one of her fantasies about what she would do if she were ever to touch this man, she threaded her fingers in his long, silky locks, unaware that he had paused with his lips a fraction away from hers.

"Black Eagle," she whispered. She released a slow breath before his lips settled on hers. A whisper — a soft connection — sent shock waves through Carrie's frame. She moved her hands again to his shoulders, gripping him tightly as his found her waist, drawing her closer — just a feather's stroke before her lips parted to welcome him into the tantalizing warmth of her mouth.

At her welcome he pulled her closer, one hand stroking her back while the other moved to her hip. Deepening the kiss they moved as one closer to each other, closer until Carrie couldn't tell where he ended and she began. She cried out, ever so slightly, when Black Eagle shifted, but settled when she realized he lay down on the bed, pulling her with him.

Carrie stretched out half on top of Black Eagle, sliding her hand down his body and up to his hand. He squeezed her fingers in reassuring grip before she moved on to touch his shoulder and chest. Carrie had read about those powerful chests in her novels, but never dreamed that she could actually feel that power. The strength of his heart beating beneath her hand thrilled her—so strong, so steady—and in the recesses of her mind she knew it beat harder for her. With a brazenness she never knew she could have, Carrie slid her hand lower, to his hip, enjoying the feel of his skin, sinew and muscle where his hip joined his thigh.

There was something so sexy about that point on his body. Something she had drunk in when she first saw him and hoped to not only see again, but to touch and savor and—oh, she wanted this man. She wanted him more than she ever wanted anything in her life. She wanted to give to him—to give herself to him—all of herself. Feeling even surer of herself than she had ever felt before, she slid her hand to his cock.

He was longer, thicker and if possible harder than any man she had ever felt. And Black Eagle was real. This man was *real*. Not the stuff of her imagination or a book. He was real and if he disappeared tomorrow, if he went back in time in the flash of a flame, she would have known one truly real man. Carrie moaned at the slow descent—too slow for her hungry body—too slow, yet at the same time the most exquisite feeling she had ever experienced. As she stroked his cock, showing him the movement she wanted to feel in her between her other, very moist lips, he kneaded her breast, stroking across her nipple, drawing out a moan that shot through him, his cock jerking in her hand.

"I want you, Carrie Taylor. I want to be one with you."

"Black Eagle — oh. Black Eagle. I want you, too. Please. Now . . ."

He pulled up the long tee shirt she slept in before shifting Carrie to her back. She parted her legs to welcome him. To Carrie's surprise she came at the moment he entered her.

A shockwave of pleasure moved through her.

"Oh, oh Black Eagle, I need you, I want you soooooo, oh!"

Not content to allow him the slow steady thrusts he seemed determined to inflict on her, she grabbed his butt with one hand, her other sliding again into his hair in a demand that he move faster, harder, that he claim her as he had never claimed another. Never before had Carrie come more than once, maybe twice . . . this man brought her to the heights of pleasure over and over, until just when she thought it couldn't get any better she came hard, so hard, her inner muscles gripping him in a clench that pulled his own climax from him.

They lay entwined with each other for a long time, each in their own haze of satiated pleasure. She wasn't sure, but if asked she could have sworn she heard him say, "I love you, Carrie, wife of my soul," just before she fell asleep.

CHAPTER TWENTY-TWO

The next day passed way too quickly. Between looking for clues to Black Eagle's past, teaching him to read and write, and making love, the time flew by.

When Carrie returned to work Thursday, it was with a definite glow on her cheeks. After that long, sleepless night, she'd insisted Black Eagle move into her room with her. Not just because it was great sex. She had wanted him there, to hold her in his arms. She had fallen in love with him and fought the feeling, because at any moment, he could be called back in time. One thing she became more and more certain of was that if he couldn't stay here, she would go back with him. Somehow, some way, if he left, she would go back with him.

"Looks like that long weekend did you good, Carrie. Did the emergency get resolved?" Her friend Maria greeted her just as she walked in the door.

"Oh yeah, Maria. It was really good and everything is fine."

From behind her a voice squeaked, "If you can call that Neanderthal she picked up good."

"Dean. What rock did you crawl out from under this morning? And why are you here? Don't you have your own office to go to?" Maria demanded.

"Actually, it was a very warm and sexy female that I crawl—"

Carrie gave him a look of disgust and walked away, her stomaching turning at just the sight of the despicable jerk.

"Don't look at me," Maria told him. "I never understood

why she ever went out with you in the first place."

"She went out with me because she knew I was the best thing that had ever happened to her. I still am the best thing. Carrie? Carrie, come back here."

Maria moved to stand in front of him, blocking his way down the hallway, holding the phone in her hand as if it were a weapon. "Dean, if you don't leave I'll call the cops. Now go. I'm dialing, Dean. We don't need your kind of crap here. I'm dialing." She turned it so the keypad faced her and with dramatic jabbing motions began to dial 911.

Seeing Maria with the phone in hand and dialing 911, Dean backed towards the door, yelling over his shoulder. "This isn't over, Carrie. Not by a long shot. You'll see. You'll come crawling back to me."

"That sounds like a threat, Dean and I have a witness," Carrie spat.

"No threat, just telling you like it is. We belong together and sooner or later you are going to realize it. Why don't you just make it easier all around and—"

"Leave!"

He finally left, and as he walked away from the building, Carrie couldn't help but laugh as Maria walked out with a can of bug spray and pretended to spray where Dean had stood. If only it was that easy to get rid of him.

Before she left for work in the morning, Carrie had shown Black Eagle how to work the phone, doubled checked with him on the microwave—not a surprise that the remote control came to easily to him. She smiled to herself as he rapidly switched channels, looking for something of interest. Relieved the television—or rather the actors in the programs—didn't worry or frighten him, she left for work. After her fifth call in three hours he groused, "You know you are interrupting little panther every time you call."

"He sleeps twenty-two hours a day. I'm giving him a taste

of his own medicine."

"He is ill?"

"No, it's just a phrase. He wakes me all the time, so I'm showing him what it's like."

"Oh. You have many phrases, Carrie Taylor, and I thought it was me you wished to know about."

"I do. Oh, sweetie, I do."

"I am fine, Carrie, truly. I am fine. Little panther is fine, too. I have found your ESPN and like it very much."

Great, he found the sports channel. What a guy. "Good, I'm glad. I'll see you tonight, but, it's okay to call if you need anything, okay?"

"I know. I will."

The rest of the day couldn't pass fast enough for her. "I must be way deeper in love than I thought," she told her computer monitor then laughed to herself when all it gave her was a blank screen. "Normally, I'd be pretending my latest hot hero would be coming by to pick me up and laying me down. It's gotta be love, right?"

While in the past, Carrie actually enjoyed stuffing envelopes and doing mundane and routine work because it gave her time to indulge in her fantasies, today time just lagged. Of course, in the past, her imagination took over and she traveled the world over to different times and places, always with a hunky, absolutely gorgeous alpha male. Now, with one waiting at home for her — at least she hoped he was at home and hadn't ended up back in time — who needed an imaginary lover? She not only had the real deal in Black Eagle, she had a once in a lifetime man who was the most considerate, thoughtful, loving man possible.

Resisting the urge to call him — again — she called Molly who had spent the night at Vincent's. After apologizing for waking her, she asked, "You free for lunch?"

"Definitely."

"How soon can you be ready?"

Through a long yawn, she told her about an hour. "Cool. Meet you at Bodeman's for a burger?"

"Sounds good."

Meeting for lunch at the popular Bodeman's, Molly told her she simply couldn't miss the glow that still clung to Carrie. They placed their orders, picked up their drinks and sat down in a corner booth away from the buzz of a heavy lunch hour conversation. The tables were large and made of heavy oak set in a western theme. The salt and pepper shakers were shaped like six-shooters, glasses like old-fashioned beer steins and the food served on pewter trenchers. "This was a great idea, Molly. So what's the 411 on work?"

"Just fine. Julie is out of town, Leslie is the temporary supervisor, and totally cool."

"How long is the red queen out for?"

"A week from what I hear. So, tell me. Guy stuff, huh? Good guy stuff?"

"Yes — no — maybe — I don't know — but I don't want to call him."

"Don't tell me you're thinking of calling Dean. Oh, do you mean Blake? I take it you showed him how to use the phone?"

Carrie giggled, "The phone *and* the remote. I must need my head examined to have shown him the remote. When I left this morning, he was happily changing channels, and during my last call he told me he found ESPN."

"Oh, lordy. We'll never get near the TV again."

"Mmm, maybe, maybe not. He also seems to have mastered the microwave, and who knows what else he'll stumble on."

"Poor guy. Can you imagine what it would be like to suddenly have all those electronic things just there?"

"To a point. I do see what it could be like when I see how Black — Blake sees it. I've wondered a few times what it would be like not to have them."

"Are you — if there was a way . . ."

They paused while the waitress set their burgers and garlic fries on the table and checked whether or not they wanted their drinks refreshed.

Carrie fussed with her napkin and then played with a fry while she considered her answer. "I don't know. I think I would go back, if he asked me — maybe. I want him to stay, but Mol, sometimes it just hurts me when I think about what a struggle it is for him to be here."

"He seems to be adjusting pretty well."

"Yeah." She paused. Tears formed in her eyes. "Oh Molly, I'm in love with the guy."

"Girlfriend, have you been holding out on me?"

"Well," Carrie sat back in her chair, and with her fingers interlocked, stretched her arms in front of her and her legs, pointing straight out, came up off the ground. She looked like a human cat — like Taister did when he stretched after having a big bowl of cream just before a nap. "No, not really. We kissed out at the beach. Oh man, Molly, I am falling in love with him. Molly, he's everything I ever wanted and when he talks about his life in the 1800's I feel like I belong there. That's where I really belong. Not here, not now."

Carrie knew Molly was trying to wrap her mind around her confession when she asked, "Was it hot?"

"Hot?"

"Yeah, the kiss . . .was he, was it hot?"

"Oh yeah, but more than that, Molly. There's something just so special about him."

"Hey, we've known each other our whole lives. You know you can tell me anything." Molly reached out to her.

"I know, I know." Carrie drew in a deep breath and after a slow exhale asked, "You know how I'm always off reading romance novels?"

"Reading? You live them." Molly smiled as she reached for her drink.

"Yeah, well, I'm definitely living one now. Since I met him, I haven't even picked up one. He's the real deal and I just can't stop thinking about him. Can you believe I've called him like eight times today? And I can't wait to hear his voice again."

"I knew you had it bad for him."

"Yeah, I do." And he could disappear in the blink of an eye.

"Well, we'll have to double again soon. Vincent had a good time the other night with you guys."

"Did he think Blake was odd or different?"

"No. I don't think he noticed anything. Guys don't get into the same stuff we do, you know?"

"I guess."

"Something else?"

"Uh, huh, well, we made love."

"At the beach?"

"No, the night before last. Apparently he'd been coming into my room at night feeling a little unsteady about being here and I had a hard time sleeping that night and when I woke up he was there."

"And?"

"And it was all right. It was right. I wanted him there. Molly, I really am in love with him. And I don't feel like it's too fast. You know how I think it's supposed to take a few months to fall in love? Well I don't feel like this is too fast at all. It just feels right."

"That's a good thing, Carrie, 'cause I think he's falling in love with you too."

"You do?"

"Yup. I see how he looks at you and it's definitely like he's in love."

"Is that like what you have with Vincent?"

"Vincent? No. Not really."

Carrie mentally smacked herself in the head. She'd missed the look in Molly's eyes. She'd been smiling with her lips, but there was an underlying sadness in her eyes. "Mol, is everything all right?"

"Sure. What could be wrong?"

"Nothing. Nothing except I get the feeling something's off. Did Julie pull something again?"

"No. With her it's the same ole, same ole. It's just, well, Vincent and I seem to be drifting."

"Oh, no. What happened?"

"It's nothing specific. He just made a few comments about how taxing my job can be on our relationship."

"You mean your shift work?"

"No. That I can't help, but bitch about it whenever we see each other. I try to keep it down. I try not to think about that stink-hole when I'm away. It's just that every now and then something comes up. I've been trying to keep from focusing on it because it brings me down, too."

"If you need to vent, you know I'm there."

"I know, I know. I'm really okay. Honest. You'd better get going. I'll see you later."

Heading back into work, Carrie didn't know how she was going to make it till the end of the day, but it finally came and she rushed home. Lunching with Molly was good, but how could she have missed her best friend feeling out of sorts? Was she that caught up in Black Eagle, or was Molly getting good at hiding her problems?

Before she was out of her car, her expectant euphoria crashed when she saw Dean standing out front of the house. She considered grabbing the tire iron before heading up the walkway to the house. Thinking better of it—after all, killing him would just create more problems—she strode up to the house glaring at him. "*What* are you doing here?"

"Just wanted to talk, Carrie."

"I've already told you, I have nothing to say to you."

"Aw, come on. Give me a chance, huh?"

"No."

"How about we go to dinner? That little Basque place you like so much."

"No."

Grabbing her arm, twisting it painfully, he pulled her close. "I want you back, Carrie. I want to be with you. Don't you understand? I need you."

She tried to pull away, but he only moved her arm further upward. "Dean, let go of me!"

"Not until you listen to me."

"I won't—" She swore she heard the door slam at the same moment Dean seemed to go flying down the pathway.

"I have had enough of you, little man. The lady asked you to stay away and you did not. She asked you to let go. You did not. Now you will deal with me."

Black Eagle was a sight to behold. His long black hair flowed free, his jaw set in determination, his bare chest flexing as the powerful muscles bunched when he clenched his fists. Barely able to take her eyes off that smooth as satin-over-steel chest, Carrie couldn't help herself. She'd been mesmerized by checking out the butts of guys in tight jeans before, but the way Black Eagle filled his out, the material showcasing his tight butt and powerful legs—and with the top button undone—oh yeah and goody—.he was just so hot.

He stalked after Dean, who had managed to stand and begin to back away only to trip and land on his butt again. "Look, man, she came on to me today. You know she comes on to guys, right? She does. Tell him, Carrie, tell him you like a bit of an edge. Go ahead and ask her."

"That is not my way," Black Eagle ground out.

"Well then, it's not going to work, man. Really, she came on to me, invited me over—"

"You lie, you jackass. Get the hell off my property!" Carrie spat.

Just before Black Eagle reached for him, Dean managed to crab walk away, turned over onto his knees and shakily began to run once he managed to stand again.

"Let him go, Black—Blake, just let the chicken poop go. He's not worth it." Carrie shook her head.

Black Eagle stopped, his hands clenched in fists at his sides. When Carrie caught up to him and put her hand on his back he looked down at her, his dark brown eyes inscrutable. Taking his hand, she pulled him towards the house.

Inside the door he drew in a long, deep breath. "Did you really seek him out today, Carrie?"

Turning in surprise to him, Carrie went to take both his hands in hers. He pulled back. "Did you?"

"No! How could you even think that?"

"He said—"

"He lied. Black Eagle, it's you I want, it's you I want to be with."

"And what if I am drawn back in time, Carrie? Will you return to him?"

"You won't be."

"We do not know that, Carrie, we don't know."

"I do. *I* know. Remember, I've read the books and, and the time traveler stays in the new time. You'll stay." *You must stay. You must . . .*

She barely heard his softly spoken "Carrie," before he picked her up and carried her towards the bedroom. Laying her gently on the bed, he ran his hands along her arms while he lowered his head to take her lips in a searing kiss. Like a man who has just crossed the desert his lips melded with hers, his tongue tasting each corner and surface of her mouth.

Her hands came up to his waist, rubbing along his flat abdomen before settling on the zipper to slide it down. Her hips thrust up towards his while she pulled at his jeans, drawing them down. To her delight, he didn't wear the briefs she'd bought him. There was something so utterly sensual about him wearing only those form-fitting jeans over that smooth bronzed skin of his. At the same time he pulled at her clothes, unbuttoning the blouse and releasing her bra so he could taste her breasts. She chanced a quick look into his eyes, and in that brief moment saw desire, awe and a passion hotter than any she had ever seen. It just got better and better with Black Eagle. She fell harder and harder for him with each passing day.

A short time later, they emerged from the bedroom and went in search of some dinner.

Taister immediately shared his opinion on how rude it was of them to make him wait for his meal, and all the things he had to do while waiting. Entering the kitchen, Black Eagle reached for a can of the cat's favorite food, sat down with the cat on his lap and proceeded to feed him by hand.

"You're spoiling him." Carrie couldn't help but smile as she opened a can of soup.

"He prefers to eat from my hand."

"I see that. Like I said, you're spoiling him," she said with a shake of her head, cutting some chicken and vegetables to add to the soup.

"Carrie, are you afraid I will leave and little panther will miss me and not understand I have left?"

Her hand over the pot, she stopped and thought for a moment.

"Carrie, I will not leave you. I promise."

Finished adding the extra ingredients, she turned and moved to stand before him. "How can you promise that?"

"In my mind, I do not know. In my heart, I do. I will not leave you, Carrie. That is a promise I will keep."

With Taister on one knee, he settled Carrie on the other. "In fact, I have decided that I need to find some work here in your time."

"Work? We've only started to teach you to read and write and — and — you don't have any identification."

"We will find some. When your Mr. Merle returns, we will visit him and maybe he can help."

"Yeah — maybe."

Chapter Twenty-three

Friday night finally arrived and Carrie and Black Eagle double dated with Molly and Vincent. Carrie hadn't yet introduced Black Eagle to Chinese food, and the time to do so had come. It only took about twenty spins of the Lazy Susan table for Black Eagle to let go of his fascination for it. Or rather, it was only twenty spins or so before the waiter brought the first dishes. Egg rolls, crunchy fried wontons, and sizzling rice soup started their meal. Rather than be embarrassed at the compliments Black Eagle had for the dishes, Carrie was pleased he enjoyed them as much as he did. If Vincent noticed that the shrimp fried rice, broccoli beef and Kung Pao chicken were new to Black Eagle, he didn't let on. Although Carrie did blush deep and red when they read his fortune cookie.

"Not even time and space will keep you from the one you love."

After, they went to play miniature golf. That, however, had Vincent curious about Black Eagle. He couldn't believe someone had never played the game. Despite Molly's assertion that Vincent was the last true devotee of the game, he still thought Black Eagle was pretending he had never heard of it — especially when he won, hitting a hole in one at just about every hole.

Carrie suggested ice cream as they finished the second game. "How about Ann's? And a kitchen sink?"

"There is a problem with the sink in the kitchen?" Black Eagle asked.

Carrie and Molly both giggled.

"No," Carrie assured him, "It's called that because it has everything *but* the kitchen sink in it. You name the ice cream flavor and topping, it's there."

"It's our favorite," Molly put in. "Usually we have to get the mini-one with only six flavors and two toppings because there's no way we could eat the big one. With you guys we can. This way we can have a bite of every flavor."

"*Nagi Tanka* has truly sent me to the land of my ancestors," Black Eagle said as the waitress set the super-sized bowl on the table.

"Huh?" Vincent gave him an odd look.

"Ah, I think Blake's keeping with the theme of the Chinese food for dinner. Right, Blake?"

"Yes, the theme."

Vincent shrugged and then dug into the caramel covered butter pecan with true dedication of an ice cream fanatic.

The next morning, the foursome decided to go to an art and wine festival in the next county over. Rising early with a quick breakfast, they headed over. Carrie assured Black Eagle there would be plenty of food there to eat.

At the festival, they inspected the wares in each booth with Black Eagle commenting, quietly to Carrie, on the woodworking and how it was done in his time. Many items he thought frivolous, but commented that maybe they were not, for this present time. There were a variety of foods from different countries, many of which Black Eagle had not been aware of in his time, and he wanted to try them all. Carrie had already decided he had a cast iron stomach from the combinations and quantities he ate, so they dove in and tried everything.

Towards evening, they found seats and listened to the bands that had come to play. If Vincent thought there was something odd going on from either the comments the night before or today, he kept his own counsel.

Carrie figured Molly could handle whatever questions

came up without disclosing just where—and when—Black Eagle came from. Fortunately, Vincent was into many of the sports Black Eagle had watched—avidly, on television—so they had something in common to talk about.

Driving home after a full day in the sun, good food and some wine, Carrie fell asleep with her head on Black Eagle's shoulder.

Sunday the two couples made and ate a huge brunch together. Lingering over coffee, Vincent finally asked what he'd seemed to be wondering about the past few days. "So, Carrie, where did you and Blake meet?"

Before Carrie could stutter out a reply, Molly answered. "I thought I told you, sweetheart—they met over the Internet."

Grateful for Molly's quick thinking, Carrie nodded, while at the same time sliding her hand onto Black Eagle's thigh to squeeze it, to be sure he was on the same page with her on this.

"Yes, we met on the In-ter-net."

"Well that's cool. Met the man of your dreams on the Internet."

"I never said Blake was—"

"I told him," Molly finished for her. "It's pretty clear you guys are a good match. Who knows what the future will bring, huh?"

"So where do you come from, Blake?"

"The Dakotas."

"You think you might settle here?"

"I'm not sure. That depends on Carrie and what we decide."

"Well, good. I don't know about you guys, but I had a great time this weekend. So hey, Blake, I've got tickets to a Giants game Wednesday night. Want to go?"

Before Carrie could interject any kind of answer, Black Eagle replied, "We do not have giants in the Dakotas. I would enjoy that very much seeing them."

Uh oh . . .Carrie cast a quick glance at Molly, who winked to let her know they had time to coach Black Eagle on what to say and do at the game. She made a mental note to bring Black Eagle up to speed on just who and what the Giants were.

Wednesday came all too quickly for Carrie. Usually she looked forward to Wednesday because it meant only two more days until the weekend. This week it arrived too fast. Way too fast and then, promptly at three-thirty when she knew Vincent was picking Black Eagle up to go to the game, the clock suddenly stopped.

Instead of it taking one and one-half hours to get to five and getting off work, Carrie was sure the clock had stopped and even gone backwards for a bit. "Talk about time travel, I'm sure I've been traveling backwards," she muttered to no one in particular.

When five finally arrived, she literally ran out of the office and hurried home. Or tried to hurry home. It seemed every car in creation was out on the streets of Napa, and none of them seemed to have a gas pedal. She was sure she was losing it when she yelled at one driver, "It's not going to get any greener" when they didn't immediately hit the gas at one intersection.

There was no doubt she had entirely lost it when she yelled at another, "That's a fine shade of green. What one are you waiting for?"

Then she gave thanks she wasn't in Los Angeles, where she would have been shot for either one of those comments. Finally arriving home, almost forgetting to lock the car, she rushed into the house, turned on the TV and for the first time was glad they had sprung for that annoying sports channel. Otherwise she would not have been able to see the Giants home game. Not that she expected to actually *see* anything. It was the conversation between Vincent and Black Eagle she wanted to hear.

Black Eagle had never shown any temper. Well, except for Dean and who wouldn't lose their temper around him? But if they did, then there *would* be something to see, but not anything she wanted to see.

So there she stood, staring at the television, hoping for the best, just wanting the game to be over and for Black Eagle to be home and telling her that absolutely nothing about his past, or where he came from, even came up.

Taister wandered in and even he seemed to realize his person was not quite herself, because he didn't ask for any food. Instead he climbed up on the couch and settled in, lying against his favorite pillow, the white one that showed his black fur to its best advantage. That was where Molly found them when she arrived home a short time later, with Carrie standing in front of the television and Taister snoozing on the couch.

"At least one of you is comfortable. What's going on?" she chuckled.

"I'm watching the game."

"You suddenly into baseball?"

"No. It's Black Eagle. I want to be sure nothing happens at the game. That he doesn't say or do anything that, you know."

"Carrie, give the man a little credit, will you? He may not be educated, and he may not know what we do here in this time, but he's not stupid. And if you saw something on TV, how could you stop it like thirty miles away? It's not like you can hear what they are saying in their seats."

"I know. I know. But what if he says something to Vincent and Vincent thinks he's crazy?"

"Trust me, there is nothing he could say to Vincent to make him think he's crazy."

"How can you know that? How many time travelers does Vincent know?"

"'Cause I know Vincent. Carrie, he's into science fiction type stuff."

"Yeah, well, I read that, too. But time travel? Who is going to believe it's possible?"

"Um, we do."

"Yeah. Yeah. Vincent—"

"It'll be fine Carrie, really, just fine."

Molly turned to head into the kitchen and called over her shoulder, "No, like real sci-fi type stuff. Like, he believes in possibilities. However, I can guarantee you he won't bring it up. He's too much of a sports fan, and he's savvy enough to know people would think *he* was crazy if he brought it up. Come on, let's scare up some dinner and relax."

CHAPTER TWENTY-FOUR

At the game, Black Eagle was fascinated with all the go-ings-on. Making mental notes of what he found most in-teresting so he could ask Carrie what they meant later, he sat back and enjoyed the game. Taking his cues from Vincent, he stood and cheered when the other man did, matching him hot dog for hot dog and beer for beer till the end of the game. It seemed to him that in some respects this time was no different than his own — women chattered on about day to day things, men sat quietly and observed.

Granted, he fought his fears when Vincent drove on the free-ways, as he called them. But they were also in a black truck — not as big at the one he had seen the first day, but it was a truck and he much preferred it to Carrie's little car. The Bay Bridge was beyond belief to him until he looked over the bay towards the Golden Gate and knew he saw true majesty. He would ask Carrie to take him there to see it more closely.

Pulling in front of the house, Vincent commented that he hadn't planned on stopping in, but since the lights were on, he wanted to see Molly and at least snag himself a good night kiss.

Carrie jumped up off the couch and rushed to Black Eagle as soon as he stepped through the door. She took his hand and led him to the couch. "How was it? Did you have a good time? Anything weird happen?"

He pulled her close to him and smiled at her, waiting for her to reach the end of her questions. "It was good, Carrie. Did you watch?"

"Yes, just about every minute. So nothing odd happened?"

Molly had joined Vincent at the door and he asked as she pulled him inside the room, "Like what, Carrie?"

"Oh, you know. Anything just different."

"Nope. Good food, cold beer and a damn good game. Blake's planning on getting season tickets with me next year."

"Oh — good." Is it? That means he plans on staying, right? Okay, that's good. For sure by next year he'll learn how we do things, right? If he can stay, that is — if he isn't pulled back in time.

"Well, I guess I'll get going." Vincent quietly murmured.

"You sure you want to leave, Vincent?" Molly asked.

"Well, there was something I wanted to bring up to you."

"Was there?"

As Molly took Vincent by the hand and led him down the hall, Black Eagle leaned over to Carrie and told her, "I can tell you something sounds good to me, too."

CHAPTER TWENTY-FIVE

Three days later Carrie and Black Eagle woke early. Well, early for Carrie on a Saturday. She'd set the alarm so they could get up and go to Treasures to talk to Mr. Merle as soon as possible. "Instead of doing the whole breakfast thing, why don't I introduce you to fast food?"

"Fast food? Like Vincent's fast truck?"

"Um, well no. Carl's Junior has really yummy tater tots. We can eat on the run. It's really good. I promise."

She felt pretty darn good when Black Eagle told her that Carl's cooking did not come close to the good breakfasts she made, although, he did do the Tater Tots justice.

With breakfast done, even on the run, they headed to Treasures in the hope of some answers. The moment they entered Treasures, Black Eagle stalked past her and right up to Mr. Merle. He'd never shown any anger, even with Dean's antics. And this morning he hadn't seemed in that big of a rush to get going so she was quite surprised when he grabbed the older man and pinned him to the wall. "*You!*"

"Me? Me, what?"

"You stole my spirit and put it in your box."

"I did what? Carrie, what's going on here? Who is this man?"

"Black, Blake, please, put Mr. Merle down. He doesn't know what your Mr. Merle did, and no one stole your spirit," Carrie patiently explained.

Warily, Black Eagle let the older man down.

As he did, Mr. Merle stepped away, rubbing his shoulder,

while keeping an eye on the dark haired man. "Carrie, you know this man?"

"Yes. Mr. Merle. This is Blake Eagleston, and we have a few questions if you have time."

"Of course, Carrie, I always have time for you." He looked at Black Eagle again before telling Carrie, "Let me post the 'closed' sign, and put up some tea. We'll talk."

"Are you sure? It's early. We can come back."

"No problem at all. It seems you have something mighty big on your mind."

"Thank you." She nudged Black Eagle, who also offered his apology and thanks, albeit grudgingly, to the Treasures proprietor.

Sitting in the shop's little kitchen a bit later, Carrie began. "Mr. Merle, remember that photograph you gave me a few weeks ago?"

"The old tintype? Yup, sure do."

"Well, remember I told you when I got it home that night I thought I noticed there was something different about it? I'd see, like, a camera flash in it, or happen around it."

"Yes, I remember something like that. Did it happen again?"

"Happen again? Mr. Merle it more than happened again! One morning I work up and Blake was in bed with me."

Black Eagle stood, his fists gripped so tight his knuckles were a definite white. Seeing his movement, Carrie put a reassuring hand on his arm. "It's okay, Blake. Let's see if we can explain this and what Mr. Merle thinks, please?"

He slid his chair closer to Carrie. "You woke up with this young man in bed with you? What does that have to do with the photograph?"

"A lot, Mr. Merle. The bright light. Well that only happened the one time and then suddenly — well, okay, do you notice anything about Blake here?"

"No, can't say I do."

"Doesn't he look familiar to you?"

Mr. Merle studied the younger man a moment, stroking his chin. "He a model from one of those books you read?"

"No, Mr. Merle. No. The photograph you gave me. The man in the photograph?"

"Yes?"

She was going to sound certifiable. She knew it. There was no doubt in her mind she was going to sound crazy. "Well, I—I—at first I thought Molly or Dean played a joke on me, but it became pretty clear, Mr. Merle, you can't tell anyone about this. Promise me you won't repeat it."

"'Course not, Carrie. Go on," he encouraged.

"Mr. Merle, it's going to sound crazy. It's going to sound like I'm totally nuts. Heck, I think it's nuts."

"Well, let's hear what you have to say and then we'll decide how crazy it is, all right?"

"All right. When I woke up, like I said, at first I thought he was part of a joke Molly or Dean was playing on me. It became pretty clear—pretty quick—that it wasn't a joke. Blake was here, only his name isn't really Blake, it's Black Eagle and he's the warrior in the photograph—only he's not in the photograph anymore."

Carrie reached in her purse and pulled out the photograph and waved it in front of the elderly gent. "See, this is where he stood and now he's not there anymore. He's here. Right here, see?"

Mr. Merle took the photo, caressing the space where Black Eagle had been with his thumb. He studied the photo for so long Carrie wondered if maybe he had fallen asleep.

"Mr. Merle?"

The older man looked up slowly and turned to Black Eagle. "Carrie, I've got to admit, that does sound, well odd. What makes you think such a thing could happen?"

"I—well—my books, my romances, my time travels. See, well, the time—Black Eagle says he is from . . ." She was not going to cry. She wanted to because she sounded so nuts, but crying wouldn't solve her problem. She wasn't going to laugh, either, no matter how ludicrous she sounded.

"Carrie speaks the truth, Mr. Merle. I am the man who was in your photograph, and somehow you have made magic to bring me here."

Mr. Merle shook his bowed head. "It doesn't make sense. Blake is it?"

"I have taken the name Blake to live in your time."

"Blake, then. This, what you are telling me, it doesn't make sense. You think somehow you came through the photograph to this time? And you think *I* had something to do with it?"

"I do not know for a certainty that it was your photograph, but I believe very much it was."

"How could that be?" Almost as an afterthought he raised a bushy white brow.

"You did so. When you captured my spirit in your box."

"I? What box?"

"When you took my photograph. You took my spirit and put it—"

"You really think you are a man called Black Eagle who lived in another time?"

"Mr. Merle, I know I am the Black Eagle from your photograph and it is true, Carrie, he took my spirit and put it—"

"That's not going to help us." Carrie stood and paced the short distance to the back door of the shop, and looked out the Dutch door window a moment. "Mr. Merle, for argument's sake, can we say that Blake here is Black Eagle and he came from the past?"

"Of course we can, Carrie. I believe you both believe it. What a wonderful thing if it is true."

"You'd really think it's wonderful?"

"Of course. I remember what it is like to be young and in love. I remember what it's like to wonder if your special someone is going to find you. I cannot think of anything more romantic that someone braving time and space to be with the one they are meant to love."

"Thanks Mr. Merle. I knew we could talk to you about this. And it is romantic, isn't it? So Black Eagle, please, tell Mr. Merle what happened to you, after the picture was taken."

He swallowed and closed his eyes a moment before beginning his story. "*You*—or as you have told Carrie, your ancestor took my photograph. My *wanagi*." He put his hand up. "I know you do not believe this. I do. I went back to my village and dreamt of the *winyan* I would—a woman. I thought of a woman. Despite my search, I had not found a *mitawin*, my wife. There were many women from my village to choose from. None that captured my heart. You knew this, Mr. Arthur Merle. We had spoken of this."

When Mr. Merle did not respond, Black Eagle nodded and continued. "Many nights I watched the stars. Many times I watched the ones that fell to Earth. One night I could not sleep. The one thought I had was of the woman who would come to my life. I went to the lake near our village, sat on a rock and looked to the skies. Only a short time passed before I saw one star fall, more brilliant than the rest. It looked as if it would come right to my feet. I saw colors, many colors and then blackness. When I woke, I realized I was no longer in my village. I woke in Carrie's room with her beside me."

Carrie broke in. "I gotta tell you, Mr. Merle, it sure scared me. You know, waking up with a strange man in bed with me."

"I imagine it would, Carrie dear. You aren't that kind of girl."

"No, Mr. Merle, she is not." Black Eagle assured him, "She is a good and decent woman. One any man would be proud to have as his wife." He took in Mr. Merle's look before the older man closed it off.

"So," Carrie began, "once I got control of my feelings — once I could breathe again — you know, it's kind of freaky waking up next to a strange man. Well, after I caught my breath, I looked at my photograph and the Indian in it was gone. Poof! Nothing. As if he was never there. I know it sounds crazy, but the Indian in the photograph is Black Eagle and he turned up in my house. This is the man from the photograph."

"I'll give you that, Carrie. This man sure does look like what I remember of the man in the photograph. Are you maybe his descendant?"

"No. I *am* the man in the photograph. I was in it. Somehow the *iktomi* or your magic brought me here. Now I do not stand in the photograph. I live and breathe in your time."

"Well then, tell me, what is it you want from me? How can I help you?"

"I want to know how it happened. How did he get here? I want to know if anyone else from that photograph is going to end up in my room!"

"And I, Mr. Arthur Merle, want to know how to be certain I will stay here, in this time," Black Eagle calmly informed him. "And, I wonder as does Carrie, will any of the others from when you took my spirit, will come to this time."

"Well, I can't say I know anything about how this happened. If what you say is true — if you are from another time — well, I don't think anyone else is going to come to this time, if that's what happened. If they were, I think they would have arrived by now, don't you think? It's not like they'd show up one at a time."

At Carrie's nod in agreement, he turned to Black Eagle. "And you, son, if you really did come from the past, do you want to stay here in this time?"

Carrie didn't realize she was holding her breath until she saw Black Eagle's strong nod in the affirmative. "I did come from the past. This is not my time. But yes, this is where I will stay. It is my wish to remain here with Carrie. I love her and I have no desire to leave her."

"Well, that's good news."

"Good news, yes. But how do we make sure he can stay?" Carrie asked. Carrie watched closely as Mr. Merle considered his next words, covering his hesitation to answer by pouring more tea and shuffling the plate of cookies towards Black Eagle.

"I think it's safe to say if Black Eagle was going to go back in time, he would have already gone. You say he's been here over two weeks? Then it would seem he's here to stay."

Carrie exhaled and offered a tentative smile. She wasn't sure if Mr. Merle was being nice and pretending to accept the revelation that Black Eagle really came from the past or if he really believed it. What counted the most was that Black Eagle would stay with her. "That's what happens in my time travel books. Either the hero or heroine goes to another time and stays. Well, most of the time. But they always find each other again. Somehow they find each other again. You sure you really want to stay here, Black Eagle?"

"This is my home now, Carrie. I mean to make it here, with you. I miss my home, yes. Very much at times, but my home is now here, with you."

"Well that's good, as long as you treat Carrie good. She's a special girl."

"Yes. She is," Black Eagle agreed. "Mr. Merle, are you sure you do not know me?"

"Without a doubt, I don't know you, Blake. I'll tell you this. Many people think all the members of my family—the Merles—look alike. Strong family resemblance, I suppose. So I can see where, if you really are Black Eagle, you'd confuse me with my ancestor."

"Well that makes sense, doesn't it, Black Eagle?" Carrie asked, running her hand along his arm. "It does. Now we must ask about the other problem."

"Other problem?" Mr. Merle asked.

"Yes, Mr. Merle, we have a little problem."

"What's that, Carrie?"

Noting her friend seemed more relaxed than he had since they arrived, Carrie also felt a little better. And she had a little test for him. "Well, he doesn't have any ID. He can't prove he exists and, well, if he wanted to—"

"I wish to find a job, Mr. Merle. Carrie says I need this I-D to find one."

"Yes, you do. You certainly do."

"Can you help us, Mr. Merle? I mean I know it's not legal and all, but . . ." Carrie asked.

The elderly man paused, stroking his chin. "You know, I think I can. Yes, I can. I'm pretty sure I can get you some ID. Give me a day or two, Tuesday latest. That work?"

"Yes. Yes, it would. Will it not, Carrie?"

"I think so and you know, we have an opening for a mail guy, an inside messenger at work. I'm pretty sure I could get you in there. It's not exciting, pretty routine, but it's a job and we'd sort of be working together."

"Carrie, what I do is of little importance to me. What is important is that I have a job and if it would be with you that would be much better."

"Then let's plan on it. What do you need from us, Mr. Merle?"

"Well, as much as I think Black Eagle is going to object, I need to take his picture—for the driver's license."

"That is good. Then I can drive." Black Eagle grinned.

"Uh that would be a no. Not without learning to, you can't." Carrie informed him. "But we can use it for ID. It's a start."

"That's all I need. I can get anything else you need with that picture."

"Then let us take it," Black Eagle told him.

Carrie took a few minutes to help Black Eagle situate himself and took a few moments to arrange his long dark hair so it would look more in tune with what her company would want. He had mentioned having it cut, but Carrie quickly dissuaded him from doing so, telling him how much she enjoyed entwining her fingers in it. Her job wouldn't mind long hair. It just needed to be neat. Black Eagle had admitted that he enjoyed having her grab hold of his hair when they made love, so the matter of having his hair cut or not was settled. She figured they'd deal with what to do if and when he got the job.

Once they were done with the mini-grooming, Mr. Merle grabbed a camera and prepared to take the photo.

Black Eagle interrupted him. "Mr. Merle. Will this new box take my spirit again? Will it go to another picture in another time?"

"Son," Mr. Merle told him, "cameras can't take your spirit. That's the truth. If you really did travel here from another time, it was by some other means."

The picture taken, Mr. Merle led them to the door. "I'll call you Monday, Carrie. I might have it all done by then."

"Great. I'll ask at work on Monday about the job."

CHAPTER TWENTY-SIX

Watching the couple as he locked up and checked to be sure the sign on the door still said '*Closed*', Arthur Merle assured himself he had done the right thing. Mumbling to himself as he turned out the lights, he spoke to the departed couple.

"Carrie, Carrie, I hope you see I had to do *something*. You deserved better than those jerks you kept meeting, especially that Dean. You ought to have someone to love you for yourself, who will treasure you, care for and spoil you and be ready to lay down his life for you. And you, Black Eagle, you are a good, caring man, always were and it was a damn shame for you to have died without having had the love of a good woman. Besides, it's nice to see a couple that belongs together be together for a change."

Glancing at his image in the antique mirror, he assured himself, "Arthur Merle, you did do the right thing. They just need to decide if they want to be together now — or then."

An image appeared behind him in the mirror. "Are you sure you did the right thing? Or are you still trying to undo that disaster from so long ago?"

"Vivianne." He turned towards her. "You've returned. Not that I'm not glad to see you, 'tis just not like you." He glanced to the door and quickly made an inventory of the shop to ensure no customers were inside."

"I promise you, I would not have appeared were anyone around. Sometimes I think what I miss most of our time is the belief in magic. Of wizards and witches and magic."

"Ah, Vivianne, it will come again. You know this as well as I. When our darkest days come, the magic will return."

"It would seem the dark days are returning."

"The world has had more difficult times than what we see now."

"Perhaps. If that is so, then why do the signs show the return?"

"You mean the movement at Glastonbury?"

"Yes. And, dear friend, how do you know that if someone were to come to this time, that everyone involved would come at once? You must consider this if things are moving at Glastonbury. As your Indian friend asked, if one wakes, will they all at once? Or as they are needed?"

"If it comes to their awakening, I have no doubt it will be all at once. As to the Tor, it is merely the earth moving as it always does. You know, what these modern scientists call earth plates moving and ley lines. I'm sure of it. You stood beside me, did you see more?"

She shook her head and gestured toward the wall. "No. Yet I cannot help but feel . . .and look to the sword, do you not see it glows more brightly?"

"The cast of the sun. Those days are gone. We live now. Just us, you and I."

"As you say. Still, I cannot help but feel something is happening. So your friend, Carrie, she is happy with your magic?"

"It seems so. She deserves it."

"I hope it works out, dear friend. I hope it works out." She nodded again towards the case. "Glastonbury calls." With that her image shimmered, fading to nothing save a few sparkling motes on the floor.

Turning back to the mirror, the white-haired man thought of the other time and place and couple he tried to bring together. A couple that should have been together, but unforeseen forces had interfered. No, not unforeseen, just a force he had not reckoned on. A force he hoped stayed back in that long-ago time. He stood thinking, if all was well with Carrie and Black Eagle, then perhaps it was time for him to do something about that vile Julie Prince, the woman Carrie told him had been making Molly's life a living hell. He'd do it for Carrie.

One thing Arthur Merle had learned to live with was that he could send others through time and space, but he himself could only move through space. And, some things couldn't be undone. Once set in motion, they just couldn't be undone. Placing his hand flat on the mirror, he drew in a long, deep breath, closed his eyes and in his mind saw himself inside the local Department of Motor Vehicles.

Within moments he was inside the building and before the computer that would soon contain the information on Blake Eagleston. It wasn't the first ID he had helped with. After all, Black Eagle wasn't the first man or woman he'd help move through time to be with their one true love. Not that he'd admit that he could do that. If anyone knew, even the couples he helped, it would ruin some of the magic of the relationship. The mystery of how two people who belonged together found each other added something special to the union. No, this was not his first identification, nor he suspected, would it be his last. Finished with Blake's identification, Arthur waved his hand about the room to clear away any traces of his presence, and in the blink of an eye, was back in his shop. Once back inside, he pushed on a panel in the mirror and extracted a ledger from within, sat down and made some notes. Looking at his notebook he thought about the others he wanted to help—so many people with so many dreams, fine dreams, that he would help come true.

CHAPTER TWENTY-SEVEN

Carrie and Blake, as she was getting better at calling him, went shopping for a few new items for him to wear to work and she coached him on current money, how to greet people and whatever else she could think of to help him at work. In particular she liked the matching eggshell fisherman's knit sweaters and tan corduroy jeans they bought. Comfy, cozy clothing to wear on a chilly fall day.

And they made love. Carrie admitted to herself that what they shared was more than simply hot sex. No, they made love like she'd never made love to any other man before. Oh, it was still very hot, but it was more, much more. With each kiss, with each caress, it was clear he was the man she'd waited her whole life to meet. Black Eagle was the first man who had taken the time to cuddle with Carrie after making love and oh, did he cuddle.

One morning, he rose from the bed after he'd held her so gently following their sweet lovemaking, and went to stand at the window. She watched him with the pale morning light highlighting the shadows and curves of his muscular body as he stood there looking so lost. Finally rising, she went to join him, placing her hand tentatively on his shoulder, a gentle whisper of a touch.

"Blake?"

It wasn't pain, but confusion, she saw on his face and in his eyes. "Blake?" Pulling slightly on his shoulder, she softly asked, "Black Eagle?"

He finally turned to her. "I'm sorry, Carrie. I was lost in my thoughts. I could not stop them from running through my mind."

"What's wrong?"

"Nothing and yet, something." Putting his arm around her, he pulled her to the heavily cushioned chair that sat in her room. Pulling her onto his lap as he sat, he drew her head down to give her a kiss.

"Blake? Blake, what is wrong? What did I do? Did I hurt you? Offend you? Please, tell me wha —"

Shaking his head, he rained light kisses along her jaw and cheek, finally silencing her questions with his lips on hers. "You have done nothing. I am only confused. Carrie, there is no doubt in my mind your Mr. Merle is *my* Mr. Merle."

"How can that be? He'd be almost two hundred years old, or more, if they were the same. Didn't you say your Mr. Merle looked as old as mine? And mine's pretty old. If anyone was *that* old it would be in the news. Don't you believe him?"

"I do not know how I know, but I do know he is the same man. He looked exactly the same when he came to my village in 1860. Do you think he may be a time traveler, too?"

"Blake, how can you be sure of that? Think about it. Don't you think if he could time travel he would have told us? Especially when we asked him how to make sure you can stay here?"

"No normal man does. There was something about him. I remember something about him that was different when he came to my time. A twinkle in his eye gave the impression that he knew some magic that no one else knew."

"Well, yes, he does have a twinkle in his eyes, but when he gave me the photo, he said his ancestor took it. A lot of relatives look a whole lot alike. Remember he said that was a family trait — that the men look alike in each generation. You saw your Mr. Merle one hundred and sixty or so years ago. Memories can fade."

"No, Carrie, I saw him maybe a month ago in my time. You forget I saw him when he took my photograph, then a couple of weeks later I arrived here, in your time. That is no ancestor. That is the man I know."

"Then, well, what do you think? Blake, it's not possible. A man can't make time travel happen. I mean, it happened because you are here. I just don't think someone can make someone else do it."

"Based on your books, a man cannot make time travel happen? Or do you know for certain some other way?"

"My boo—are you making fun of my books?"

"No, Carrie, never. What happened to me, to us, is not the stuff of your books. This is something that really happened to me and I believe that man made it happen."

"But how?"

"I don't know. Maybe, as my people believe, the camera took my spirit and he somehow brought me to live here. Carrie, let me ask you something. I know you think hands are hands. That I cannot remember my Mr. Merle's hands, but I do. Did you ever see your Mr. Merle do something like this?"

Black Eagle repeated the movements he had seen the Mr. Merle of his time do when he took the picture, the same waving of his hand with the palm down one way and palm up on the other, just as he saw each night in his dreams. Carrie thought about it a moment. "Yes! I *did* see him do something like that when I brought him the photograph. But that probably doesn't mean anything. After all, it could just be a family thing. Like the Masons have these signals and all. Maybe it's a family thing that they pass down to each other."

"Carrie, I know not these Masons. Even if it were a family signal, don't you find it odd that both of our Mr. Merles would do it around my photograph?"

"I guess. But, the way you are talking, are you—are you sorry you are here?"

"No, Carrie, I have waited my whole life for you. I love you and will not lose you now. That is why I must understand what happened. So that I can stay here with you. If he did bring me here, will the same hand movement send me back in time?"

Wrapping her arms around his neck and shoulders, she clung to him. "I want you to know I love you, too. I love you so much and I don't want to lose you, either. These weeks with you here have been the happiest of my whole life. Are you sure you want to stay here? That you'll be okay if you are here? I'd go back with you, to your time. I know some things were hard back then compared to now, but I like how simple you make life sound. I would love to be in a time when life is easier, not so much clutter."

"Of all these hard things, you know acceptance with you as my wife would be the most difficult. I will stay, Carrie. It does not seem I have a choice. I cannot say there will not be times I am sad to no longer be in my home. It would not be honest if I said otherwise. Yet those times will mean nothing if I am with you. I do want to stay here with you. Therefore, we must know what Mr. Merle, both yours and mine, have done and how he or they did it. Only by knowing how it is done can we make sure we will stay together."

"Okay, I see that. But he can't be the same man. Don't you see? He'd be ancient. No one can live that long."

"Carrie, if he can move one man through time, why not two? What if in my time he found a way to come to the future and brought me with him?"

She considered that. "Then if that is so, he can move other people through time. We could just pop in here and there whenever we wanted. He would be a genius and the government would want him. Other governments would want him. That makes it even more interesting. Like a James Bond movie."

"I do not know this James, but if that is so, Carrie, then you and I could be in as much danger as him."

"Bingo," Dean said to himself. He'd seen the couple return home and rather than attack the big guy again, he thought he'd hang around and see what he could learn. Maybe figure out a way to break them up and make it look like it was Carrie's idea. Physical confrontations never quite worked out for him, but mental mind games always hit the spot. At first a bit disgusted with himself for watching Carrie and Blake make love, he quickly found it was interesting to observe. In fact, it turned him on a lot more than some of the movies he rented that he had delivered to a post office box in the next town over. Under another name, of course.

He wasn't sure why she called the guy two different names, at first, but that was Carrie. What he heard after was just what he needed to know. Not that he had any grand plans, not at first. He just wanted to get Carrie to marry him so he could get his promotion at work. But what he'd heard, *that* opened up a ton of other possibilities. Heck, he might not even need to marry Carrie. If he could somehow use this information to get money — a lot of money — he didn't need that promotion, or anyone else. That time travel thing certainly had intriguing possibilities. Okay, Carrie always acted a little loopy. All those smut books of hers drove him nuts. But for that partnership he could deal with it. Besides, he only had to be married, not involved with her. Yes, he could certainly use that time travel business. The question was how . . .

CHAPTER TWENTY-EIGHT

"Molly?"

"Hey, Carrie."

"I know you're looking forward to going back to nights and weekends, but I gotta tell you, I'm going to missing hanging out with you. Is Vincent coming over later?"

"Nooooo," her roommate warbled.

"Oh no, what's wrong?" Carrie sat beside her and with a hopeful glance to Black Eagle her man left the roommates alone.

"Everything. Nothing. Life."

"Did you guys break up?"

"Not exactly. He said he needed some guy time, and I asked him if Blake was going with them, and he said no. Just some of his friends."

"Well that's not a bad thing. After all, you and I go off and still do girl things."

"No. Carrie. No. Since we met we've done something on Friday nights. Even if it's just to hang out at home together before I leave for work. You know that. Remember how you joked with me about it in the beginning, about how you never saw me awake on Fridays."

"Yes."

"This is the first Friday in ten months he hasn't wanted to see me. Something is wrong."

"Did he say it was?"

"Not in so many words. He's just not calling as much and making plans with his friends instead of me."

Black Eagle returned with tea and some ginger snap cookies on a tray. "I thought this might help. On the television the other day, one of the women was upset, and her friend made tea."

"Th-th-thank you, Blake." Molly sniffed. "It smells really good. At least there's one man out there who understands."

"What happened, Molly?" Blake sat across from her, leaning forward, his hands on his knees, studying her.

"Well, Julie came back to work Monday and was in rare form. That bitch, Kris, screwed up again over the weekend and this time it was pretty serious. This woman called because some man was looking in her daughter's window."

"Oh, my god," Carrie blurted out.

"What did the woman do?" Black Eagle asked.

"Well, the parents are divorced and it was the father's weekend with the daughter and she went home on Monday and told her mom what happened. She told her father when it happened, and he went and looked around outside, but didn't do anything about it and didn't tell the mother. So when the girl told her mother, the mother wanted a police report. I put it in. Kris decided that because it was a day late, different house and no witnesses she wasn't going to send an officer and just closed out the request. Didn't call the mother or anything. When the mother called back, justifiably angry, Kris said it was my fault because I didn't offer any options like a phone call. The woman wanted to talk to an officer, she requested one and if there was a question it should have gone to a sergeant, not Miss High and Mighty Peanut Butter legs."

"Peanut but—" Black Eagle looked confused.

"What she means," Carrie told him, "is her legs are so spreadable they are incredible."

"Ah, she gives away her favors."

"Big time. Anyway, because old PBL can't do anything wrong, I got written up. I was so upset I called Vincent and he listened, like he always does, and said he'd call me later. He didn't call, hasn't answered my emails, nothing. I called again last night, to see what was up, and he said he had made plans for tonight."

"His loss. We'll do something, the three of us."

"I don't want to bring you guys down."

"You won't. And we have some good news about Blake."

"Really? So Mr. Merle is back?"

"Back and going to help Blake get a job with me. But Mol, what can we do for you?"

She thought about it and smiled. "You know, nothing. I like being with my roommie and her guy."

Monday, Carrie rushed to get in to work a little earlier than usual and stopped in to see Mrs. Carmichael, her supervisor, before she even went to her desk. Juggling her purse, book bag and lunch, she walked into the woman's office, "Hi, Mrs. C. How you doing?"

"Pretty good, Carrie. And you?"

"Fine. Things are going well."

"Good. Is there something I can help you with?"

"Actually, yes."

"Well then, come in and have a seat."

Carrie walked further into the office and settled into one of the flowery cushioned chairs Mrs. Carmichael had dotting the room. "Do we still have that opening in the mail room?"

"As a matter of fact, yes, we do. Do you have someone in mind?"

"Yes. I have a friend who arrived from out of town and he wants to settle here and needs a job."

"Why don't you have him come in and fill in an application and we'll set up an interview?"

"Great. Actually, I can bring it home with me tonight and

have it to you by morning."

"That will work well. Any chance he's free to interview tomorrow?"

"I think so. I'll know better tonight, but I'm pretty sure he'll be free."

"So how about elevenish tomorrow and then, if you want, you can show him around and go to lunch."

"Sounds good. Thanks, Mrs. C. I'll see you in the morning."

Mr. Merle called later in the afternoon to tell her he had the identification ready to go and to come by after work to pick it up.

After dinner, Molly and Carrie coached Black Eagle on how to act and what to say at the interview, although Carrie felt certain he was a shoo-in.

Black Eagle drove in to work with Carrie the next morning and said he would visit with Mr. Merle before the interview. There were some questions he wanted to ask the older man and maybe, without Carrie there, he would get his answers. However, while Mr. Merle welcomed him, there was little time at all to visit and ask any questions, as the shop seemed particularly busy that morning. Customers wandered in and out and the old cash registered rang a merry tune with sales. One woman came in who seemed to find fault with everything she saw and finally huffed out the door. Shaking his head Mr. Merle whispered to Black Eagle, "You ever see that one coming steer clear, she's trouble."

Blake Eagle asked, "Who?"

"That would be Julie Prince, the bane of Molly's existence. Interesting that she would come by on the very day I was thinking about her, and what could be done to help Molly. If you watch her, she seems to flounce rather than walk. Always acts like she's better than everyone else. From what Carrie's told me, that woman has made Molly's life a living hell. Well, Molly and everyone else that works for her."

"I do not understand why she would come here. To me it seemed she found fault with almost every thing she saw."

"That's her. She's made life miserable for people in this city and the next one over for years. She works in the next county over as a manager for a police dispatch department and her greatest pleasure in life seems to be writing employees up for the most unbelievable things. She's even been known to write people up for things that happened on their vacations. From what Carrie has told me, that Prince woman only gives the good jobs to young women, those under thirty, usually blonde, who will sleep with the police officers. Someone like Molly who is a little older and doesn't have loose morals would never get one of the good jobs. Now if this was the old days, like when my ancestor was around, she would have been tarred, feathered and run of town long ago."

"I do not understand the manager and dispatching."

"Oh well, you see . . ."

"That is of no matter. Carrie will explain to me. What I would like to know is why do they not tar and feather her kind now?"

Mr. Merle chuckled. "Good question. Thing is, in this time, no one really gets run out of town anymore and rumor has it she has something on someone high up in the police department so they can't get rid of her."

"Something on . . . ."

"Yeah, she knows something about someone that she keeps a secret so she and whoever it is, can keep their jobs."

"Then if she cannot be run out of town, can you still tar —"

"Nope. Much as people would like it, especially her employees, we don't do that anymore, either."

"One day she will be repaid for her cruelties. This I believe."

"I hope you are right, Blake. Well, looks like it's time for your interview, you did say eleven, right?"

"Yes, eleven. And then Carrie and I will go to lunch."

The elderly gent shuffled over to the cash register and pulled out what appeared to be a small card and handed it to Black Eagle. "So here is your ID."

Black Eagle studied it and nodded to Mr. Merle. "Thank you. It is good to see my photograph and yet I still stand before you."

Shortly before he was due for his interview, Black Eagle walked up the street to Carrie's office. Though a bit nervous, he felt much better when Carrie came to greet him and took his hand. "Right on time! Mrs. C is waiting for you."

A short time later, Black Eagle emerged from the interview with the news that he would be starting the next day. Not that Carrie was surprised. She was very pleased for him. He was a proud man, one who was a leader and she knew that part of his homesickness came from not having a purpose. It wasn't a job like leading a whole village, but it was a job.

Still pondering how he could use the information he'd learned over the weekend, Dean spent his lunch hour sitting in front of Carrie's building. Eating a Limburger cheese sandwich with fresh onions, he flicked off the crumbs of the white bread on his jacket and cheese lingering on his sparse little mustache. He knew he'd smell pretty bad later, but that would be Lisa's problem, not his. As long as Turdberg didn't call him in, it wouldn't matter what his breath smelled like. Considering Carrie, he thought to himself, *Yup, with that info I can get the girl and the partnership and get rid of you, Tonto, in one shot. And I gotta get rid of you soon, so I can get caught up on all those stupid cases.*

Kneeling there in the dirt, Dean considered how best to use the information, and various scenarios went through his mind.

He could get rid of Blake by proving he was nuts. After all, who in their right mind thought they were an Indian from another time period and that they time traveled to here and now? Dean could just see Blake telling the authorities his story and ending up in the nut house. That would be one down. While he was proving Blake was nuts, he'd be 'protecting' Carrie from the deranged man. Clearly Blake was deranged, right? After all, who thought he traveled through time? Really.

In exchange for being rescued and safe, Carrie would gratefully marry him. He'd get his partnership and then . . .oh, oh, oh, this was too good! After an appropriate time, he'd start to make noises about Carrie not acting quite right. After all, she believed in the time travel bit, too. Oh yeah, he'd get her to talk about the time travel business and be put away, too. Different nut house, though. Couldn't let the two of them plot together. That would solve his problem of being stuck with Carrie, and his partners would feel so sad for him they would rally around him and understand completely when he divorced her. Oh, that was just too richly good!

Then there was that Mr. Merle. Not that he was a real problem, but somehow he was connected to Carrie leaving him in the first place and he was even more connected to that Blake guy. He'd have to think about what to do with Mr. Arthur Merle. So, how to put it all in motion; where to begin . . .

When he returned to his own job after lunch, Turnberg called him in. *That* totally ruined his day. Fortunately Lisa kept some mints on her desk and a handful later he answered his boss' summons. "Mr. Turnberg, you wanted to see me?"

"Yes, Dean, yes. I've been waiting to hear. You pop the question to that sweet little Carrie yet? I told my wife you were thinking of doing it this past weekend and I've been waiting to hear."

"Uh, no, umm, not yet. I've been waiting—"

"Time's a-wasting there, Deano."

"I know, but I'm not really wasting it."

"No?"

"No, see," he shifted on his seat, uncrossing one leg and crossing it over the other, "my plan all along has been to propose on her birthday. She's a very romantic type girl, likes a lot of romance and I thought that would be real romantic. You know, do the whole bit with roses sent to her house early in the day, bring her more when I get there, rent a limo to go to dinner some place romantic in San Francisco and then have the ring in a special dessert. I've been planning this for a long while now."

"Well now, that *does* sound like a plan. When is her birthday? Partnership decisions are being made . . ."

"Uh, oh, in two weeks, actually."

"You hurry and do it, Dean. No one makes partner if they aren't married."

"Yes, sir. I know. Thanks for the advice."

Dean cursed to himself when he left the office. Turnberg was such a pompous ass. Didn't that guy know that half of his partners were screwing around on the job? That their wives played the field, too and no one was into the serious marriage thing? Heck, he'd seen Turnberg's wife going into one of the local hotels, into a room, with another woman! Things were difficult as it was with Carrie, now with that Blake or Black Eagle guy there—well, he'd have to amp it up, that was all—and get Carrie to buy into changing her birthday for him.

Chapter Twenty-nine

The next morning, Carrie and Black Eagle headed off to work together. She'd carefully selected his outfit, then changed it, then changed it again and then again. She was about to pull out another shirt when Black Eagle made a sound that came out suspiciously like a growl before he reached over to pull out the first outfit she'd chosen for him. His presence reminded her of how excited she was when she got her first job her senior year of high school. "You'll be fine," she assured him, more for herself than for him. After a restless night, she was pretty nervous.

Black Eagle, on the other hand, seemed calm and in control. What his body did for the olive green Dockers and form fitting pale green button down cotton shirt distracted some of her nervousness. His assurance came through when he told her, "I expect to be fine, Carrie. After one has prepared for and returned victorious from the hunt, going to work in a comfortable building, knowing your woman is nearby, is very easy to do."

As it turned out, it wasn't his being a success at doing the job itself that was a concern. It was the other women in the office, even seventy year old Edna Brewster, eyed him like a slice of Triple Threat Chocolate cake made with Godiva chocolate. She swore she'd have to spend her lunch hour getting sponges with chinstraps, the way some of them looked him over. The upside was that everyone was more than happy to help him find things and seemed pretty vested in his success. *Well, who wouldn't be? Who wouldn't want to come to work and look at that package . . .my package, every day?*

Choosing to be generous—at least she told herself it was generous—she invited Maria to join them for lunch. Black Eagle, as usual, was charming. His smile warmed Carrie to her toes and did other things that needed to wait till they were home that night, to happen in her body.

"So, Blake, any more at home like you?" Maria casually asked.

Carrie almost spit the swallow of coffee she had just taken across the table, but managed to just sort of choke on it as Black Eagle patted her back.

"No, at my home now I am the only one of me. But at my home I came from, I have many brothers."

"Big family, Blake has a big family, right, sweetie? His dad was one of those ones who wanted to field a baseball *and* football team." Carrie answered for him.

"My father—"

Putting her hand on his thigh in a movement he was coming to learn meant she wanted him to agree with her, Carrie broke in, "Remember, you told me?"

"Yes, yes I do." He nodded as if trying to remember the earlier conversation.

Fortunately, the rest of the afternoon seemed to pass quickly. Over a baked chicken dinner, Carrie and Black Eagle shared their versions of the day with Molly. Black Eagle clearly was thinking it a big success because all the women smiled at him, omitting the glowers a few of the men gave him. Carrie was concerned that he may have slipped about where he came from.

"It sounds like your first day was a huge success," Molly told him.

"I believe it was. But tell us, Molly, do you hear from Vincent?"

"No. But he knows during the week I work so, well, maybe later."

When they turned in for the night, Black Eagle pulled Carrie into his embrace. "I think your real worry today, woman, was that another would catch my eye."

Carrie sputtered, squirmed and sputtered again. "I had no such worry!"

"No?"

"Don't you laugh at me!"

"I do not laugh at you, I laugh alongside you."

"You *are* laughing at me."

"No, no. I am pleased. Do you have any idea how much it means to me to know you think me that desirable? Do you?"

"So you flirted on purpose?"

"Flirted?"

"Yes flirted . . . made goo-goo eyes at the other wom—"

"Goo?"

"Love eyes, like you wanted them."

"I did not. Carrie, they were kind to me, helped me, but there is only one woman for me. Only one I want to see each night right before I close my eyes, and who is the first sight I see each morning. The woman I love as I never thought to love a woman."

"Really?"

"Yes, really."

CHAPTER THIRTY

Things went well.

Until Friday afternoon anyway.

Just as Carrie and Black Eagle returned from lunch, there was a commotion in the front lobby.

"Let me in. I'm here to expose a fraud," a male voice squeaked.

Just those few words were all Carrie needed to hear to know Dean had come into the building.

"Just tell Carrie I'm here. She'll want to see me."

"I don't think so, Dean-ster," Maria said with a glower in her eye.

"Maria, ever the watchful friend. Just get her," Dean spat.

"Dean, we do not appreciate that tone here, I suggest you leave until you get that temper of yours under control," Ms. Templeton, the office manager, firmly stated on her arrival.

"Thanks, Ms. Templeton, I'll handle this," Carrie told the quickly growing group of onlookers.

Dean smiled, clearly believing he'd won, when Carrie walked into the lobby and seemed to take charge.

That smile, rather than diminish when he saw Black Eagle, grew even more broadly, which immediately put Carrie on guard.

"Well, hey there, Tonto."

Amid several gasps, Black Eagle questioned, "Tonto?"

"Yeah, Ton-to."

"I know no Tonto."

"Everyone knows Tonto. He was the Indian who followed

the Lone Ranger around."

"Who?"

"Well, everyone who grew up with television would know. You didn't though, did you, *Tonto*? They didn't have it in the eighteenth century, did they?" Dean rudely poked at Black Eagle's chest as if that would bring his point home.

"Eighteen century? The Lone Ranger went off the air before half the staff here was born. Dean, what are you talking about?" Maria asked.

"1860, even you should know that's the eighteenth century."

"Gees, Dean," Carrie interrupted, "the 1800's were the nineteenth century."

"Oh, no. Eighteen is eighteen. Just like seventeen is the seventeenth and we're now in the twenties something or other."

"Whatever. Understand this though, Sir D, not everyone watches the television." Black Eagle glowered at the shorter man.

Everyone snickered, and Dean glowered. "What are you saying, Tonto? What do you mean by 'Sir D'?"

Black Eagle answered him, "If I remember what Carrie told me, it refers to a part of a man's body which you do not have much of or not at all. It is Sir Dickless she calls you."

As several more snickers erupted, Carrie cut in. "What you want, Dean?"

"I think you'll want to hear this privately, Carrie."

"You can tell Carrie anything you need to here," Ms. Templeton interjected.

"Okay. If you want it that way. You'll be sorry. Humalated and sorry."

"Humalated?"

"Yes. Humalated."

"Um, Dean, do you mean humiliated?"

"Whatever. I have a police officer outside and he'll be very interested in what I have to say."

When Dean motioned the two officers in, both looked decidedly uncomfortable.

"That does it. Officer, this man," Carrie pointed at Dean as she tried to explain what was going on, "has been calling me, following me and now threatening me. If you could please do something about it, I would very much appreciate it."

The first officer glanced at Dean, who all too calmly pointed at Black Eagle. "That is the man who has the fake ID. He is an Indian from another time and he came here to the future and got this old guy, Mr. Merle at the junk store, to make him false identification. Carrie Taylor there has been aiding and abetting him."

"Say *what*? Are you certifiable?" Carrie was surprised at how calm she sounded.

"No, I'm telling you, that man, he calls himself Blake Eagleston, but he's an Indian named Black Eagle and he came from the past. He was living in a photograph for ages, until he somehow got out and moved in with Carrie."

The officer squinted one eye and shook his head. "Look, bud, if you brought us here as a joke, it's not very funny and if you called us in to harass this young lady, we will take *you* in for filing a false police report."

"No! I'm telling you, look. Check his ID. It's a false ID."

"Dean, give it up," Carrie told him.

"No, no! I'm telling you! He's from the past! He's a *time traveler*."

Carrie chuckled. This may be the best thing that ever happened in the course of her relationship with Dean. "Time traveler? And you think I'm weird for reading romance books?"

As Dean's claims that Black Eagle was from the past became more strident, the officers decided enough was enough. With one officer on each side, they cuffed him. Of course, he was so delusional he didn't seem to realize the officers had handcuffed him.

Leading him to the door, one of the officers assured him, "Yeah, sure, we'll check his ID in a few minutes. You folks make sure he doesn't time travel anywhere while we take this gentleman to a nice, restful room with comfy padding on the walls, okay?"

Amid giggles, a few of Carrie's co-workers walked past, telling her that it looked like Dean finally got what he deserved. They were sure that he'd be away for more than a seventy-two hour hold period. When the entertainment provided by Dean died down, Black Eagle followed Carrie to her office and asked her what this seventy-hour business was.

"Oh, a 5150. It means he's crazy and they can usually keep someone who is unstable in the hospital for no more time than that. In Dean's case, though, everyone's thinking he's going to be put away for a long, long time. Let's hope so."

Upon understanding what had been done with Dean, Black Eagle wanted Carrie to call Molly. "She should hear the good news as well." So she did.

"Oh Carrie, that's hysterical. I know what I thought when you first told me about Black Eagle, but it was pretty clear you guys were telling the truth. Dean must have seemed like a total nut case."

"Yeah. 5150—can't beat that. And you know how he was always saying it was my *perception* when I didn't see things his way, or thought he was wrong?"

"Yup."

"Well, I guess *his* perception on this was a little skewed!" Carrie laughed so hard her stomach hurt.

"So, you and Black Eagle want to grab some dinner to celebrate?" Molly asked

"Sounds good. How about Bodeman's? It's just a bit up the way from Treasures."

"See you there about six."

When they hung up, Black Eagle asked what was this 'perception' thing that had Carrie laughing so hard.

"Dean couldn't handle anyone disagreeing with him, or thinking he might be wrong. So if you said something he disagreed with, or you didn't see things his way, he would say," she cleared her voice and tried to lower it, "'Now Carrie, that's just your perception.' I started to *hate* the word perception. So, you see, he perceived things all wrong today." At the last, Carrie started to laugh so hard her tummy not only ached, but tears rolled down her cheeks.

"So we are free of him?" Black Eagle grinned.

"For seventy-two hours, anyway, maybe more. Hopefully he'll get it now. I do think we need to be sure your ID is really good to go, though."

CHAPTER THIRTY-ONE

After work, Molly in tow, they stopped in to see Mr. Merle, inviting him to join them for dinner, to share what had happened and double-check on the ID. "Mr. Merle, you will never guess what happened today!"

"Something pretty good, from the looks of you two."

"Oh, yeah. Come to dinner with us and we'll fill you in on all the details."

"You sure you want an old man tagging along with you young folks?"

"We sure do. You were part of this. And Mr. Merle, you aren't old. You are my friend as much as Molly and Black Eagle are, so come on."

"Well all right then. I look forward to it. Let me just close up here." He turned to walk towards the kitchenette. From beyond the beaded curtain that separated the shop from the kitchenette they heard him call out, "Vivianne! What? No, don't go in there."

Curious at what could make the normally calm Mr. Merle sound a tad agitated, Carrie peered through the curtain to catch sight of whoever this Vivianne was. Apparently the petite, dark haired woman with an amazing shade of blue eyes knew Mr. Merle, or rather he knew her or they knew each other, had popped into the shop without Mr. Merle seeing her. At a look from Black Eagle she shrugged and turned to browse among some of the objects in a glass cabinet. Mr. Merle knew all kinds of people and the woman dressed in nuvo-chic hippie was no concern of hers. In the glass reflection she saw Molly smile at Black Eagle as if to say, "Don't ask me." Studiously studying the glass, with an ear towards the kitchen she heard a few stray words — Gareth — Glastonbury — now — where? But could make no sense of it.

Her attention was drawn back to Molly when she heard her roommate whoop. "Well beans! You startled me!"

Carrie spun around to see a tall, light haired man with eyes that looked like molten emeralds staring down at Molly. It wasn't the shoulder length blond hair that looked like liquid gold that caught her attention. It was what the man was wearing.

She looked up at Black Eagle, "I guess I should be used to guys in odd clothing by now, but that's a bit much, even for someone getting ready for the renaissance faire. Check out that suit of armor."

Black Eagle gazed towards the man, brow quirked to let Carrie know he wasn't sure what she found so odd.

"I'm so sorry," Molly gushed. "I can't believe I didn't see you there. Is your foot all right?"

The blond giant stood staring at Molly, his tongue laving a quick switch across his lips, the look in his eyes about the way she felt just before digging into a huge banana split. It seemed pretty clear to her he was about to devour Molly. "Lovely Lady, my foot is quite well. 'Tis my heart, mayhap, which needs attention."

She pushed lightly on the metal-like vest the man wore, "Are you — does your chest hurt? Do you need us to call 911?"

"My chest doth feel a spark, if pain there be, 'tis my need to have you, lady."

"Uh. Right." Molly stepped back, squinting her eyes at the man.

"Nice suit there." Carrie stepped up. "Taking a break from ballet rehearsal?"

"Ballet? I know not this word. However, if it doth please

my fair lady."

"Gareth!" The woman Mr. Merle called Vivianne rushed from the kitchenette toward the man. Looking over her shoulder, she admonished Mr. Merle, "I told you he walked among us."

Carrie was certain that when the woman first rushed into the room she'd been wearing a long white gown trimmed in gold and some jewelry. She blinked as the woman advanced, the gown seeming to shimmer and become a dark burgundy turtleneck sweater and form fitting black jeans—just about the exact outfit Carrie was herself wearing.

The man smiled a wolf's grin at Molly, "My lady. I would have you join me."

Just before he grabbed her arm, Mr. Merle took hold of it, "*Gareth*, I've been waiting for you. The package you requested is in the kitchen."

"Mer—"

Carrie watched as both Mr. Merle and that Vivianne woman made some odd sort of fluttering motion with their hands, basically shutting the man up just before they pulled him towards the kitchen.

"My nephew, Gareth," Mr. Merle called over his shoulder just as he, Vivianne and the big blond guy crossed the threshold to the kitchen.

"Mol, Black Eagle, did you see—that woman had—she—her dress—jeans. *One minute she was in a long dress and then bam! She was in my outfit!*"

"Did you see that guy, Mr. Merle's whatever? He was *hot*! And that accent. I *love* an English accent." Molly gushed.

"He looked like a man, Molly," Black Eagle stated, as if the other man's appearance was nothing out of the ordinary.

"Something really weird is going on here. Where did he come from? I didn't hear the bell above the door ring. Suddenly he was just there, talking medieval weird to you, Molly, and that woman, I swear she was wearing like an evening gown when she started walking in here and suddenly she was in the same outfit I'm in." Carrie looked from one to the other.

"Please, excuse me," Mr. Merle told them, returning from the kitchenette. "I'd like you to meet my sister, Vivianne and her nephew, Gareth."

From the kitchen they heard the woman say, "You shouldn't be here. For now you must listen and do as Merl—your uncle says."

"As you wish, lady."

"Ah, here they are. Vivianne and Gareth. Please meet my friends Carrie, Blake and Molly." Mr. Merle smiled as he led Vivianne and the younger man back into the shop.

"I hath already met the fair Lady Molly. 'Tis my greatest wish to know her better."

"Yes. Well. Maybe later, Gareth. Your aunt has a few things for you to take care of."

"Aunt? Vivianne? Nay, I think—"

"Your uncle is correct. We will see you shortly." The petite woman pulled the sun-color haired man from the room once again, surprisingly strong for one so small.

"Well. Family. Huh? What can you say? Shall we go to dinner?" Mr. Merle gestured toward the door.

"Ah, sure, Mr. Merle. Um, wouldn't your sister and nephew like to join us?"

"Perhaps another time, Carrie. They need some time to, ah, well yes. Time." He herded the group towards the door, looking over his shoulder to make sure the man and woman did not follow. "You said Bodeman's right? I'm starving, let's go."

Inside the restaurant, after the waitress took their orders, Carrie could hardly contain herself another minute. "It was a pleasure to meet your sister and nephew, Mr. Merle. We have some news, too. Dean showed up at work today. Not just work, and not just Dean. He brought the police with him. At first I was kind of nervous, because he was going on about Black Eagle having a fake ID and that he was going to get you and him arrested. But then the police showed up and—"

"Fake ID? Carrie, how did he find out about the ID? It's not fake, you know."

"It's not?"

"No. That's a real driver's license. I also arranged for a real Social Security card. You know you can't tell anyone though, right?"

"Definitely, Mr. Merle. It's our secret. I don't know for sure, but I suspect Dean was lurking around the other night when we were at your shop. He does that, or did that, hung around eavesdropping. He thought no one knew but I'd see him all the time skulking around. I don't know what I ever thought I saw in him."

"I'm going to pretend I'm not hearing this. It wouldn't do for me to be party to a crime like that you know," Molly told them.

"Important thing is you did see Dean for what he is, Carrie." Mr. Merle told her.

"I know. Interesting thing is, the police thought he was just nuts and took *him* 5150."

"Now that is an ending even I couldn't have anticipated. How wonderful."

"It is. So Mr. Merle, you didn't know your family was coming?"

"My family? Oh. Vivianne pops in and out. A world traveler of sorts."

"Your nephew talks like the characters from some of Carrie's books," Molly observed.

"He's a Shakespearean actor. I'm sure you saw his costume. He's rehearsing for a play," Mr. Merle told them.

"Which one?" Carrie asked.

"Which one?" Mr. Merle asked.

"Which play? We'll have to go see it."

"I'm guessing Romeo and Juliette," Molly gushed.

"Exactly," Mr. Merle told her.

Throughout the rest of the meal, Carrie and Black Eagle entertained Mr. Merle and Molly with a lively rendition of what had happened during Dean's arrest earlier, Mr. Merle studiously keeping the attention off his family. Black Eagle devoted himself to the variety of dishes they had ordered, seeming to enjoy each bite more than the last.

After dinner they walked Mr. Merle back to his shop and bid him goodnight before heading home.

Watching the threesome head off, he once again thought over his decision to bring Black Eagle to the future. Not that he'd ever admit he'd had anything to do with it. Magic and all that just didn't fit in today's world. After watching the couple together over the evening, he had no doubt Carrie and Black Eagle belonged together. Now with Dean out of the way for possibly a long time, they would have the kind of life they deserved.

For too long it had bothered him that a man as good and decent as Black Eagle could die alone and unloved. Now he had Carrie. He seemed to be adjusting to living in the future fairly well, although a few times over dinner he did seem a little sad and perhaps even a bit homesick. With Dean out of the way, he was certain the twosome would move things along and Black Eagle would be content and not look back. He'd accomplished what he'd set out to do—to bring Carrie and Black Eagle together.

"At long last you return," Gareth growled from behind him.

"Did he behave?" Mr. Merle asked Vivianne.

"He tried." Vivianne smiled at the younger man.

"Did he tell you how he came to be here?"

"*He* is here in the room with you. *He* should thank you to speak to him and not over him," Gareth informed him.

"Tell me then, how did you come to be here, in California?" Mr. Merle squinted up at him.

"To speak the truth, I know not. One moment I was saddling my mount preparing for battle, and the next in this place."

"If this is true, then the others may soon arrive. Vivianne, we must prepare."

Arriving home, Molly went off to call Vincent, and Carrie and Black Eagle wandered off to her room. Climbing into bed, Carrie leaned over to kiss the man who had taken her heart. Instead of giving in to the passion that they usually shared, Black Eagle pulled her into his arms and held her close as if he might lose her if he let go.

"Black Eagle, are you all right?"

"I am fine, Carrie. I just miss my home. Since I have been here in your time I have thought little of my village or my time. For some reason, tonight though I miss my home more than ever."

"Do you want to go back?"

"No. I could not leave unless you were with me."

"I'm glad, because I don't ever want you to leave. Black Eagle . . ."

"Yes, Carrie."

"I want you to know—well I think you do—but just in case . . ."

"Tell me, Carrie. What concerns you?"

"It's not a concern. It's that—well—I want you to know, I love you. I love you so much and sometimes I can't believe you are for real. And—and—if something ever happened I'd try to find you again. Really."

"I am very real, Carrie and I want you to know, I love you, too. You are the woman I have longed for, the one I have wanted in my life. You are my heart, Carrie. It is my wish to spend my life with you."

"I'm happy, so happy. And now with Dean out of the way, we can really concentrate on us, our life."

"That is good. I like this concentrating on us."

"Just think, all it took to get rid of him was for you to come here and him to talk about it. Good thing I didn't think about having someone pretend to be from the past before."

"Yes, a good thing."

CHAPTER THIRTY-TWO

The next few weeks passed fairly peacefully, with Carrie at her job and Black Eagle there beside her. By Friday night, however, Carrie noticed Black Eagle becoming pre-occupied and asked what was wrong.

"The past few days it seems I miss my time more and more. Carrie, it is almost as if I am being pulled back there. Your time is interesting, some things are easier like your microwave and car, but at the same time you are busier. You work in your office all day, we come home and we sit here in your house, we watch the television and go to bed. The next day is more of the same."

"How—how was it different in your village? You told me once everyone worked. Everyone had a job to do. How is what we do here—now—different?"

"We were outside, in the air. We worked, yes, but we sat, we talked to each other. We listened to each other's thoughts and cares. Children ran free and the entire village looked out for them. There were no locked doors, no one worried about stealing from another. I do not think many of your time know the peace of just sitting and looking at the sky."

Carrie sat and thought about his words. Her heart felt almost as if it was going to break if she wasn't very careful. "Do you—if you could—would you go home? Have you changed your mind about wanting to stay here?"

"I've said many times before, this is now my home, Carrie."

"But if you could go back to your time, would you?"

"Sometimes, I think yes. To visit maybe. I think yes I would, but not without you, Carrie. Sometimes I worry that I will wake in my own time and not have a chance to say good-bye to you."

"You mean like you would go back in time without knowing it was going to happen?"

"Yes. I did not know I was coming here. How can I know whether or not I will return to my time?" He held her a few minutes and finally, taking in a deep breath, asked, "If I were to go back in time, would you try to come back to find me?"

"You know I would, don't you? Black Eagle, you are my life now. You are everything I ever wanted in a, a boyfriend. If you suddenly ended up back in time, somehow, some way I'd find my way back to you."

When they made love before sleeping that night, there was a different level of tenderness, combined with a toe curling passion Carrie had never felt before. Not even with Black Eagle. He held her as silent tears coursed down her cheeks afterward. "What is wrong, Carrie?"

"I don't know. I just—Black Eagle, I love you so much, so much sometimes I feel like my heart is going to burst with how much I love you."

"I feel this too, Carrie. It is as if my heart beats with yours."

As they fell asleep, Taister climbed up on the bed between them and cuddled up to Black Eagle, his little black head on the warrior's shoulder, his paw extended as if in an embrace. It was as if even Taister felt a change in the air.

While the couple slept, a streak of lightning flashed in the distance. No thunder or rain followed—yet another flash came shortly after, only this one came from within the photograph.

In that instant Carrie stirred and moved to snuggle closer to the man beside her but her hand only met with Taister's furry little head. "Black Eagle? Black Eagle, are you here?"

Coming quickly awake, Carrie reached to turn on the light, her hand knocking his photograph to the floor. Its clatter brought her fully awake. Turning on the lamp while at the same time reaching for the photograph, she called again, "Black Eagle?"

"Noooooooooooooooo!"

Chapter Thirty-three

A moment later, Molly rushed into Carrie's room. "Carrie, what's wrong? What's going on?"

The tears flowed down Carrie's cheeks in a torrent, her breathing in broken gasps so painful she could only look to her roommate and hold the photograph out to her. Taking it in her hand as she sat by her friend, Molly gave it a quick glance before pulling Carrie into her arms.

Knowing the answer, yet not wanting to really know, Molly asked, "Where's Black Eagle?"

Despite the intense shaking from the sobs coming deep from within her chest, Carrie could only point to the photograph. Molly lifted it to look at it again, to finally see what had upset Carrie so. Black Eagle was back in the photograph, but his expression was no longer that of the bold warrior she knew. Instead, his look was one of utter despair and a loss of hope. "Oh, Carrie, we'll bring him back. I promise we'll bring him back."

"No, oh no, Molly, I don't think we can. I think he came only to help me get rid of Dean and now that Dean is gone . . . Oh, Molly, what am I going to do without him?"

Molly sat holding Carrie until morning and then reached for Carrie's phone to call in to her work to let them know Carrie was sick " . . .and I can't believe this myself, but Blake got an emergency call from his family last night and had to rush back to Wyoming . . . No, no I don't know when or even if he'll be back . . .Yes, I'll have Carrie call you when she wakes and see if she knows his plans."

A few hours later, Molly managed to get Carrie up, some coffee in her and told her they were going to go to Treasures. "Maybe Mr. Merle knows what happened and maybe he can undo this."

Taister sat on the chair beside Carrie's while she drank her coffee. Even he seemed to be missing his new person because he simply sat there. He didn't demand any treats or groom himself. He sat beside her, as if he too were deep in thought.

"No, Molly, he's gone. He can't come back. He was only here to help me get rid of Dean."

"No, Carrie, he was looking for and wanted a wife. Look, even Taister is upset. If not for you, then at least for Taister we need to see if Mr. Merle can help."

"All right."

Entering Treasures a few hours later, it was Molly who called out to Mr. Merle. One look at Carrie and he knew what had happened. Even Gareth who seemed to still be in town although he'd traded his tights and armor-like top for jeans and a form fitting tee shirt, was somber when he saw the sad looks on the women's faces. "Ah, Carrie, I am sorry. I am so sorry."

"Mr. Merle, how did it happen? Why did it happen? Where did he go? You said he wouldn't leave!"

Again turning the sign to '*Closed*', he led the young women to the kitchen. "I'm not sure I can explain, Carrie, Molly. But let me try . . ."

He considered a moment before going on, "So here's how I think it works. I'm not an expert. These are just my thoughts about time travel. Some things are present in more than one time. The photograph was real both in the 1860s and now. It was real twenty years ago, and it was real every year from when it was taken, until now. It's a tangible thing that exists in both times. So the photograph doesn't move. It always exists. Now, I'm not admitting to anything here, understand.

The way I see it though, Black Eagle existed in the 1860s. When he made his wish for a wife, magic happened and his wish brought him to the present, here with Carrie, who also had a wish for a good man. A man she could love for all time. Even though he made his wish in the past, that's all it was, a wish. There was no one to receive it or to make it come true. That situation didn't exist until Carrie got the photograph. When she got it, the photograph, that piece of paper, brought the two wishes together and brought him to the present. Do you understand?"

"You believe in time travel?"

"Unless Black Eagle just left you in the night, there's no other explanation. And, he's back in the photo, right?"

"Yes. He's back in there." Carrie sniffed.

"If anyone needs to be stuck in an old picture, it's my nasty boss, Julie Prince. Why couldn't *she* end up in a picture? Only one where she's miserable," Molly blurted out.

"That's a good question, Molly." Mr. Merle said. "Who knows, maybe one day she will. Now Carrie, you understand how I think both your wishes brought you together?"

"I think so. We both needed to exist for it to happen. And he probably didn't come to the future sooner because I wasn't ready?"

"Exactly."

"All right, so I can buy that — Black Eagle was here because he made a wish and I had to come along, but why did he fade from the photograph? Why was his picture gone?" Carrie held back the tears that threatened to spill.

"Because he existed now, in 2021. He no longer existed in the past because he was alive here, now. So time rights itself by removing indications of him being alive in the 1800s. If he wasn't there he wouldn't be in the photograph."

"So why did he go back?" Tears spilled from her eyes. Tears she thought had long passed.

244

"I don't know, Carrie, I don't know." The sound of defeat echoed in his voice. "Maybe he did what he came to do, or maybe it's a test of your love."

"So he can come forward again?"

"I don't know. I don't think so. Give it a day or two. I know that will be hard, but give it a day or two and see if he comes forward again."

"I will." She thought for a moment and then asked, "Mr. Merle, what if I was in the picture? What if we put me in the picture?"

"I don't know, Carrie. I'm not able to say how this happened in the first place, so I can't say what would happen in the future. But let me think about it and see if I can figure something out."

"All right, and, well, I'm going to try to Photoshop myself into the photo."

"That's as good an idea as any. Molly, if she does go back in time, you'll let me know? I hate to think of one of my favorite people going to another time and me not seeing them again."

"Sure."

Throughout their discussion Gareth sat quietly listening, his gazed fixed on Molly. Mr. Merle could tell from Molly's clipped 'Sure', she didn't believe any of this. It seemed she didn't even really believe Black Eagle was back in the photo.

With a heavy heart, the older man watched the two young women leave. He glanced to the sword, shaking his head.

"I told you not to meddle." The soft voice came from the depths of the mirror. "I told you to leave it be. Merlin, when will you stop interfering in lives?"

"I don't—"

"You did. You *do*. You could have told Uther no. Had you

done so, Arthur would never have been born. Lancelot and Gwenivere would have had the life they deserved. How many others have you brought together on a whim rather than let love run its course?"

"That is what you say, Vivianne. Arthur loved —"

"As did Lancelot. Ah, you think me cold and heartless, a creature of my mother's. Merlin, I may have been my mother's son, but I was also a companion. Why else do you think I am come now?" Gareth answered.

"You found a way to send him back as a lesson to me?" Mr. Merle turned, surprised at Gareth's words.

"No. I had nothing to do with it. This was not my doing," Gareth assured him.

"He speaks the truth, Merlin. I do not know if your magic in bringing Black Eagle forward in time has broken the magic of Glastonbury or if it is that dark time when we need the return of the Knights most. That Gareth is here is but a sign of what is to come. You know the legend as well as I. When the Earth needs the Knights the most, they will rise. It is possible meddling has set their return in motion," Vivianne quietly told him.

With that Vivianne and Gareth faded back into the glass as if they'd never stood before him. Merlin roared to the empty room. "And they did belong together. True love will find its way."

CHAPTER THIRTY-FOUR

When the women returned home Carrie immediately went to the computer and pulled up some photographs of herself and Taister. Then she scanned in the photo of Black Eagle, and for the next few hours manipulated the photograph to see if she could somehow move through time to be with him.

Molly let her be for most of the afternoon, and finally brought her a tray with some dinner. "I fed Taister. Now you have to eat."

"I can't." Tears once again welled in Carrie's eyes. "Molly, what am I going to do without him?"

"I don't know, Carrie, I don't know. I promise you, though, we'll figure something out."

Long after dark, Carrie picked up Taister and carried him into her room with her. If going through the day was hard without Black Eagle, entering her room was near impossible. The pain that had lingered in her chest most of the day still hung like a never-ending tunnel. Climbing into bed, she picked up both the original photograph and the one she had made on the computer and held them close to her. Thinking back on the things she had done right before Black Eagle arrived, she bent to kiss his visage in the picture. "Oh, Black Eagle, come back, come back to me. Please. I can't live without you," she cried.

Taister too meowed long and loud, as if he too added his plea for Black Eagle to return.

At long last she fell into a troubled sleep.

Across town, Arthur Merle carefully read each entry in his ledger. Looking over again and again at his notations on the couples he had brought together. Up until Carrie and Black Eagle, there had only been one — no, two — couples that hadn't worked out. He thought he had gotten it right this time. Maybe he was getting old. The two really big mistakes had happened when he was younger. *Funny thing for a three thousand year old man to think, but maybe I am getting old.*

"How am I going to help those two? If any two people belong together, it's Carrie and Black Eagle. Well, she said she would go back to be with him; maybe that's where they need to be to be together."

He sat by the window, looking out into the night sky, watching the stars that fell — stars like those Black Eagle described he saw when he came forward in time. As the morning sky heralded a new day, the first pink rays crossing the sky, he rose and pulled out his phone book and located Carrie's number. He waited a few more minutes before calling. Not because he was afraid to wake her. In his heart he knew she hadn't slept much through the night. No, it was because he was afraid she wouldn't talk to him because of what he had done. He gave her not only hope, he'd given her the love of a lifetime.

"Carrie, it's Mr. Merle."

"Mr. Merle." Her voice was soft and to his surprise, it sounded to him like there was hope in her tone.

"Just wanted to see how you were doing, Carrie."

"I'm alive and, and if Black Eagle is back in time, Mr. Merle, I miss him so much. I want him to come back."

"I know, Carrie, I know. Did you try to make up a photograph yesterday?"

"Yes, I did, but as you can hear, it didn't work."

"You feel up to bringing it by today?"

"Sure. I'll come by on my lunch hour. Somehow I gotta get myself in to work today."

Mr. Merle watched Carrie leave his shop after she had brought the photoshopped image she'd made. Locking the door, he stopped before the mirror and looked at his own blurred image in it, back to a time when his white hair flowed long and he wore druid's robes. Moving towards the back, he picked up his ledger and made a few notes before returning it to the secret cubbyhole in the mirror. A flash across the glass with his hand, a few words of old spoken and a glimmer of light appeared in the mirror. Satisfied he had done all he could, with a weary sigh, Mr. Merle returned to cataloging some new acquisitions.

She didn't know how she did it, but Carrie managed to go in to work. Fortunately, everyone believed Molly's story that Black Eagle had to return home for a family emergency, and didn't say much else to her, except for to tell him they were thinking of him.

At lunch she went to see Mr. Merle, left the picture she'd made on the computer, and returned to work.

The end of the long day couldn't come soon enough for her, and after feeding Taister, she picked up a book, went to her room and crawled into bed. She couldn't read but only sat looking at Black Eagle's photograph. A short time later, Taister ambled in and joined her on the bed and he, too, gazed at the photograph.

The rest of the week went by all too slowly for both Carrie and Molly. Worried about her roommate, Molly was relieved, rather than upset, that Vincent had once again made other plans for Friday night.

Not that Carrie noticed. As with every other night since

Black Eagle left, she had gone to her room and sat, staring at his photograph as if she could call him forward to her once again.

Saturday afternoon, Molly woke for her first shift back on graves and stretched, surprised she had slept so long. What surprised her even more was how quiet the house was. Even Taister wasn't yelling for his breakfast. Once Black Eagle had arrived and while he was there, Carrie had been different. Different in a good way — she had more energy, smiled more, had more confidence. She was still the same Carrie, just more of the good parts of her. She even got up early on weekends, mostly due to Black Eagle's prodding and wanting to see all there was in this new world for him.

The past few days had been heartbreaking. But, based on the sounds she'd heard from Carrie's bedroom when she came home from work about four in the morning — maybe he'd come back. Maybe all that magical mumbo jumbo was just a trick with mirrors, and Black Eagle had returned. No wonder they had slept in as well. Molly padded into the kitchen and had started her coffee before she realized something was very out of place — no Taister. No matter what else was happening in the world from rain to an earthquake to hot sex in the bedroom, Taister never missed a meal or a snack, even when it wasn't meal or snack time. Just the possibility of someone passing within five feet of the kitchen was his clue that it was time for a treat.

"Taister?" Her tentative call seemed to echo through the house. "Taister, you in here?" No response. *Where is he?*

Oh no, it couldn't be . . . the little guy was a stoic little go-getter. Did he sneak out of the house? She hurried to Carrie's room and wasn't too surprised by the rumpled bed, but no sign of Carrie, Black Eagle or Taister. Not that Black Eagle was going to come back. It would take a miracle for that although there were the sounds she heard the night before.

Carrie's purse sat, as usual, on her desk, a few items of

clothing scattered about on the floor. There seemed to be a slightly acrid smell in the room, almost like a whole book of matches had just been lit. She glanced at the strewn about clothing. It wasn't exactly like someone undressing in a hurry; it was more like a windstorm had swept through the room. Molly sat down on the bed and absently picked up the photograph. Without really looking at it she thought back on the night before . . .

Where had Carrie gone? Was she so upset that Black Eagle had gone back that she just took off with Taister? Or would she have kept watching the man who really loved her exist only in the photograph, back in time?

There had been something different in the air last night, almost like an electrical charge. She swore she heard Carrie and Black Eagle laughing and teasing for awhile and then total silence — but that was after he had gone. Deep in thought, she searched the room, as if the answers lie somewhere on the walls. But no answers came. Absently she once again glanced down at the photograph in her hands. There stood Black Eagle. No longer was his visage the sad one filled with despair they had seen when he first went back in time. Instead, there was a happy, wide smile on his handsome face and next to him stood . . .

"Oh my God!" Next to him stood Carrie, the brightest, happiest smile imaginable on her face. And in his arms, "Well, what do you know?" In his arms, sitting like an Egyptian God, sat Taister. She just knew, she just knew, he had that little grin on his face, the one they joked about him having as if he'd just heard a funny joke. There they were, in the photograph — together, in time, forever. Carrie had made it back to her man.

The End

About the Author

From earliest childhood Regan was an avid reader and upon discovering Alexander Dumas and Charles Dickens she was hooked on books that carried the reader away to a different time and place. Preferring the quiet of her room and a good book to spending time with people she traveled far beyond those four walls.

It was while working as a police dispatcher, first for the California Highway Patrol and then her local police department, she began to write fiction, primarily time travels and romantic suspense. In the spring of 2009 she returned to the day job she always liked best, working as a legal secretary. Although, curled up in her bunny slippers with her furfaced children, Missy, Lulu and Ollie, while writing is one of her most favorite things to do.